KU-725-999

SIX
GRAVES

BOOKS BY ANGELA MARSONS

Angela
MARSONS
SIX GRAVES

bookouture

Published by Bookouture in 2022

An imprint of Storyfire Ltd.
Carmelite House
50 Victoria Embankment
London EC4Y 0DZ

www.bookouture.com

Copyright © Angela Marsons, 2022

Angela Marsons has asserted her right to be identified
as the author of this work.

All rights reserved. No part of this publication may be reproduced, stored in
any retrieval system, or transmitted, in any form or by any means, electronic,
mechanical, photocopying, recording or otherwise, without the prior written
permission of the publishers.

ISBN: 978-1-83888-739-1
eBook ISBN: 978-1-83888-738-4

This book is a work of fiction. Names, characters, businesses, organizations,
places and events other than those clearly in the public domain, are either the
product of the author's imagination or are used fictitiously. Any resemblance
to actual persons, living or dead, events or locales is entirely coincidental.

This book is dedicated to Mr Derek Church.

This wonderful man contacted me on Facebook a while back to tell me to 'crack on with the next Kim book before he carked it'.

At 93, Derek claims to be my oldest reader and is now responsible for sending me my daily joke to set me up for the working day.

Derek, you are a legend!

PROLOGUE

Bryant averted his gaze from the hole in the ground. He couldn't force himself to imagine the coffin descending into darkness.

He shrugged further into his jacket as the cold wind gusted around the small group of mourners at the top of Powke Lane Cemetery. The coffin was being placed into the hearse for its final journey up the hill to where they awaited its arrival.

Nice spot, people always said about the highest point of the cemetery. Mourners drew comfort from a good view from where they buried their loved ones. He suspected that the dead didn't care.

He knew his mind was rambling away with inconsequential thoughts to avoid facing what was actually going on right in front of him.

Was Stacey doing the same thing? he wondered as she met his gaze. Their eyes locked for a moment. Each wondering how they had got to this point. Both of them were original members of the team; the fourth one buried already after heroically saving a young boy's life. He wasn't surprised to see tears forming in the detective constable's eyes before she broke the hold of their gaze. Their thoughts were also with the late Detective Sergeant Kevin Dawson.

Not far away from Stacey stood Alison Lowe, a behaviourist who had consulted on numerous cases, during which she had formed a strong bond with Stacey. A few sideways glances at her best friend offered quiet reassurance.

His eyes moved across to Penn and noted the stoicism in his demeanour. The most recent addition to the team and a man Bryant felt to be emotionless and cold with a sprinkling of weird. Recently he had come to know him better and understood him a whole lot more. The man was not as infallible as he'd once thought. Before they'd walked into the service, he had taken Penn aside to reassure him that he hadn't fucked up during their most recent case.

She would have wanted him to do that.

Two feet away from Penn stood Woody – DCI Woodward, their boss. His arms had not moved from his side, and his gaze remained fixed ahead. What memories was he reliving right now? Bryant wondered.

His gaze swept across the rest of the mourners. Local pathologist Keats stood to the right of Woody. To his right was Doctor A, the Macedonian forensic anthropologist who had assisted them on many cases. Beside her was their lead forensic technician, Mitch, present at every crime scene. A gap of three feet separated him from Ted Morgan, a child psychologist, now in his seventies, and as much a part of this family as any one of them.

And that was it. The total number of people surrounding the grave.

Bryant was struck that they had all chosen to stand singly. There were no small huddles. It was as though they had all spaced themselves evenly around the grave, forming a barrier, protection.

He shook the thought away. It was too late for that now.

The minister finished the prayer and stood aside to reveal a temporary wooden cross. Bryant's breath caught in his throat. His conscious mind knew what they were here for – what they had come here to do – but his brain wasn't ready to see the black-and-white proof of it. His gaze passed over the dates and went to the words inscribed into the wood.

Even through the tears in his eyes, he could make out the name and, once again he asked himself one question:

How the hell had they ended up here?

ONE

THIRTEEN DAYS EARLIER

Kim's voice got lost against the cloth that was tied loosely around her mouth, but the tie wrap that bound her hands behind her back prevented her from pulling it away.

She growled in desperation at her powerlessness and her inability to help prevent her team from danger.

Danger of coming last at this rate, she realised as she spat out the gag.

'Bryant, make the same knot as Stacey,' she cried. 'It'll be stronger.'

The outburst earned her a stern look from the course coordinator, Jock, a short-haired, strapping ex-SAS member who now taught teams how to work together more effectively.

'Last warning, Stone,' he said as he placed the cloth loosely back into her mouth.

How the hell removing her ability to instruct her team was going to help anyone she had no idea. Of course she got the logic of it all – cut off the head to ensure the rest of the body could function – but it wasn't like she was planning on going anywhere.

When they'd arrived the previous morning, or what felt like

three weeks ago, they'd checked in to the camping site on the outskirts of Hay-on-Wye, where Bryant and Stacey had walked to the top of the hill to peruse the view of Black Mountain and beyond to the Brecon Beacons.

Three other police teams had eventually rolled up before Jock had arrived with his small team and told them what the weekend would entail. When one of the members of the other teams had asked for an express ticket to 5 p.m. the following day, Kim had finally understood that all four teams were here to tick boxes.

She had argued her point with Woody. Her team didn't need to grow closer or bond over a campfire and marshmallows. They were perfectly cohesive, and their statistics should speak for themselves.

Woody had told her to look closer before instructing her that it was not negotiable.

The rest of her team had been delighted with the idea of a weekend away, sleeping rough and living off the land. Not exactly true; they'd been supplied with a state-of-the-art tent, basic cooking facilities and enough tins to feed a family for a week.

Woody didn't know what he was talking about, she'd thought as they'd pulled up into the car park. Her team was tight.

The first activity had been a hike up Black Mountain. The camaraderie and good humour between the four teams had been eviscerated once Jock had explained there were prizes for the fastest and consequences for the slowest. Each team had slinked away from each other. Kim's team had arrived at the finish line a minute and a half before the second team and had earned themselves four sleeping bags.

Since then they'd built a rock pile to the required height before anyone else, thanks to Bryant's dogged determination and motivation. They'd transcribed a coded message from enemy forces ten minutes before the other teams, thanks to Penn. Last night they'd been given a logic problem to ponder overnight and, thanks to Stacey, they'd had the answer before any of the other teams were awake.

Each member of her team had performed out of their skin. They had all excelled in areas that she expected – Bryant's stability, Penn's statistical brain and Stacey's logical application to a complex problem.

She'd seen it all, and she'd also seen something else.

Woody was right.

There was a disconnect between two members of her team that she hadn't noticed before. It didn't present as open hostility, which was one of the reasons it had stayed hidden for a while now. It displayed itself as indifference, dismissal, a frown, a shake of the head, an eye-roll.

On a daily basis, while sifting clues and following leads, Bryant's impatience with Penn had been hidden by long days, warped minds, challenging crime scenes and a need to get the job done. Away from the familiar, she had seen the frustration in Bryant's face when Penn had detailed how he was going to have to unlock the code of his own task, and she'd listened as Bryant had snapped at Penn when Penn had offered himself as a listening post to Stacey, who'd wanted to talk through her logic problem.

Kim hadn't seen Bryant slap him on the back when he'd done a good job or have a private laugh with him about something either she or Stacey had said. There was not one ounce of man banter between them.

It narked her no end that her boss had seen something she hadn't, so she'd endured every activity in the hope some common ground might be found.

Right now, the three of them were on the bank of Llangorse Lake, trying to make a raft formed from four empty drums, four planks of wood and about a mile length of string.

And she could hardly bear the pain of watching them quietly working separately as the three other teams appeared to be communicating effectively and working on one joint at a time.

Her team was going to lose.

She spat the gag out of her mouth for the second time.

'Bryant, Penn's right. Your knot is going to—'

'Okay, West Mids is disqualified,' Jock shouted from behind.

She and her team turned to look.

He wasn't joking.

'Bloody hell, I was only—'

'Telling them what to do,' he said, reaching her. 'Which wasn't the object of the exercise. I gave you the benefit of the doubt once, but you just couldn't help—'

'Don't punish them for my—'

'You were warned.'

'I want to lodge an appeal,' she said, seeing the annoyance on the faces of her colleagues.

'Go ahead, appeal,' he invited.

'To who?'

'Me.'

'Well that's not gonna work, is it? You're the one who—'

'Appeal heard and decision upheld. Still DQ'd,' he said as team Cheshire launched their raft into the water.

'Damn it,' she said.

'They weren't even doing a bad job,' Jock said, glancing over at the abandoned raft. 'I reckon they'd have been second in the water and would have got across first.' He lowered his voice. 'There's a fair bit more weight on the Cheshire team.' He shrugged. 'You should have trusted them to—'

'I have total trust in my team,' she snapped, putting an end to the jokey banter.

'You trust them to do things your way. There's a difference,' he said as her team approached.

She scowled at him, and he sidled away.

'Okay, guys, I'm sorry. I should have kept my mouth shut,' she said, hearing the sound of a siren in the distance. Although a common sound back in the Black Country, it seemed out of place bouncing off the Welsh mountains.

'We were almost there, guv,' Bryant said, wiping his hands on his jeans.

The siren grew closer.

'The knots were all sound,' Penn added.

'I just wanted you guys to be first in the water.'

Stacey shook her head. 'Boss, we were... where on earth is that coming from?' she asked, turning towards the road that ran alongside the lake.

Everyone else had turned to look as a squad car screeched into the car park.

'A bit extreme, Jock. Disqualification wasn't enough?' she asked as the course leader moved to stand beside them.

She idly wondered who amongst the other teams had been up to no good.

'It's one of ours, guv,' Bryant said as two police officers exited the vehicle.

'What the hell?' Kim asked as they both headed straight for her.

'DI Stone, can you please come with us?'

She turned to her team. 'Am I being punked, guys?'

Their expressions told her this had nothing to do with them.

The rest of the police teams had left the water and were watching with interest.

'Jock?'

He shrugged and shook his head.

'Marm, we really must insist that you—'

'Insist all you like,' she said, squaring up to them. 'I'm not going anywhere until you explain what's going on.'

'We have instructions, marm, strict instructions from DCI Woodward to collect you and bring you back to—'

'Where's my bloody phone?' she asked, turning to the others.

'Back at base camp,' Jock answered.

Damn it. She needed to call Woody to find out what the hell was going on.

'Get him on the radio,' she ordered the taller of the two males – the one who had done all the talking.

'Marm, if you could just cooperate and get in the car...'

'I've told you. I'm not...' Her words trailed away as the talking officer took her elbow.

'Get your fucking hands off me,' she said, shaking her arm from his grip. 'And I dare you to touch me again.'

She could see his discomfort growing. 'Marm, please...'

'I don't even know you,' she said, taking a step back.

He took out his ID. 'Sergeant Tovey, officer with the tactical driving unit, and we have instructions to return you... by force if necessary,' he said, reaching for her elbow again.

'Guv, you'd best just go,' Bryant said as she dodged the officer's grip.

'Thanks for your support,' she snapped, although she wasn't sure what exactly she expected him to do.

'Marm, DCI Woodward warned us you wouldn't come quietly, but he did say he would explain everything once we get you back.'

Explain what? her mind screamed as he reached for her for the third time.

'Don't even think about it,' she warned.

The second officer appeared to be doing little more than admire the scenery.

She sighed heavily.

'Okay, I'll come but don't touch me again.' She turned to her team. 'Guys...'

'We'll be right behind,' Bryant answered. 'Once we've packed everything up. We'll see you back at the station.'

Kim began walking towards the squad car, trying to make sense of the situation. Why hadn't Woody just called her phone? She would have got the message eventually. If it was a new case that needed their attention, why not contact Jock and tell him to send them back immediately? What possible situation could warrant this type of urgency?

She slid into the back seat of the squad car as the talker took the driver's seat.

The silent one took a last look around the area before getting into the front passenger seat.

He nodded and the talker started the car.

She hadn't really taken much notice of the second officer. He hadn't spoken or interacted with her in any way. She took a good look now and saw what Bryant had already noted.

The silent officer was armed.

TWO

'Sir, would you like to tell me what the hell is going on?' Kim asked before her new minders had even closed the door behind them.

It had taken less than an hour to blue light her back from the Welsh countryside into the heart of the Black Country.

After her seventh attempt at gleaning a clue from her companions had been met with stony silence, she'd given up and counted down the miles until she could ask for herself. They had taken Woody's instruction seriously and deposited her in her boss's office.

'Sit down, Stone.'

'Sir, we have this same conversation every time and I've told you I prefer—'

'I said sit.'

She hesitated for just a second. Better to get it over with so she could make a start on whatever it was she'd been summoned back to do.

'You know one of them was armed,' she said, nodding towards the door.

'At my request.'

'You gave instruction to shoot me if I didn't get in the car?'

She saw the ghost of a smile pass over his lips. She blinked and it was gone.

'The armed officer was not for your cooperation. He was for your protection.'

'From what? I haven't yet met anyone who warrants that level of—'

'Symes has escaped.'

'Wh... What?'

'He's free. He's out there, and as far as we know, he hasn't forgiven you. We both know you're still top of his list.'

Kim sat back in the chair. Symes was by far the single most evil person she had ever met. He was a man that made her arch nemesis, Alexandra Thorne, look like a teddy bear.

Every muscle in Symes's body was driven by anger and hate. His only joy came from inflicting pain.

Their paths had crossed a few years back when he'd been involved in the abduction of two nine-year-old girls. For all his time and effort, the man's only demand had been the promise of inflicting as much pain as he wanted on the little girls once the money was received. He wanted no share of the ransom though, and his interest was not sexual. His payment was the pure enjoyment he would receive from causing pain.

Luckily, she and the team had foiled the plan and returned the girls to safety before he could harm them, but the physical struggle between herself and Symes – and a piece of glass from a broken light bulb – had resulted in him losing the sight in one eye.

He had never forgiven her, and while imprisoned he had become obsessed with getting revenge. She'd become aware of a previous attempt to escape and track her down which had been thwarted when another sicko from her past had chosen to recreate the most traumatic events of her life. She'd thought that was the end of it, but she should have guessed that Symes's hatred of her ran deeper than that.

'It appears he began work on his new plan immediately. He's been very busy getting rehabilitated.'

'Rehabilitation isn't an option for Symes,' Kim said.

'Agreed, but his many hours with the prison chaplain paid off when his wife died two weeks ago.'

'What wife?'

'The one he married nine months ago knowing she was terminally ill.'

'You are kidding me?'

Woody shook his head.

She was sure it was as much a mystery to him as it was to her how much female attention men attracted while incarcerated. It was fair to say that Symes was not a looker. At six feet four inches, bald, and carrying around twenty-four stone in weight, he was no catch. The broken nose and glass eye did little to improve matters, and yet his fan mail had outnumbered every other prisoner at Featherstone.

'He married her just because he knew she was going to die?'

Woody nodded. 'The prison chaplain and psychologist were in agreement that attending the funeral was in the best interest of the prisoner, to help his abandonment issues and his deep-seated fear of rejection and—'

'Sir, you have to be joking?'

'I wish I was, Stone, but they really felt he was genuinely grieving.'

'Don't suppose an "I told you so" memo will put him back in the box, will it?'

'I'm afraid not.'

'Have the families of Charlie and Amy been informed?' she asked. He'd been promised the lives of two little girls and, despite the fact they were now in their teens, it was hard to know what warped direction his revenge would take.

'They have. They'll be taking precautions.'

'How long has he been on the run?' she asked.

'Twenty-four hours now.'

'Jesus, he could be anywhere.'

Even if his time inside had softened him, he was ex-forces and well trained in survival techniques.

She stood. She needed a minute alone to digest what he'd told her.

'Okay, I'll take—'

'Sit back down, Stone. We're far from done.'

The drama involved in her return to the station made more sense as she realised something.

She sat back down. 'They have no idea where he is, do they?'

Woody hesitated before shaking his head. 'He feigned chest pains on the way to the cemetery, and they stopped the van to administer first aid.'

Kim shook her head in disbelief at the naivety. 'Overpowered them both?'

'One is in intensive care and the other has a serious concussion. Onboard cameras caught most of it, but they obviously didn't catch which way he went. There was a report on the lunchtime news, so he's not going to be free for long.'

Kim raised an eyebrow. The man was resourceful. He'd think nothing of murdering an entire family for a good meal and a bed for the night.

She'd been completely ignorant of the whole situation in the Welsh countryside; no phone, no television, no news. She was glad to be back in spite of the circumstances.

'Okay, sir, I'll—'

'They don't expect him back, Stone.'

He let the meaning of his words settle between them before continuing. 'Before he left, he gave all his possessions away to other prisoners.'

'He doesn't mind getting killed in the process of what he aims to do,' she said.

'I'd say he expects it. There's only one thing he feels that strongly about and that's you.'

'Enough to carry out a suicide mission?' she asked.

'Looks that way.' He folded his hands together in front of him. 'You need to disappear for a while; go and stay with a family member.'

'Got none of those.'

'Friends.'

'Got even less of those.'

'Someone who can stand to be around you for long periods of time?'

'Nope. Sorry. I got nothing.'

'Come on, Stone. There has to be someone, somewhere you can go to stay out of the way for now.'

'Sir, there's no one, and even if there was, I wouldn't go. I have a job to do and he's not going to chase me out of it.'

'The job is no good to you if you're dead, Stone.'

'Absolutely, sir, but I don't plan on getting dead any time soon. I'll be extra careful, and I'll even let Bryant follow me home if it'll help.'

The end of her sentence was met with a knock at the door.

'One minute,' he called.

'You won't even consider taking a leave of absence until he's safely behind bars?'

'Only if you can persuade the criminals to take that same leave as I do.'

He sighed heavily and shook his head.

'Sir, I'll do whatever you tell me to. I'll take any kind of precaution you want to throw at me. Just don't stop me doing my job.'

He tipped his head and narrowed his eyes. 'Any precaution?'

'Yes.'

'And you'll follow instruction?'

'Absolutely.'

'Somehow I knew this would be your response, so I took the liberty of arranging a little extra protection for you.'

'Sir?'

'Come in,' he shouted at the door.

It opened and revealed the person behind it.

Kim threw back her head as genuine laughter forced its way from her stomach and out of her mouth.

THREE

Kim was still laughing when Leanne King closed the door behind her.

She quickly became aware that no one was laughing with her. Any hope she had that Leanne's presence was an elaborate hoax to take the sting out of the news about Symes was fading fast.

'Is this some kind of sick joke?' she asked her boss as Leanne crossed the room.

He shook his head.

'You're putting me in the care of someone who hates my guts. Good call. She'll be sitting outside my house with a flashing neon sign and one of those massive pointing fingers shouting, "She's right here. Come and get her."'

'No, she won't.'

'Well, okay, maybe not the finger but—'

'I mean she won't be outside. She'll be in your house.'

Kim shook her head. 'Oh no.'

'If you want to keep working, you have no choice.'

'What's she gonna do, sit on the end of my bed? A little bit creepy.'

'That's a thought that's just as disturbing to me, Stone,' Leanne said, offering her a stony look.

'And you can be quiet,' Kim said. 'But, sir...'

'You have a spare room. Consider it taken for a short while. The minute Symes is back in custody, you get your house back.'

'Sir, I really don't want—'

'Fine, there's a nice little safe house in Norfolk that we use...'

'Okay, okay. She can stay.'

'Well, thank you for such a gracious invitation,' Leanne offered.

Kim looked at her properly for the first time. There was no amusement in her expression or her tone.

It was safe to say the two of them had not hit it off when they'd met on a recent case.

From the outset, Leanne had obstructed their investigation into the murder of a man they later learned was in the witness protection programme. She had continued the charade of being a family member instead of a witness protection officer long enough to have Kim's team chasing their own tails. In addition, her cold, stubborn demeanour had done nothing to endear her to anyone.

'Why you?' Kim asked pointedly.

'It's my job.'

'No rapists, murderers or mob bosses available at the minute?'

'No.'

'Quite the talker, isn't she?'

'I'll let you continue this conversation somewhere other than my office,' Woody said, standing to signal the meeting was over.

A movement outside caught his attention. 'And I think your team just drove into the car park.'

'Thank you, sir,' Kim said, standing, although she wasn't sure exactly what she was thanking him for.

She waited until the door closed behind them both before she turned to Leanne. 'So, how is this gonna work?'

'You do everything I tell you and we'll be fine,' Leanne said with a shrug.

'Well, that's your first problem, but I meant the fact we can't stand the sight of each other.'

'I haven't much liked any of the people I've been responsible for,' Leanne admitted.

'Comforting. Also, that one of them is dead, but hey ho, we all have bad work days, I suppose.'

Kim was rewarded by a flash of anger in Leanne's blue eyes and a line of tension in her square jaw.

Kim understood more now about protection officers than she had before. She knew that they were responsible for the safety of some of the sickest people in the country. She understood the tight emotional rein needed to put your own life on the line, sometimes for quite despicable characters. She also understood that they worked solitary and in complete secrecy, unable to share any details with friends or loved ones. One slip and an entire family could be wiped out.

'So, you're gonna follow me everywhere?' Kim asked, taking the stairs down to the squad room.

'Yes,' Leanne answered, keeping step with her.

'Well, ain't that gonna be a barrel of laughs?'

She entered the squad room and wasted no time.

'Hey guys, remember Leanne? Feel free to be as pleasant to her as she is to you.'

Both Penn and Stacey raised a hand in greeting while offering her a questioning glance. Bryant's back was to her, as he was on the phone.

'Our old friend Symes has escaped custody and, instead of getting himself off to the South of France, he's gonna come looking for me. He's gonna try and break every bone in my body, but don't worry because Leanne's gonna stop him.'

Their expressions took on equal measures of shock. She knew she was being flippant and blasé about the whole thing, but she had barely been given time to get her head around what was going on before Leanne bloody King had been thrust back into her life. The hits just kept on coming.

Her team responded as expected.

'How the hell...?'

'What the...?'

'Doesn't matter. He's out and he's not planning on getting caught. More later, but, most importantly, did we win?'

Penn held up a small silver cup with a plaque engraved with the word 'Winners'.

'Quite right,' she said as Penn placed their hard-earned trophy on the windowsill next to the coffee machine.

'Yep, won by a country mile. The second team only—'

'Hey, guv,' Bryant said, ending the call, 'we're wanted—'

'Thanks for putting your phone down to—'

'It's your phone actually,' he said, tossing it towards her.

She caught it as he turned a frown on Leanne.

'I just finished explaining to the—'

'Save it,' he said, holding up his hand. 'Explain in the car. That was Keats. He's got a crime scene in Pedmore, and it's got our name all over it.'

'Not so fast,' Leanne said, holding up her hand. 'It's imperative that I carry out a full initial briefing with you and your team.'

'Err...' Kim said, looking towards Bryant.

'Guv, we gotta go. Apparently this crime scene is growing old already.'

'Umm...'

'Stone, your team needs to understand the dangers from the outset.'

Kim suddenly felt herself caught between a rock and a hard place.

'Okay, everyone to the car. We'll do it on the way,' she said.

Oh, this was all going to work out well, she thought, heading for the door.

FOUR

'And Leanne is what stands between you and Symes – a man that kills people with his bare hands?' Bryant asked, heading out of the town centre.

'I am here,' Leanne offered from her position in the back seat of the car, sandwiched between Stacey and Penn.

'That was more about Symes than you,' Kim offered.

Leanne said nothing.

'No offence intended,' Bryant agreed. 'I can think of no single person who can stop that man.'

Kim could see the concern etched into his features and she appreciated it.

'What are the options?' she asked.

'Army, National Guard, SAS, all of them, or better yet hide you in a cave somewhere until he's safely back behind bars.'

'Yeah, cos I'm all for that option,' Kim offered.

'Ditto,' Leanne added.

'Boss, how do you even prepare for something like this?' Stacey asked from directly behind her.

'Good point,' she said, turning in her seat. 'Leanne, the floor is all yours. Brief away.'

'Okay, well, basically as you're the people that spend most time with the target, you're all at risk now. From what I understand, he'll use anything he can to get to the target, and if he has to grab one of you to force her out of the woodwork, he will. You all need to take precautionary measures until he's caught.'

'Such as?' Penn asked.

'Change your journey routes to and from work. Try to make sure you're not alone at any time. Don't visit unfamiliar places. Make sure your homes are secure and that you're aware of any changes to your surroundings. Don't answer your doors if you're not expecting any visitors, and if you suspect anything at all is amiss, call it in immediately.'

Kim was forced to acknowledge, if only to herself, that Leanne seemed to know what she was talking about.

'Should I tell anyone in my street?' Kim asked.

'Don't tell anyone anything until I've done a full home assessment – but you should inform family and friends to call if they're planning to visit.'

Kim turned to Bryant. 'You planning on visiting?'

'Nope.'

'Done,' she said as Bryant began to slow the car down. The five miles from Halesowen to Pedmore had passed in a matter of minutes.

Bryant pulled into a driveway that still wasn't full despite the ambulance, fire engine, squad cars and forensic vans. Beyond a row of elaborate topiary structures was a mock Georgian property with a three-car garage to the right.

They all exited the car, and Kim jumped when she found Leanne standing right behind her.

'Really?' she asked, waving her hands around the area. There were more uniforms than a passing-out parade, not to mention her own team members.

'Where you go I go,' Leanne said simply.

'Okay, but be prepared to see what real police officers do.'

Kim couldn't help the barb before it came out of her mouth. It still rankled that as a fellow police officer she'd done nothing to help one of their previous investigations.

'Ah, here she is,' Keats said, stepping out of the tent that had been erected at the front door. 'Along with what looks like half of CID.'

'Safety in numbers,' she said.

'And who is your friend?' he asked, looking at Leanne.

'Not important,' she answered.

'Did you bring her back from the idyllic Welsh country-side?' he asked. 'Where you couldn't even stay quiet when bound and gagged.'

'How the hell do you know about...?'

'I have friends in high places, Inspector.'

'Claiming a direct line to God is a little fatuous, Keats, even for you.'

'Jock is an old friend of—'

'Good for you,' Kim said. Enough time had been wasted. 'Now what do we have?'

'Report of smoke coming from the residence at 7 a.m. this morning.'

'Keats, it's 6 p.m. on a Sunday evening. Why am I only hearing about it now?'

'Only cleared for entry an hour ago, which is when we found them.'

Kim looked up at the property. Two storeys and two dormer windows. A family home.

'How many?'

'Four. All deceased.'

'Shit.'

'Adult male, adult female, teenage boy, teenage girl.'

Jesus, a whole family wiped out by the looks of it.

'Any idea what caused the fire?' Kim asked, understanding her role in this tragedy. The manner of death needed to be agreed on by the pathologist and herself before the removal process could commence.

'Don't know,' Keats answered as Mitch appeared in the doorway.

'Where did it start?' Kim asked, taking steps forward to enter.

'Not sure yet.'

'Keats, are you trying to be obtuse?'

He shook his head. 'Waiting for Nigel Adams to arrive, but it's not going to help us any. It wasn't the fire that killed them. Gunshot wounds, every one of them. Looks like murder-suicide to me.'

Kim stopped walking. She had assumed a house fire had claimed the lives of the family.

'You're telling me that Dad got a gun and shot up his whole family.'

'I'm telling you it looks something like that, except the person holding the gun was Mum.'

FIVE

Kim followed Keats into the house once attired in protective clothing. The pathologist had refused entry to more than two of them, and there had been no question that those two were herself and Bryant. Stacey and Penn had been dispatched to search the exterior of the property and check in with the constables on witness statements. Leanne had been instructed to remain outside. The woman had attempted to argue with Keats, and Kim had silently wished her luck. There were few things Keats guarded more fiercely than an active crime scene.

As she passed through the tents, she was still processing what he'd told her. Although she'd never attended a murder-suicide scene, she knew that in cases such as these it was normally the father that took the life of his family, often due to guarding a secret or financial ruin.

She immediately thought of a case in Shropshire in 2008. A fifty-year-old man had shot dead his wife and teenage daughter along with their horses and dogs before setting alight their million-pound home. The investigation had quickly determined that the man was heavily in debt, and had most likely killed his family in an effort to protect them from the certain poverty they were going to face.

Looking at the house, Kim immediately wondered if they were going to face a similar story here.

'All family members are up there,' Keats offered.

Kim mounted the stairs, realising that she was heading away from the fire damage, as the lingering smell of smoke grew weaker, and she saw no damage to the lower hallway or the winding stairs that deposited her at a spacious landing.

Attractive cupboards and drawer sets were placed against the wall spaces between the numerous doors. Each piece of furniture held either a decorative lamp, delicate ornament or framed photo. No surface was cluttered, just styled yet homely.

Although the carpet was good quality, a trodden path could be seen leading to all of the rooms, with only the outer edges retaining its former glory.

'Where first?' Keats asked.

'Can we follow her likely path?' Kim asked, finding the use of the female pronoun jarring in such a situation.

'Impossible to know at this stage, but this first door here is the room belonging to Rosalind Daynes, seventeen-year-old daughter of Helen and William.'

Kim took a breath and entered the room, aware of Bryant's presence behind her. Twenty-four hours ago this bedroom had been filled with life and was now prematurely still.

'Jesus,' Bryant whispered.

Like her, she suspected his gaze had gone straight to the bed.

A girl with black curly hair lay on her back with the quilt cover gathered at her waist, exposing her upper half. The thin-strapped, white vest top had a red circular stain with an epicentre right between her breasts. Trails of blood had crawled away from the circle and seeped down into the bed covers.

She wore only a delicate chain around her neck and a Fitbit

watch on her wrist. Ear pods were visible, and a phone rested on the pillow beside her head.

The bed wasn't scuffed and there was no evidence of a struggle. Rosalind Daynes appeared to have been shot at close range while she slept. Kim guessed her death had been instant and that she'd been spared seeing her mother's face looking down at her. But how had her mother looked down at her resting child and pulled the trigger?

She tore her eyes away from the body that could have been a normal sleeping teenager, if only the quilt was pulled up a little higher. Along with the sadness, she couldn't help feeling relief that the girl hadn't known who had done this to her.

The room itself was unremarkably normal. The wallpaper was a little dated but covered with posters of what appeared to be rap stars with lots of gold jewellery and single names. Small piles of clothes littered the floor around the wardrobe and a tall chest of drawers.

Kim wandered over to the desk, which looked as though it was used for just about anything other than studying. A high-tech computer and video camera were surrounded by piles of cosmetics and hair clips, combs and slides. Everything left haphazardly with every intention to return.

Kim felt a stab of sadness that the teenager had never made it out of this room. At seventeen she'd been on the cusp of adulthood, but she would never experience life out there on her own.

'It's not going to get any better, I'm afraid,' Keats said gravely as she headed for the door.

She crossed the hallway and entered a slightly smaller bedroom that was just a little bit messier than the one before.

'Bloody hell,' she whispered at the sight of the teenage boy, lying face down, dressed in blue Fortnite pyjamas, limbs akimbo, with a similar bloodstain on his back.

'Lewis Daynes, turned fifteen a week ago,' Keats offered from the door.

Unlike his sister, Lewis appeared to be a messy sleeper. The quilt was entangled in his lower limbs, and his arms were flung either side of him. A game controller rested by his right hand. She could imagine he'd fallen asleep, his mind still racing through the games he'd been playing with his friends online. Had there been any clue that he wouldn't wake up and play those same games again? There were no headphones like his sister and Kim wondered if Lewis had been the first to die.

'What the hell was going through her mind?' Bryant asked beside her.

She didn't have an answer. There was nothing she could conjure that made any sense.

The sadness of the scene she was witnessing was weighing heavily upon Kim as she moved towards the master bedroom.

This scene was more chaotic than the previous two. No area of the other rooms even hinted at a struggle, but in here, her gaze took in the fallen items from the bedside cabinet. The body of a male was at the corner of the bed dressed only in boxer shorts. From the discarded quilt, it appeared that he'd got out of bed and was heading towards the door.

The woman appeared to have shot him from the doorway before placing the gun underneath her chin and blowing a hole in the side of her head. The gun lay by her side with her finger still on the trigger. Her three-quarter-length nightgown fell just below her knees.

'Mr and Mrs Daynes, I presume.'

'It is indeed,' Keats answered.

'May we?' Mitch asked from the doorway. The photographer stood behind him.

Kim took one last look before heading back into the hallway.

'Any signs of an intruder?' she asked the techie.

He shook his head. 'All doors and windows locked or closed,

and the fire crew broke the deadbolt on the kitchen door to gain access.'

Kim nodded her understanding.

Forensic evidence gathering was going to be a nightmare for Mitch and his team. Three separate crime scenes to comb.

'How long until you can remove them all?' Kim asked.

'At least the early hours of the morning,' Keats answered.

Kim understood the delay. There was a lot to process first.

'We'll start background tomorrow to try and—'

'Boss, could you come down please,' called Penn from the bottom of the stairs.

She heard shouting from outside.

Oh, please God, not yet, she thought heading down the stairs. There was no way she wanted relatives in the house.

'May I help you?' she asked, stepping out of the property to where two men were being contained by Penn, Stacey and a couple of officers. Leanne had moved to the side and offered no assistance at all.

Both men were slim and attractive, one dark-haired, one light.

The fair-headed one took a step forward. Penn's arm instantly raised like a car park barrier. The man looked at it with disgust and knocked it away.

'Zachary Daynes,' he said by way of introduction. 'Where's my family?'

She looked to the dark-haired male who had put a steadying hand on the other man's shoulder.

'Gavin Daynes,' he offered in a calmer tone.

'Brothers?' she asked.

Gavin held up his left hand to display a gold band. 'Husbands.'

'Got it, Mr Daynes. Would you please come with me?' she asked gently.

He shook his head and lurched for the barrier. Bryant was ready and pushed him gently back.

'Let me through,' he hissed, and for the first time Kim got a whiff of alcohol on his breath.

'Please, Mr Daynes, come with me.'

She needed to move him away from the doorway before he saw or heard something he didn't need to.

With Gavin's help, she was able to steer him towards a park-style bench just out of the cordon area.

'We had a call from the neighbours,' Gavin offered. 'Something about a fire,' he said as she raised the tape for them to exit.

'I have to help,' Zachary said, turning back, but Kim had a firm hold of his arm.

'Mr Daynes, I'm afraid that there's nothing you can do for them now.'

'Wh-What?' he asked, looking from her back to the front door.

She shook her head.

His legs buckled and he all but fell onto the bench.

'Are... are... you saying they're dead?'

'I'm afraid so,' she said, delaying even for a moment the inevitable. One piece of horrific detail at a time was enough.

Gavin's hand had tightened on his husband's shoulder as his mouth fell open.

'Rozzie and Lewis?'

'I'm sorry, Mr Daynes.'

'Jesus Christ,' Gavin said as Zachary's head fell forward and his body began to shake.

'I'm so sorry,' she said.

'From the fire?' Gavin asked, blinking away the tears.

The inevitable had arrived much sooner than she'd hoped.

'Not directly, no.'

Zachary's head shot up. 'Wh-What do you mean?'

'It would appear that the death of your family is not linked to the fire, but I can say no more at the moment.'

Zachary's tears ceased for a second before rage filled his face. He stood and stepped into her space.

'Officer, I demand to know the truth. They are my fucking family.'

Kim took a step back. 'I understand that, and you will be the first to know once we fully understand what took place here, but you can't enter the house at this time.'

Gavin pulled his husband back a step.

'I don't understand,' Zachary said, shaking his head as the tears started again. 'How have they died? Were they all in the same room? Was it a gas boiler or...?'

'Mr Daynes, please go home for now. A family liaison officer will be sent over to your address, and we'll update you as soon as possible.'

Her glance backwards at Bryant signalled her invitation to him to approach.

As Gavin offered her colleague their address, Kim placed a hand on Zachary's arm.

'We will update you as soon as we possibly can, Mr Daynes.'

'Got it,' Bryant said, closing his notebook.

'Should we speak to anyone?' Gavin asked, continuing to support his husband. 'Zach has a twin sister.'

'Immediate family members only at this point and we'll speak with you the minute we can give more information.'

She offered a look to Gavin, who appeared to be a steadying influence despite fighting his own emotions.

'I'll get him home,' Gavin said, guiding his husband away from the house.

'Never gets any easier, eh, guv?' Bryant asked as Gavin supported Zachary back to the car.

She watched as the pair got into the car and Gavin pulled his husband towards him to comfort him.

'Lots of external cameras, boss,' Stacey said as they all drew together.

Kim nodded her understanding. The action all appeared to have taken place inside the house.

'Only one set of neighbours within a quarter mile. Their statements have been taken and are on the way back to the station.'

'Okay, guys, little more we can do tonight,' she said as the engine to the Dayneses' car kicked into life.

As the BMW pulled out of the drive, another vehicle came into view.

'Aww... shit,' Kim said, knowing only one person who drove a white Audi TT.

Kim watched as *Dudley Star* reporter Tracy Frost parked right next to Bryant's Astra Estate, meaning they had to pass her to leave.

'Want me to have a word?' Bryant asked.

Kim shook her head. 'Frost is a spot best squeezed before it gets the chance to fester.'

Knowing Frost would wait them out to get her story, Kim headed towards the cordon. There was no more she could do here until the bodies had been removed from the scene.

Tomorrow would be soon enough to piece together the tragedy that had unfolded here.

She didn't bother to look for Leanne, knowing she wouldn't be far behind.

'Ah, here comes my favourite detective inspector,' Frost said, leaning against her car and blocking Kim's path into Bryant's car. 'And her band of merry men... and women,' she said, casting her gaze over the whole team.

'And here's my least favourite reporter.'

'Who's your friend?' Frost asked, ignoring the jibe.

'Reporter for the *Worcester News*. All access.'

'That's bollocks, but even if it were true, I'd wish her the best of luck.'

Kim was unsure if Frost would ever fully recover from being present at one of the most horrific crime scenes Kim had ever witnessed. Seeing a naked man spread-eagled on a roller cage with most of his skin missing was not a sight that went away easily.

'Not really interested anyway,' Frost said, dismissing Leanne with a glance. 'More interested in what went on here.'

'What makes you think something went on here?' Kim asked, glancing back at the collection of emergency service vehicles, squad cars, activity and tents blocking the front door.

'Intuition,' Frost shot back.

'There was a fire,' Kim said, walking around the car to get to the door that Frost wasn't blocking.

'And here was me thinking the fire tenders were here for a stranded cat. I can smell the bloody smoke myself, Stone.'

'Keep up the good work, Frost. You'll make a good reporter one day,' she said, opening the passenger door.

'What about the gunshots?'

Kim paused. 'What shots?'

Frost shrugged. 'I heard there were shots.'

Kim moved closer. 'There were no shots. If any shots appear in your initial report, you'd best hope that car of yours can—'

'You know, Stone, you should be sick of threatening me by now.'

'Oh, that'll never grow old, but there were no shots, got it?'

Frost sighed heavily. 'You might want to put a gag on the Porters next door, who seem happy to share everything they saw and heard.'

Kim glanced at Bryant, who took out his phone and moved away. He would ensure an officer was dispatched next door to advise them not to talk to anyone.

Kim knew where her first port of call was going to be in the morning.

'No shots,' she repeated.

Frost rolled her eyes. 'Okay, family tragedy it is until the press conference.'

'Where you will get first question,' Kim said, appreciating the heads-up on the neighbours.

'Careful, Stone, folks will be thinking—'

'Now fuck off. There, that should stop any thoughts,' Kim said, swinging the car door open, leaving Frost with no choice but to move.

She stifled her irritation. She could expect no better from the reporter. Of course she'd manipulated a conversation with the neighbours who obviously knew no better than to speak to anyone about what they'd heard.

Bryant ended his call and nodded in her direction, signalling that it had been taken care of. An officer had been dispatched to advise them accordingly.

'Okay, what's the plan now?' Kim asked, once the five of them were in the car. She turned to Leanne. 'I'm assuming your car is parked at the station.'

Leanne shrugged. 'What would you normally do now?'

'Bryant's not normally on carpool duty with the whole team in the car, but as Penn has no vehicle because we've just returned from Wales, I assume he'll drop these two at home before taking me home, ready for a 7 a.m. briefing tomorrow.'

'Then that's what we do. Everything stays the same for now except that I come along too.'

Kim turned back in her seat.

That was the only part of the plan she had a problem with.

SIX

It was almost eight when Bryant pulled up outside her house.

'Guv, do you want me to...?'

'I'm fine, Bryant. Get off home and I swear I'll call you if I need to.'

He didn't look reassured, but he nodded his acceptance anyway.

She waved him off before putting the key in her front door.

'You're not really prepared for this, are you?' Kim asked. 'No case, no overnight bag, no change of clothes.'

'I'll be fine.'

'Okay, but prepare to be mauled once I open this door.'

'No offence, Stone, but you're not my type.'

Kim looked for any evidence of humour in her face, but it gave away nothing.

Everything about her day was temporarily forgotten once she laid eyes on Barney, who was wagging his tail and turning in circles.

'Come here, boy,' she said, lowering herself to the ground. She hadn't seen him since dropping him at Charlie's at the

crack of dawn the previous morning before heading off to
Wales.

'Good boy,' she said, capturing him and hugging him tightly.
He raised his head and offered low growly noises as he trampled
her legs. She didn't mind it one little bit.

For a brief moment she forgot there was anyone else in the
room.

'You sure love that dog, eh?'

'Oh yeah.'

'Get rid of it,' Leanne said, walking past her.

'Excuse me?' Kim said as her hand stilled in Barney's fur.

His tail stopped wagging as though he understood Leanne's
words.

'Ignore the nasty lady, boy,' she said, ruffling his fur. 'She
doesn't understand I'd get rid of most of my team before I got
rid of you.'

'He's a vulnerability. It's my job to rid you of as many of
those as I can.'

'Then your job sucks. Move on to the next thing cos Barney
ain't going nowhere.'

'Have it your own way, but if Symes wants to hurt you that
badly, he'll think nothing of killing your dog. He'll do it just to hurt
you, to get a reaction, even just to throw you off your game, distract
your focus. Where's the dog been while you were in Wales?'

'I have a neighbour, Charlie, that takes care of him.'

'Then you're putting him in danger too – and all of those
things are bad enough, but that's not even the worst thing he
could do.'

'Worse than kill my dog?'

'Yep, he could use your dog to lure you somewhere because
I'm pretty sure you'd go.'

'Absolutely.'

'Then get rid of it.'

'Stop calling him *it*. His name is Barney and he already fucking hates you.'

'I'll live. He's your biggest vulnerability. One of the few things you care about.'

Despite herself, Kim could see the logic of her words. If Symes ever got hold of Barney... well, it just didn't bear thinking about.

'I'll take him to Charlie's in the morning.'

'Not good enough. Symes will soon work that out.'

'Charlie visits his sister in Prestatyn every month.'

'That'll do. Get him to go now and take the dog. Where are the keys to your window locks?'

Kim shrugged. 'Dunno – they're around somewhere.'

Leanne blew air out of her cheeks as she continued to walk around.

Kim followed Barney to the treat cupboard and took out a pig's ear – a rare treat but she'd missed him.

'You want coffee?' Kim asked, trying to get used to someone else in her space. Her last guest had been a stay-over mercy mission for Frost. It had been one night but had felt much longer. She sure hoped they caught Symes soon. At least she'd grown a smidgeon of respect for the reporter.

'Got anything herbal?'

'Water.'

'But hot?'

'Hot water.'

'I'll take coffee.'

Good, cos that was pretty much all she had.

She noted that Barney's eyes followed Leanne wherever she went despite his focus on his big treat. Kim felt the exact same way as Leanne paused at the bottom of the stairs.

'Anything up here you don't want me to see?'

'No, I keep all my sex slaves in the garage.'

'Get 'em dressed cos that's my next stop,' she said without missing a beat.

'No sense of humour,' Kim said to Barney.

'But excellent hearing,' came the response from the stairs.

Kim shook her head. They'd been in her home five minutes and it felt like hours. She briefly considered asking Woody if she could join the task force searching for Symes. The quicker they found him, the quicker Leanne would be gone. If he was caught by morning, she wouldn't have to send Barney away.

The thought of that prompted her to busy herself making a pot of coffee until Leanne reappeared.

Without speaking, Leanne headed through the kitchen door into the garage.

Kim followed, realising that the woman barely noted the contents of the property while she looked only for vulnerabilities. She probably could have had a couple of sex slaves in there and Leanne would only have noticed if the chains weren't secure.

'Did I pass?' Kim asked as Leanne brushed past her back into the kitchen.

'I don't suppose it's any coincidence that the most secure part of your house is where you keep your motorbike?'

'Probably not,' Kim admitted.

The Kawasaki Ninja was her second love, coming only after Barney.

Kim pushed an empty mug towards her. 'Help yourself to coffee; milk and sweeteners on the side.'

Leanne took the mug to the machine as though in a self-service restaurant.

'And to answer your question, you failed miserably. Your door locks are as old as the house foundations. Your deadbolt chain is broken. The windows upstairs barely lock. You have no motion sensors, no CCTV, no door camera, no external lighting, no door contacts or—'

'Kitchen drawer,' Kim said suddenly.

'What?' Leanne asked, sipping her coffee.

'Window keys,' she said, opening the junk drawer. Sure enough, a key ring full of the little blighters stared back at her.

'I'm very reassured,' Leanne said, taking out her phone.

'What are you doing?'

'I've spent half the day watching you do your job, Inspector, and now it's time for me to do mine.'

She scrolled down her contacts and hit a number before moving away from the breakfast bar.

It sounded as though the call was answered immediately. Leanne launched into a list of letters and numbers that Kim didn't understand.

'And make sure you include a number nine,' she heard Leanne say before she went out of earshot.

Kim considered following to hear more, but her own phone ringing prevented her.

'No fucking way,' she said, seeing the contact name.

Grantley Care Home was not in the top 500 of who she wanted to speak to right now.

Only a couple of weeks ago she'd learned from her arch nemesis, Alexandra Thorne, that her mother was terminally ill.

The phone stopped ringing.

The home for the criminally insane was under strict instructions only to contact her if her mother passed away.

She understood how heartless she appeared, but her mother was solely responsible for the death of her twin brother, Mikey, who had died of starvation in her arms while they'd both been handcuffed to a radiator in a flat on the Hollytree Estate. Her mother's intention had been to kill them both.

The phone started to ring again.

Same number.

Perhaps it was the call she'd been expecting. Was she ready to take that call?

She grabbed her phone after spotting Leanne talking animatedly while walking round her back garden.

'Hello,' she answered shortly. The blood was pounding in her ears.

'It's Mary, Kim.'

'Yes,' she said, thinking, *Say it. Say it.*

'Kim, I'm ringing because she hasn't got long left. We're talking days.'

Kim said nothing. She'd readied herself for the words and they were nowhere to be seen.

'She didn't want to go to a hospice so we've made her as comfortable as we can here.'

Kim's mind screamed at the words she was hearing. 'Want' and 'comfortable'. Who cared about the monster's comfort? Was she suddenly supposed to give a shit about the woman who had ruined her life?

'I'm ringing for your sake, Kim.'

'I know,' she answered, feeling her throat thicken at the woman's tender tone. She'd been Kim's main contact at Grantley for over twenty-eight years. She had called periodically, offering Kim the opportunity to visit, and she had only accepted once: a couple of years ago when her mother, Patty, had hoodwinked the authorities into thinking that she was safe for release. Kim's presence at the hearing had disabused the panel of that opinion, when Patty had been goaded into revealing that she hadn't changed at all and was as dangerous as she'd been thirty years ago.

'I appreciate the call, Mary, but nothing's changed. I hate her as much now as I always did. There's no forgiveness in me.'

'I understand, but I just wanted you to know where we were and that you're welcome here any time.'

'Thanks, Mary.'

'Take care, Kim.'

She stared at the phone for a full minute after the call

ended. She knew that Mary would not bother her again. The kindly woman clearly felt that it would benefit her to offer her mother forgiveness.

But it wasn't in her. It just wasn't there.

'You know the lock on your back gate is knackered, don't you?' Leanne asked, walking back into the room.

Kim put down the phone and mentally shook herself back to reality. She had enough problems in the present without going looking for ones in the past.

'There's nothing back there,' Kim said. She only kept the back garden decent for Barney.

'So you won't have noticed that the house opposite has built a rockery wall, making scaling the fence into your garden a piece of piss.'

No, she hadn't known that. But more to the point. How had Leanne?

'It's pretty dark out there.'

'Oh, glad you've finally noticed,' Leanne said, glancing at her watch.

'Feel free to turn in for the night. It's been a long day,' Kim offered, just to get her out of sight. She was sure her inspection of the house had highlighted which was the spare room.

Leanne took a sip of her lukewarm coffee.

'I'm good, thanks, Inspector, and shortly you'll understand that for tonight there is a lot more to be done.'

'Who are you, bloody Scrooge? Are the spirits coming too?'

Leanne shook her head. 'I'm sure the penny will drop soon that you've got a damn sight more to worry about than ghosts.'

SEVEN

Symes pushed himself further into the shadows of the house at the end of the road.

He had watched her return with that woman but he had no idea who she was. A friend? A girlfriend? he had wondered initially.

His brief saunter up and down the street had confirmed that there was no police vehicle in the area. The local force had to know that he had escaped and that he was coming for her.

That was when it had dawned on him that the woman was a police officer, her protection. He had almost laughed out loud. The force clearly couldn't give two shits about her if that was the best they could offer. He would probably be doing them a favour once he got his hands on her because there was one thing for sure: they weren't getting the bitch back.

Being so close without prison bars between them was tantalising. Every limb ached to go to her right now, to take her apart bit by bit.

Every waking moment in that prison had been consumed with thoughts of what he would do to her, and there had never been any doubt in his mind that his opportunity would come.

It had presented itself in the form of do-gooders; nice people were so much easier to manipulate because they believed that everyone had a decent core. His plan had started with Gloria; lovely, trusting, gullible Gloria, whose letter he had dismissed until he'd read that last bit. The part that stated she hoped to hear from him before she died. It was in that moment that the plan had formed.

He had initially wondered if he could carry it off – not the wooing and courting of Gloria; he'd known that would be easy enough, but the other part of the plan.

He had taken the letter to the chaplain, who was a good man and welcomed any genuine attempt to reach out to Jesus. They had prayed right there and then for Gloria's health, and from that moment Symes had been a changed man. He picked no fights, minded his business, went to every session where he could display remorse for his crimes. He invited Gloria to visit him and showed her that she was right. He was misunderstood, he was sorry for what he'd done, and it was all out of the absence of love in his childhood. He knew that his every move and action would all, one day, get back to the decision makers. He took every opportunity he could to pray with the chaplain. He stopped writing to other women and focussed all his energy on Gloria. They were married exactly three months from the day he'd read her letter.

Charading as a nice person had become simpler as time went on. Once he learned how to separate his thoughts from his actions, it became easier. In the privacy of his cell he could fantasise as much as he liked about inflicting pain and violence as long as he kept those thoughts to himself.

He had remained devoted to Gloria until her death two weeks earlier. The bitch had hung on longer than he'd thought, and upon hearing the news, he'd hidden his delight behind brave, unshed tears and a quiet dignity.

He had respectfully requested the opportunity to attend her

funeral, agreeing to any measures deemed necessary so that he could say a proper goodbye to his courageous, adored wife.

Every building block had led him to this point, every counselling session, every prayer reading, every time he'd curtailed his natural tendencies, every time he'd walked away from a fight, every time he'd helped a fellow prisoner, every time he'd donned the mask of a decent human being. Everything had been for this one request.

He'd already heard of the recent Home Office directive that prisoners were to be offered attendance at funerals of close family members either in person or virtually. Joining by iPad had been no good for his plan, so he'd gone to town with the tears in his grief counselling session. And Margaret had come good for him. She'd bought it hook, line and sinker and had recommended a temporary pass for Gloria's funeral.

During the journey, the coughing fit and accompanying distress had forced the guards to pull over to check him, and the rest had been a piece of cake.

There were no words to describe his elation at finally removing the shackles both literally and physically. Once the cuffs were off, he let the pent-up rage within him finally explode. Yes, he'd continued beating the shit out of the two guards, even though they were unconscious, because he was enjoying himself. Yes, he had relished the sensation of flesh being pummelled into a bloody mess and the sound of bones breaking beneath his fist. He only knew that there was no more pretending to be a decent human being and that he was once again free to be himself.

His hands drew together. His fingertips touched the knuckles. He revelled in the broken skin and bruising he felt there. The discomfort filled him with joy.

He was now where he'd dreamed of being for years. He was on the cusp of fulfilling his dearest wish. He cared nothing for what happened to him once he'd achieved his goal.

'Soon, Stone, soon,' he whispered as he slinked back into the shadows.

As he moved away, he remembered again that day she had robbed him of his reward. His only payment had been the lives of those two little girls. She had taken that away from him together with the sight in his left eye.

Had she known then that in doing what she did, in rescuing little Charlie and Amy from his clutches, that she had, in fact, exchanged their two lives for her own?

EIGHT

'Well, I'm not sure what else your night entails but I'm taking Barney for his late-night walk.'

'No, you're not,' Leanne said easily as she checked her phone.

'Okay, Leanne,' Kim said, crossing her arms, 'I think we need some ground rules here before—'

'There's only one ground rule I'm aware of which is that you do as I say or you're off to Norfolk.'

'I swear this situation is not going to end well for—'

'Hit the pause button,' Leanne said as her phone dinged a message.

The first hint of a smile rested on her face as she read. 'Perfect timing.'

Kim watched as she headed for the front door and unlocked it. Kim wasn't aware Leanne had even locked it behind them.

'What the hell?' Kim asked as Barney issued a couple of low-throated growls.

Two men dressed in jeans and T-shirts passed Leanne carrying an assortment of boxes.

'Move aside, Stone,' Leanne instructed. 'Some of these are heavy.'

Kim could feel her temper rising. One stranger in her house was bad enough, but two more carrying goodness knew what was playing on her last nerve. It was her fucking home.

'Two more,' said the first male, heading back outside.

Kim called an anxious-looking Barney to her as she glanced outside at the grey Transit van parked on her drive.

'Leanne?' Kim growled.

'CCTV and security equipment. Gotta be done, Stone. You're in the dark ages here. We've got to have eyes and ears to give us the best chance of stopping him.'

'It's eleven o'clock at night.'

'You're detached.'

'Folks have still got ears,' she snapped.

'They'll be as quiet as they can, but it has to be done. Not that fussed if a couple of your neighbours cross you off their Christmas card list.'

Kim wasn't sure if her neighbours even sent Christmas cards. If they did, they didn't send them to her.

Kim itched to take out her phone and call Woody to demand this female demon be exorcised all the way out of her house.

It wasn't the fact of it being 11 p.m. on a Sunday night that stopped her. It was that it was 11 p.m. on *this* Sunday night, the very first night she was under instruction to do as she was told. If she started making waves this soon, Woody would remove her from active duty and send her to Norfolk without a second thought.

She stepped backwards into the kitchen and took Barney with her. She could feel his tension at having so many people in the house.

Kim couldn't help but wonder how Leanne had managed to arrange this so quickly – on a Sunday night no less. She'd been at break-ins where she'd sat and waited hours for a locksmith or a window boarder. Clearly these were not normal police contractors.

'Okay, guys, I want three passives in the back garden: if a mouse ventures in, I want him lit up like he's on a football pitch. Two AV twelves at the bottom of the garden, and a PTZ on the south-facing wall.' She paused for breath. 'Two passives on the front and a door cam.' She thought for a minute. 'And put a fixed on the front facing the gate.'

'That it?'

'You wish. You're gonna be here a while. There's no alarm system so I want a motion sensor aimed at every external door, door sensors on every internal door and glass-break detectors on every window, oh and a new chain on the front door along with a deadbolt. But do the outside work first to avoid upsetting the neighbours.'

'Got it. And what about your number nine?'

'Just pop that on the table in the hallway.'

'What's a number nine?' Kim called across the room.

'Special fried rice from the best takeaway in the Midlands.'

Jesus, these guys had even brought her food, Kim thought as the guys started unpacking boxes and working silently. Barney was still resting against her leg.

Fuck this. It was one thing making her feel uncomfortable in her own home, but Barney would keep his routine.

'Come on, boy,' she said, taking his lead from the cupboard. She needed to get out of her own house, wanted to escape the feeling inside her own stomach.

She headed to the hallway and reached for the footwear she'd removed when she'd entered.

'Nice boots,' Leanne said, leaning against the door frame. 'Going somewhere?'

'Yes, I'm taking my dog for his night walk, and I heartily

dare you to try and stop me. I'll knock you the fuck out and do my time in Norfolk.'

'Wouldn't dream of it,' Leanne said, holding up her hands. 'Where are we taking him?'

Kim groaned. She should have guessed she wouldn't get to go alone, but if it meant she could leave the house for some air, she'd allow Leanne to tag along.

'And don't speak to me,' Kim instructed as they reached the pavement.

Leanne nodded her acquiescence and fell into step beside her.

It was only once she got to the end of the street that her discomfort made itself known to her. She looked back at her home and the activity within. She understood the time, money and effort going into keeping her safe.

Leanne had asked why she'd displayed no emotion at her predicament. Truthfully, she'd been convinced that within a couple of hours, Symes would be caught and put safely back behind bars. No problem. But as she considered the work now being done on her home, she had to consider that other people didn't share her view.

She hadn't lied to Leanne. She hadn't felt there was any real threat to her life. She hadn't been worried.

Not until now.

NINE

'Bryant, you should know that I like Leanne even less now than I did when you left us last night,' Kim said, getting in the car.

'Should make for an interesting day but feel free to share your reasons,' Bryant answered, pulling away from the kerb.

'She made me send Barney away. Right now, he's on his way to an undisclosed location in north Wales.' She couldn't help the sarcasm that dripped from her last few words.

'Given that there's nothing you wouldn't do for that dog, I can see why that would—'

'Traitor,' she spat. 'Here's hoping you never need my support again.'

'To be fair, guv, I've always hoped that if I'm ever in some serious shit, I've got Barney with me, cos I know then you'll get there a damn sight quicker.'

He wasn't wrong so she let his point pass.

'And she's turned my house into Fort Knox. Pretty sure if I fart I'm gonna set off some kind of alarm or sensor.'

Bryant laughed. 'Sorry, guv, but that was kinda funny, and that's also okay by me.'

Realising she wasn't going to get her colleague on side, she turned her attention out the window. Leanne hadn't said one word yet had still managed to win the battle.

It hadn't been easy handing Barney over to Charlie for safe-keeping. He was her soul balm, her best friend and the only thing that could bring her back to zero whatever kind of day she'd had. Without Barney to calm her down, the people in close proximity were in danger of feeling her wrath. Leanne was looking good for top spot.

True to her word, the woman had stayed in the lounge all night.

After a few hours of unsettled catnapping, she'd risen herself, sure that she'd dreamed of Symes but unable to recall the details.

She'd found Leanne already dressed and making coffee. Spying the large duffel bag that hadn't been there when she went to bed, Kim had questioned its appearance. Leanne claimed 'a friend' had brought it during the night. Kim couldn't help but wonder at these secret people who moved and lurked at night.

The electricians had finally finished defacing her home in the early hours of the morning, leaving her with key fobs, a panic alarm and the feeling that her home was no longer her own. The final insult had been this morning when Leanne had demanded her phone.

'Why?' Kim had asked, clutching her phone tightly to her chest.

Leanne had rolled her eyes. 'I need to install an app so you can access everything remotely.'

Reluctantly she had handed it over.

Leanne had pressed buttons, swiped, and pressed some more buttons. 'All done, and your password to the system is Barneyboyeleventwelve, capital B and no spaces. Got it?'

'What are the numbers? They mean nothing to me.'

'It's my birthday, and it's good that they don't,' Leanne said, taking the back off her phone.

'Hey, what the hell are you—?'

'Tracking device,' Leanne said, taking a small envelope from her pocket.

Kim lurched towards her. 'No bloody way.'

Leanne evaded her grabbing hand. 'Yes way and this is not negotiable. I can't trust you so it's going in or you're going to Norfolk.'

Kim stepped back and shook her head. 'Jesus, just when I thought you couldn't go any lower.'

'There are no limits to how low I'll go to get the job done,' she said, snapping the back of the phone in place. 'Here you go. All done.'

Kim snatched the phone back. First chance she got that thing was coming out.

Leanne held up her phone. 'See, you're the green dot and I can see exactly where you are.'

For now, Kim thought.

'And it has a tamper sensor. If you mess with it or it becomes dislodged, the light turns red.'

It was a shame that the first genuine smile she saw on Leanne's face was drenched in smugness.

Kim had stormed from the room to go and shower, taking her rage with her.

The fact that other people appeared to be taking the threat of Symes way more seriously than she was unnerved her.

She shook away all thoughts of Symes as Bryant pulled into the station car park.

Leanne shadowed her into the building, and Kim had the urge to throw a dance move here and there to see if Leanne would copy that too.

She headed into her office and fired up her emails. Bryant made coffee while Leanne plonked herself at the empty desk in the squad room.

By the time Kim had sent a few things to the printer, the coffee was brewing and both Penn and Stacey were at their desks.

'Okay, team, let's get right to it,' she said, passing four photos to Penn. 'And this will be a closed-door investigation.'

Penn took a quick look at the photos and closed the door.

Kim continued. 'This is Helen and William Daynes, a couple in their early sixties. Helen shot her husband, daughter and son in the early hours of yesterday morning. Keats has sent through all crime-scene photos, which I've circulated, but we'll just have these four on the board.' Images depicting minors with gunshot wounds did not need to be visible from outside the door.

'We have Rosalind Daynes aged seventeen and Lewis two years younger.'

Penn taped the photos to the wipe board and wrote the details beneath each picture.

'Right now, we know nothing about this family. There are no sensational headlines or apparent scandals. They appeared to live a quiet and privileged lifestyle off the back of their furniture company. There are two older children, Rachel and Zachary, who are twins. Bryant and I will be talking to them both in more detail this morning.'

She turned to Stacey. 'We've got Zach's address but if you can get one for Rachel that'd be great.'

'Of course, boss.'

'And do some digging. Just because there's nothing in the press doesn't mean there was nothing at all. You know better than me where to look so just do what you do.

'Penn, the post-mortems start at 9 a.m. so I'll leave that with you. Anything, however insignificant, that strikes you as strange let me know.'

'Splendid,' he answered.

Kim tried not to pay too much attention to the fact that Penn relished a good post-mortem.

'So, guys, thoughts?' she asked, pouring a coffee from the machine.

'Murder-suicide isn't that unusual,' Stacey said. 'But not all that common for the woman to be doing the shooting.'

Penn agreed. 'A study in 1990 concluded that murder-suicide was most common between married couples or intimate partners with an overwhelmingly male bias.'

'Motives?' Kim asked.

Penn continued. 'Most often carried out due to depression, marital or financial problems.'

'Maybe he was having an affair and the wife found out,' Stacey said. 'Revenge killing.'

'But why the kids?' Bryant asked.

'A fit of rage?' Penn answered.

Bryant shook his head with that barely tolerant expression. 'Her rage would be at the husband not the children.'

Prior to the team-building weekend, Kim hadn't noticed how quick Bryant was to shoot Penn's ideas down, and the two days away hadn't made the slightest bit of difference.

'She may have wanted to punish him. If she killed the kids first, he would have known that before he died.'

'Doesn't make sense,' Bryant insisted.

She respected Penn's determination in making his point despite Bryant's protestations, and she had to disagree with Bryant. In Penn's scenario, the order of the shootings did in fact make sense. William Daynes had been the only one out of bed so must have heard the first two shots. When his wife entered the bedroom and pointed a gun at him, he had to have known what she'd done.

Kim turned to the detective constable. 'Stace, priority is to check on Helen's mental health.'

She finished her coffee and grabbed her coat. With a bit of luck and a strong wind, this might be one of their quicker cases to solve. Perhaps, even by the end of the day they'd know why Helen Daynes had slaughtered her family.

TEN

The house belonging to the Porters looked to be about half the size of the Dayneses' home. A one-car garage was flanked by three vehicles. There were no electric gates, and the gravel driveway was full of weeds.

'Is this really necessary?' Kim asked as Leanne got out the car behind her and Bryant.

''Fraid so,' Leanne answered as Bryant rang the doorbell.

Kim exchanged a look with her colleague. She knew that her tolerance level would eventually be reached and that she'd be tearing into Woody's office, but she also knew that if she did it too soon, she would be bundled into a vehicle and removed from the area, just like her dog.

'Mrs Porter?' Kim said as a woman with a blunt bob answered the door. There was something about the richness of her black hair that told Kim it wasn't her natural colour. The thin lines around her mouth and eyes placed her somewhere in her late fifties.

The woman nodded without smiling as both she and Bryant offered their ID.

'And this is Leanne King, a trainee,' Kim added as Mrs

Porter opened the door. 'Any more reporters been around?' Kim asked, trying to keep the accusation out of her voice.

'No. Definitely not. We haven't spoken to a soul since that nice officer visited us yesterday.'

'Good,' Kim said, following her into a small drawing room. The furniture was plush and heavy. There were ornate edges everywhere she looked. The bay window was swamped with thick floor-length velour curtains, the space heavy with maroon-coloured walls. It had the grandeur but not the space to show it off. The result was a dark, cramped room.

'Mrs Porter, may—'

'Della, please,' she said, sitting on the edge of a single seat.

Kim and Bryant had taken opposite ends of a three-seater sofa that seemed to drop by a foot once she sat on it. Bryant's expression told her that he too was wondering how he was going to get back up. Leanne lingered somewhere beyond the doorway.

'Okay, Della, we know you've all given statements, but can you tell us in your own words what happened yesterday morning?'

'Am I under arrest?' she asked, crossing her feet at the ankles.

'For what?' Kim asked.

'For questioning.'

'We don't need to arrest you just to ask some questions about what you witnessed. You did alert the emergency services, didn't you?' Kim asked, wondering if she'd got her facts wrong.

She nodded vigorously.

'Okay, if you could start from—'

'Do I need my lawyer here?' she interrupted.

'Della, unless you've committed some type of crime or you're planning to obstruct our investigation, I'm pretty sure we're okay to just have a chat.'

'Okay, but let me just call my husband.'

Kim tried to hide her irritation as Della rushed out of the room. At this rate they'd be lucky if they were out of here by lunchtime. And yet she'd been more than happy to talk to the press.

'This is my husband, Alec. He's retired recently so we get to spend lots more time together now.'

Alec's expression as he offered his hand said that his wife was much more excited about that than he was.

'And what did you do, Mr Porter?' Kim asked as Bryant shook his hand.

'Social care, vulnerable adults,' he replied, reaching for his wrists. Kim recognised the gesture. He was reaching for shirt cuffs that would have been pulled back down after extending his arm. Here was a man who had clearly worn formal clothes for most of his working life. His plain blue sweater was well made and fitted perfectly, but it wasn't a shirt and tie.

'I'm not sure exactly what I can tell you. I didn't see or hear a thing,' he admitted.

'Della?' Kim asked as the woman retook her seat.

'I was getting myself a glass of water. He snores. I prodded him. He wouldn't turn,' she said, nodding towards her husband. 'I was getting annoyed, so I went downstairs,' she said, offering her husband a withering look. He rolled his eyes slightly, and Bryant offered him a sympathetic glance.

'I heard the first shot at around 3 a.m.'

The first shot – son, Lewis Daynes.

'The second shot came soon afterwards.'

Second shot – daughter, Rosalind Daynes.

'The third was a minute or so after that.'

Third shot – husband, William Daynes.

'And an even longer pause before the fourth shot. Five minutes at least, maybe more. Long enough that I thought they'd gone.'

Fourth shot – Helen Daynes herself.

'Did you call the police at that time?' Kim asked, confused. Her understanding was that the call had come much later.

'No, I took my water and went back to bed.'

Kim could barely contain her surprise. 'Hearing four gunshots in the middle of the night wasn't suspicious?'

Della coloured as though it should have been.

'Not round here, Inspector. We have a residential travellers' site at the bottom of the lane. They come up here with lurchers and shotguns rabbiting at all hours of the night. We've reported it to the police many times, but they're a law unto themselves.'

Kim's mind was racing. Why had there been a long pause between Helen shooting her husband and shooting herself? Had she hesitated in the final part of the plan? Had she wondered if she really wanted to die despite killing most of her family? Had she struggled with positioning the gun? Had she broken down with remorse for what she'd done before taking her own life?

'And you reported a fire at 7 a.m.?'

'Yes. I didn't see anything, but Reece had seen it on his morning run.'

'Reece?'

'Our boy. He'd noticed it and told me to call the police.'

'And Reece is?'

'At work. Early mornings. Road gang.'

Bryant had already noted the basics of the timeline in his notebook – now she needed to put some meat on the bones.

'And what were they like?'

'Are you not going to tell us what's going on?' asked Mr Porter.

'Not at the moment, I'm afraid.'

'You used the past tense. Are they all dead?' he pushed.

'I can only confirm that there's been an incident. Now, please, can you tell me a little more about the family?'

'Not really,' Della said. 'We don't know them that well.'

'You've lived here for how long?'

'Thirty-two years.'

'And you don't know your neighbours?' Kim asked, trying to understand.

'They're not very sociable,' Della answered.

Well, neither was she but she'd lived in her own home for around ten years, and she knew that Louisa over the road smoked outside the porch door when her husband wasn't home. She knew that a young couple who'd moved in along the street fought like cat and dog every few nights. She knew that Mrs Trevin on the corner kept the Fiat Panda on her drive for show, to give the impression she wasn't home alone even though she hadn't got behind the wheel for a couple of years. She knew these things even though she never spoke to any of them.

'You know nothing about the family after all these years?' Bryant asked doubtfully.

'I didn't say I didn't know anything about them. I said I didn't mix with them. They don't really mix with anyone.'

'So how do you know about them?' Kim asked.

'Reece has done odd jobs for them. He's heard stuff here and there. Arguments between William and Helen. Helen crying and having days she couldn't get out of bed. Rozzie being spoiled and without direction. Lewis spending all day in his room and not doing great at school.'

Della was imparting this news as though it was hot gossip of scandalous proportions. If that was the best she'd got on the kids, it wasn't a lot. Sounded like typical teen behaviour to her. The only not normal part was Helen's behaviour.

'Any reason you know of for Helen's depression?'

Della shrugged. 'Not a clue, but I've heard she had a full-on breakdown around twenty years ago. Found walking the grounds in the middle of the night with an empty pushchair, screaming a child's name. I mean, don't quote me, it's only what I heard.'

No wonder the family kept to themselves if this was how they were discussed.

Della was looking at her with a 'that's all I've got' expression. It seemed to her that Reece knew more about the family than anyone.

'Would you ask your son to come to the station when he's got a minute? We'd like to speak with him.'

Alec opened his mouth to speak, but Della got in first.

'Why? He hasn't done anything. He was just out running.'

Kim frowned at the woman's instant defence of her son. 'He appeared to know the family well. He may be able to help.'

'Oh, okay, I'll tell him.'

Kim climbed out of the sofa and stood. She took a card from her pocket.

'If you think of anything else, please give me a call.'

'I will,' she said, placing the card on one of the side tables.

Kim headed for the door with a feeling of unease that she hadn't had when she'd walked in.

ELEVEN

Symes shovelled a heaped tablespoon of cereal into his mouth and chewed noisily. He really had fallen on his feet here – a comfy bed, hot showers and a great choice of food in the cupboard. When he'd seen the surveillance equipment being fitted to the bitch's house last night, he had considered finding another Edna somewhere else, but it was a decent set-up, and being four doors down from the bitch, he was confident the camera on the front of the house was aimed at her front garden gate. Yeah, she was a copper, but she still couldn't record the comings and goings of the whole fucking street. Nah, just down the street was the last place they were gonna look for him, and Edna was looking after him just fine.

'Got any bacon?' he called across the room.

The elderly woman offered no response. The gag in her mouth prevented her from speaking, and the rope binding her wrists to the chair prevented her from moving. Admittedly, it wasn't a very ladylike position for a woman of her years, but he didn't really care. Clearly, she had soiled herself between him strapping her to the chair last night and him waking up this morning.

The bruise on the side of her face was prominent where he'd given her a good thump to knock her out. It really hadn't been that hard, but he guessed old people bruised easily. Never mind. It had given him time to secure her to the chair and gag her with a pair of her own knickers. While she was unconscious, he'd fixed himself a sandwich and taken a good look around the house.

Initially, he'd planned to use the place as a one-night-only kind of deal. A bit like a Travelodge: check in, eat, sleep, shower, renew energy, kill the homeowner and fuck off. But as he'd walked through the home closing curtains, he'd noticed only one bed upstairs and a distinct lack of family photos. Only one old picture of what he assumed was her wedding day was evident on her bedside table. He'd realised he may be able to hole up here for longer than he'd thought.

He carried his cereal into the middle of the room and shovelled another spoonful into his mouth as he kicked her foot.

'Oi, wake up.'

Her head came up and her eyes widened with terror.

He stepped away, out of the stench of piss.

'You got anyone coming today?'

She remained still except for the trembling that had overtaken her body.

It always amazed him how vulnerability came at the beginning and end of life with no clue at the woman she'd been in between. Had this frail woman once been formidable, direct, ambitious, spirited? His own maternal grandmother had been a total bitch. Every relative and neighbour had been terrified of her. Nobody fucked with Biddy Evans. He hadn't seen her for years until he'd heard she'd suffered a massive stroke which had robbed her of her speech and mobility. He'd visited her in the home to see for himself. The rumours were true, and she'd been unable to react when he'd spent the entire visit pinching her and causing her pain. It had been a good visit.

He sighed heavily.

'Lady, if you play dumb, this is not gonna end well for you.'

It was a given that it wasn't anyway, but he liked his victims to cling to one shred of hope. It made his life easier if they thought being helpful would earn them an escape.

She shook her head slowly.

'Good, it's just us then,' he said before emptying the contents of the bowl into his mouth.

'So, you got any fucking bacon?'

She shook her head.

He sighed and stepped away. A decent bacon sandwich had been on his wish list for years, but it was good to know he didn't have to rush.

The plan for Stone had been formed long ago. He wasn't going to deviate from it, however desperate he was to feel his fist pounding against her flesh. If he could pull it off, it would exert maximum pain in more ways than one. There were things to put in place first, and the timing of snatching the bitch had to be just right. He'd know exactly when that was, he thought, wandering into the pokey kitchen, because if he just moved the curtain a fraction and stood on tiptoe, he had a perfectly good view of the bitch's front door.

TWELVE

The home of Zachary and Gavin Daynes wasn't what she'd been expecting.

Their flat was located on the top floor of a small development on Timbertree Estate, built where the estate pub of the same name had once stood.

Kim turned in her seat as Leanne undid her seat belt. 'Not this time. These are grieving family members. You can keep watch from here.'

Kim readied herself for an argument that she was perfectly happy to have. It was one thing intruding on her life, but these people had lost most of their family.

'Feel free to report me to Woody.'

'Don't be so dramatic, Stone. I get it.'

Kim got out of the car a little disappointed she'd won that round quite easily.

'Do you feel like we're missing something?' Bryant asked as they walked towards the lift.

'Yeah, the weight that's been sitting on my shoulders for the last eighteen hours.'

Bryant chuckled as he hit the button for the top floor.

'And if you were wondering if she's just as sour faced away from the office, I can confirm that she is.'

'Don't really care how sour faced she is as long as she's good at her job.'

Kim closed her mouth. She was obviously getting no empathy from him.

'Who's the FLO?' Bryant asked as they approached the door.

'None.' The assigned family liaison officer had been an officer in her mid-forties named Hilary. 'They sent her away after an hour,' Kim answered.

Not every family welcomed a family liaison officer. The email she'd seen in the car stated that they hadn't been unpleasant about it – they just wanted to keep their grief to themselves.

And when Gavin Daynes opened the front door to the flat Kim guessed there was a secondary reason.

'Good morning, Inspector. Please come in,' Gavin said, forcing himself against the wall to make room. The hallway was little more than a cubbyhole with four doors leading off it. She was guessing it was a one-bedroom property. Unless one of these doors led to a further hallway, she could see every room in the place from the front door.

'Zach's through there,' he said, nodding towards the door that was straight ahead.

The room was more oblong than square, which made the arrangement of furniture quite haphazard and clumsy. A two-seater fabric sofa rested against the longest wall. Zach sat in a single leather chair close to the window. A miniature Yorkshire terrier sat on his lap. It occurred to her that their pet was proportionate to the property, just like the television and other furniture. The only things that appeared to be out of proportion were the painted canvasses on the wall.

'Zach did them,' Gavin said, standing behind her.

His husband's voice roused Zach and his eyes opened.

Kim made no comment on the artwork. She'd never understood art. She didn't want to have to interpret anything she put on her walls. Although she didn't get art, she was still able to appreciate fine use of colour or the skill involved, but the daubings she saw on the wall appeared to possess neither.

'Please, may I get you a drink?'

'Coffee would be great,' Kim said, surprising her colleague.

It only took him a second to catch on.

'In fact, I'll give you a hand,' Kim said, following him into the boxy kitchen. She certainly understood not wanting anyone unnecessary in this space.

'How is he?' she asked, standing in the doorway.

'He's barely spoken,' Gavin said, filling the kettle. 'I mean, obviously he wants to know what's happened, but he mainly cries and stares.' He grabbed four mugs.

'Okay, so what do you really want to ask me, Inspector?' he said, turning to face her. 'I've seen enough cop shows to know what's going on. Please don't beat around the bush. Just ask whatever you want.'

His voice was warm, and his invitation was open.

'Okay, I'll ask again. How is he?'

Zach had barely looked at her when she'd walked in the door.

'Tenuous,' he answered honestly. 'He suffers from anxiety and sometimes paranoia set against a backdrop of clinical depression. No one knows from day to day how he's going to be. Some days he's angry, some days he's sad and other days he's the man I fell in love with.'

Gavin turned away on those last words.

'Not sure of your experience living with someone's poor mental health, but it's not easy.'

Not at all, Kim thought. *And some days they even try and kill you*. The picture of her mother degrading in a bed came to mind, but she pushed it away.

'Was he close to his family?' she asked. Her visit to the lounge had been brief, but she hadn't clocked the presence of family photos.

'Oh, Inspector, that's a big question. I'm not sure they ever fully understood him. He didn't do well at school, dropped out of college, lazed around for a few years and then hopped from passion to passion.'

'The paintings?'

'A couple of years ago. The need to express himself through art was burning inside him. It fizzled eventually, but I keep the paintings up to inspire him and to show that he can achieve his goals. His most recent passion is photography.'

'And how does he earn his living?'

Gavin hesitated as though he didn't want to answer.

'He doesn't,' he said eventually.

'But you do?'

He smiled. 'Someone has to keep a roof over our heads, such as it is. Luckily, my work as a paralegal supports us both. Just.'

'No help from the parents?'

'He's a fully grown man. Not many twenty-nine-year-olds rely on their parents.'

'Of course.'

They rely on their husbands instead, Kim thought and then caught herself. It wasn't her judgement to make.

'He wasn't particularly close to his younger siblings. The age gap meant he had little in common with them.'

'His twin?'

Gavin rolled his eyes. 'Love, hate in equal measure. Let's just say they're explosive. Milk and sugar?' he asked as the kettle boiled.

'Not for me, and just milk for my colleague.'

He finished making the drinks and picked up two mugs, nodding to the other two.

'Inspector, is he going to be able to deal with whatever it is you've come to tell us?'

Kim grabbed the remaining two mugs. 'I think he's going to need you close by.'

Gavin nodded his understanding, and she followed him back to the lounge. Zach's eyes were closed again, and the dog had moved to Bryant's lap. Her colleague shrugged, indicating that Zach hadn't said a word.

She took a seat on the sofa, placing the mugs on a side table. Gavin sat on the arm of the chair and took Zach's hand.

He opened his eyes but said nothing. His skin was an unhealthy grey, and his cheeks appeared gaunt. The man was suffering. She immediately felt bad for the less than charitable thoughts she'd had in the kitchen. Nothing she had to say was going to make him feel any better.

'I'm afraid I have bad news for you.'

'What, they're more dead than they were yesterday?' he asked.

Kim ignored the jibe that was borne of pain.

'We need to discuss the circumstances of the incident, Mr Daynes.'

'Zach, for God's sake. Mr Daynes died in a house fire yesterday.'

She and Bryant exchanged a glance which Gavin caught and frowned at. He placed his arm around Zach's shoulders. Kim only wished the gesture offered some kind of protection against the words she was about to say.

'Zach, the fire never reached your family. It was extinguished before it got anywhere near the upper level of the house.'

Both men's eyes widened, and it was the most alert she'd seen Zach.

He waited.

'There was a shooting. All four of the victims – sorry, your family members – suffered fatal gunshot wounds.'

Zach began to shake his head. As if that wasn't bad enough, there was worse to come, and she had to get the words on the other side of her lips.

'It was your mother who was found holding the gun.'

Now Gavin's head shook in disbelief too. 'Helen, with a gun?'

'Are you saying my mother shot people, her own family?' Zach asked incredulously.

'The gun was found in your mother's hand.'

Zach looked to Gavin as though he was going to make everything right. Seeing the disbelief on his husband's face, he turned back towards her.

'You can't be serious. You can't really think she could have done such a thing?'

Kim remained silent for a moment, allowing the enormity of what she'd said to find its place in his mind.

She'd expected denial. It was difficult for family members to accept suicide in general, but add the taking of three other lives as well and it became near impossible to digest.

'My mother, a murderer?' he said, before laughing. 'You really can't begin to understand how ridiculous that is.'

Kim was surprised he'd attached that label to her quite so quickly, but of course it would be a title that would be attached to her forever more. Helen Daynes, mother and murderer. The word would be in every news report, every online article and the Wikipedia page that was sure to appear. It would follow her everywhere.

'Zach, I completely get that this is difficult to digest, but we understand that your mother was depressed and—'

'Who told you that?'

'Your parents' neighbours said—'

'You've spoken to the weirdos before speaking to me?'

'They raised the alarm,' Kim explained. 'We had to get a timeline.'

Clearly, he didn't like the neighbours much, and yes, she had to admit they were a bit strange.

'Were they lying about your mum's depression?' she asked gently. She needed Zach to reconnect to what she was saying.

He shook his head. 'She's always suffered with depression, but that doesn't make her a bloody murderer.' He snorted. 'She's had issues since I was a child so why now? Why would she do such a thing now?'

'We were hoping you could help us with that, Zach.'

He opened his hands expressively. 'I've got nothing. She loved Rozzie and Lewis. She would never hurt them.'

'Were things good with your father?'

'They weren't all over each other, but they seemed content enough.'

'Any financial problems?'

Zach shook his head. 'My parents never discussed money in front of us.'

'When was the last time you saw them?'

'Last Sunday,' Gavin offered. 'Monthly roast for all the family.'

'Anything strange or out of the ordinary?' she asked.

Gavin thought for a moment before shaking his head. 'Helen was a little quiet, but she normally is around this time.'

'Why's that?' Kim asked.

'Didn't the weirdos tell you?' Zach asked.

Kim shook her head.

'Mum struggles around March. It's the twenty-year anniversary of the child she lost.'

Kim waited.

'Cot death. A girl.'

Kim had wondered at the twelve-year gap between the twins and seventeen-year-old Rosalind.

'I'm sorry to hear that,' Kim said. 'It must have been a difficult thing for the family to take.'

'It happens,' Zach said dismissively. 'She had two more.'

Kim hid her surprise at his tone. Despite the benefit she was affording him due to his grief, she wasn't really warming to Zachary Daynes.

'We'll need a family member to identify the—'

'No,' Zach cried and looked to Gavin, who squeezed his shoulder.

'Is that something I can do, Inspector?'

Kim nodded and took a card from her pocket. She stood and handed it to him.

'Give me a call later and we'll arrange a time.'

He took the card and nodded.

She didn't sit back down, and Bryant took the hint. He placed the sleeping dog on the sofa and stood.

'Just to let you know that we'll be giving a press conference this evening, but we won't be revealing all the details. It'll come out over time.'

Zach had already closed his eyes and returned to shut-down mode, but Gavin indicated his understanding. Kim appreciated his assistance.

'Again, we're sorry for your loss,' she said when she reached the front door.

'Thank you, Inspector.'

'Our next visit is to Rachel, so I'd imagine she'll be in touch once we've left.'

'Good luck with that one, Inspector,' he said before closing the door.

What the hell did he mean by that?

THIRTEEN

Stacey reached for a chocolate brownie from Penn's Tupperware box. She'd reminded him to take it from his manbag before he dashed off to attend the post-mortems. Somehow, she'd known she wouldn't find them so appealing if they'd spent a few hours in the morgue. She hummed as she chewed, still buzzing from the trip they'd taken at the weekend.

Unlike the rest of her team, she'd been excited at the thought of a night away, bonding around a campfire. Especially when it fell on Devon's night shifts. They were long nights when her wife was working hard as an immigration officer.

Okay, so they hadn't exactly had the bonding moment she'd been expecting. Outside of the station, Bryant had appeared even snappier with Penn, but it had been refreshing to see her colleagues outside of their normal constraints and yet still acting completely within their normal personalities. Solving puzzles and working together without a dead body relying on them had been liberating. She'd found herself enjoying the company of her colleagues. Even the boss had been a little more relaxed, except for when they were in competition with the other teams. Then she'd been in full-on DI mode.

She'd lasted longer behind that gag than Stacey had expected. She smiled at the memory, but the smile faded when she remembered they'd returned to a horrific incident and an escaped psychopath who wanted to kill their boss.

In all honesty, she had mixed feelings about the boss remaining in place. Part of her wanted Woody to insist that she be removed from sight and guarded by all three armed forces until Symes was safely back behind bars. On the other hand, she didn't want the boss so far away that they couldn't check on her themselves.

She wasn't too fussed about having to change her own routine. There was already enough variety in her journeys to and from work. Sometimes she caught the bus, other times a taxi and there were times Devon dropped her off too. Devon had finished her night shifts on Sunday morning, so she wasn't going to be alone when she got home from work. Knowing how the boss felt about Leanne, Stacey felt a bit like teacher's pet for following all her rules, but she did seem to know what she was talking about. If the force had entrusted her to keep the boss safe from Symes then she had to respect the woman's direction.

She shuddered at the thought of Symes, instantly feeling the need to shower. He was truly one of the most sadistic and terrifying killers they had ever dealt with. Stacey hated to think what he would have done to Charlie and Amy. How much would he have tortured their nine-year-old bodies if the boss hadn't caught him in time?

'Just get him quick,' she said to no one as she typed the last email to the doctor's surgery.

All four members of the Daynes family were covered by the same practitioner, but she had to make separate applications for each record. She'd sent the request for Helen Daynes first and marked it high priority.

Stacey couldn't even imagine what might drive a woman to kill all her family before taking her own life. Had she suffered some kind of sudden breakdown? Had she had some kind of delusion? Had she felt her family needed protecting from something? No matter how much she thought about it, her brain couldn't compute an answer where this solution was the best resolution to the problem.

'Aah, maybe this'll help,' she said to herself as the financial records lit up her inbox. The family appeared to keep everything with one bank, which made life easier for her.

Attached were the most recent statements for the business account, joint personal account, savings account and pension.

She opened the business account first and frowned immediately. She could see there was no financial issue there. The business was showing a healthy six-figure balance with good cash flow. The outgoings appeared to be mainly equipment and salaries, and the deposits ranged from a few hundred pounds to tens of thousands.

She closed the document and opened the latest joint account statement. A quick perusal told her there was no issue here either. Although they didn't appear to spend frivolously, there was a buffer of twenty thousand pounds that when touched sparked a cash injection from the business.

The savings account was just as healthy and would have kept her in chocolate muffins for the rest of her life.

There were no monthly payments on a mortgage, so the home was owned free and clear. They paid their taxes on time, made payments to various charities, and didn't spend unnecessarily.

Stacey sat back in her chair. The family had more wealth than she was ever going to see in her lifetime, but they weren't out spending like there was no tomorrow. There were no payments for flash new cars or expensive holidays. It was as if the couple had never expected to make this kind of money. Either that or they had a very cautious accountant.

So financial problems could most certainly be ruled out.

There was no irregular spending or large bills that needed to be explained.

As she closed the last of the documents from the bank, a reply to the priority request for Helen's medical records pinged her inbox.

She opened the electronic record and started at the top with current medication. The neighbours were right. She was on quite the cocktail for anxiety and depression.

Stacey scrolled down the record.

Her cursor chewed up the years as it headed south on her screen.

Helen Daynes not only suffered with depression and was heavily medicated, but that had been the case for a very long time.

FOURTEEN

'No offence but what you've told my brother is bollocks, Inspector,' Rachel Hewitt said as she opened the door, giving Kim no chance even to introduce herself.

'I assume Zach has spoken to you,' Kim said, showing her ID anyway. Rachel barely glanced at it.

'Of course – he's my twin.'

Kim was unsure of the need to add the obvious statement of fact.

'May we come in and discuss it?' Kim asked when Rachel made no move to step aside.

Kim nodded to Leanne in the car before stepping inside a house that was much closer to what she'd expected of the Daynes children. The cul-de-sac was a hidden collection of eight houses just off the main Stourbridge to Wollescote road. All detached with double driveways, she guessed they were looking at roughly half a million in value, and Rachel Hewitt matched the house in which she stood.

Her raven-black hair was sleek and shiny and stretched all the way down her back. Her face was fully made up with red lipstick that stayed on the right side of tasteful. Either she had help or she was an expert in how to make the most of her face.

'In here please,' Rachel said, pointing to a formal lounge that was drowning in beige. For some reason Kim found herself disappointed in the woman's creativity. She would have liked to see colour, personality, something that matched the fire with which they'd just been met, but she saw decor that matched the house and not the person.

'What you told my brother is absolute bullshit,' she said, standing behind a caramel velvet chaise.

'We heard you the first time, Mrs Hewitt, but the facts remain that your father, brother and sister were shot, and the gun was found in your mother's hand.'

'Are you sure it was that gun?'

'I'm sure the ballistics report will return a positive identification.'

'It's impossible. I'm telling you.'

'Your mum didn't shoot guns?' Kim asked.

'Yes, she shot. Nothing live. She couldn't stand the thought of killing an animal, but she shot tin cans in the paddock. My father insisted she learn how to use one because of living rurally.'

Kim said nothing. It wasn't impossible as she stated and she knew it.

'It couldn't have been accidental?' she asked, twirling the chunky chain around her neck.

'Your siblings were shot as they slept, Mrs—'

'Rachel, please. And my father?'

'Your father appeared to have tried to defend himself.'

'He wasn't asleep?'

Kim shook her head. Rachel probably wanted to believe that none of her family members had known what was going on.

'We believe that the first two shots to Lewis and Rosalind—'

'Rozzie,' Rachel interrupted. 'She abhorred her name. Everyone called her Rozzie.'

Kim nodded her understanding. 'The sound of the first two shots appeared to wake your father, but he couldn't get to your mother before she shot him.'

She visibly paled at the pictures that were forming in her head.

'Sweetheart, I just need to— Oh, sorry, I didn't realise.'

A suited man Kim assumed to be Rachel's husband had burst into the room.

'Police officers,' Rachel explained and then looked him up and down. 'You can't possibly be going into the office.'

'Pleased to meet you. Daryl Hewitt,' he offered in their general direction before turning back to his wife. 'I have to, love – the team needs reassurance. I'm sure they've all heard the rumours. We need to steer a steady ship in the face of the shock—'

'What about my shock, Daryl?' Rachel asked as her eyes filled with tears. 'How can you leave me at a time like this? I'm not a bloody employee. I'm family and they're all gone. I need you here. Mia needs you here.'

'Mia is sound asleep,' he said, crossing the room and taking her in his arms. Kim should have felt embarrassed at being privy to the tender moment, but she didn't and she quickly understood why. It wasn't a moment where a husband was offering genuine comfort or support. He wasn't shouldering any of her anguish. He was simply giving her a hug as he stared over her shoulder. His body was wrapped around his wife, but his spirit was already halfway out the door.

'My husband works for the family business,' Rachel said, taking a handkerchief and wiping her eyes.

'Managing director,' he corrected, as though his title mattered to them. Quite honestly, she didn't care if he was the tea boy.

'William left the running of the business to me when he retired.'

'Okay,' Kim said. 'And how well did you know Helen?'

'Rachel and I have been together seven years, married for five, so I'd say I knew her quite well. Helen was a wonderful woman, who could be unpredictable at times. I'm sure you know that her mental health was—'

'Daryl,' Rachel snapped. 'You can't honestly believe that my mother was capable of—'

'It's what your brother said they were told,' he said, edging back towards the door. 'I assume these officers know what they're doing. They know—'

'And I know my mother,' she screamed and then waved her hand towards the door. 'Just go look after the precious business.'

'I promise I'll be back as soon—'

'Just go,' she snapped, turning away from him.

He turned his attention their way. 'Is there anything else I can help you with?' he asked, as though finishing a customer service phone call.

'No, we'll talk more once the pathologist releases the bodies.'

She saw Rachel positively blanch at that word.

'And then you can arrange the burial,' Bryant added.

Daryl frowned. 'Are post-mortems necessary?' he asked. 'Surely it's obvious how they all died.'

'Standard procedure in these circumstances. It won't delay the process for too long.'

He nodded, then turned towards his wife. 'Just an hour or two, love – just to settle the troops.'

'Just go,' she said, turning away from him and folding her arms.

Kim waited until the front door closed behind him before continuing.

'Arrangements have been made to identify the victims; unfortunately, your brother wasn't able to bring himself to consider—'

'Of course he wasn't,' Rachel sneered. 'Zach can barely wipe his own arse. Gavin offered to do it, didn't he?' she asked as her eyes softened just a little.

Kim nodded.

Rachel stared at the door, as though realising her own husband had made no such offer before rushing off to work.

'I swear, Zach wouldn't be able to remember his own name if Gavin didn't remind him every day. He doesn't bloody deserve him.'

Kim wondered at the animosity between the twins, but family dynamics was not her forte or her responsibility.

'You do know that even if you showed me footage of my mother committing the act I wouldn't believe you.'

'We understand that your mother had a difficult anniversary coming up?'

'Yeah, same anniversary that came every year.' She raised an eyebrow. 'You're not claiming that's the motivation for all this?'

'It may be a contributing factor,' Kim said. 'Your mother's mental health was—'

'Jesus Christ,' she said, throwing herself into a chair. 'She suffered with depression. Had done for years. Millions of people suffer with it, but they don't just murder their entire household.'

'And sometimes they do,' Kim offered.

Rachel shook her head. 'There's nothing you can say to convince me. My mum had way too much to live for. My dad had finally retired. They had plans, and that's not even mentioning Jonathan.'

That wasn't a name they'd heard come out of anyone's lips.

'Who is Jonathan?'

'Jonathan is a seven-year-old boy that my parents fell in love with, a foster child they were due to take in next week. Does that sound like someone who's considering murdering their husband and children?'

That wasn't the first question in her mind.

Why hadn't this been mentioned by Zach?

FIFTEEN

Penn watched as Keats made the Y incision into the flesh for the second time. The horizontal line cut through the site of the bullet hole at the centre of the chest.

So far Keats had turned the body of fifteen-year-old Lewis Daynes inside out.

Penn's whole team knew he was intrigued by the mechanics of the process, but he'd only witnessed it being carried out on adults. There was something unnerving about watching Keats deconstruct a body that hadn't even finished growing yet.

Right now, it was Rozzie's turn. Her young, naked body exposed coldly on the table was a sorry sight. Both of these kids had barely even started their lives. They were like a car that had ignited and spluttered before dying completely without ever having a good run.

Normally he was able to watch every move that Keats made, but somehow the line of instruments waiting to be used seemed far more invasive on the bodies of these teenage children. He didn't want to see Keats reach for the toothed forceps, rib shears or bone saw.

'No, it's not the same,' Keats said, as though reading his

mind. 'Everything is different when it comes to children so don't expect to remain as emotionless as normal.'

'It bothers you still?' he asked.

'Of course. I'm human, and I would be more concerned if it didn't affect me in some way, as you should be.'

He paused before continuing. 'The first child I ever worked on was an eighteen-month-old boy who had been killed during a car ride with his father late at night. The story was that the father had taken his son out to drive around in the car to soothe him and calm him down. The boy had an ear infection and wouldn't stop crying.

'The moment I touched the child's flesh with the scalpel I wanted to run away. The whole time I swore I was going to retrain in another field. The emotion overwhelmed me, but it also energised me. The anger fuelled me. It made me alert. It made me focussed and, twenty minutes into the process, I found the truth,' he said, pausing to point at his throat. 'I was able to examine all tissues of the neck, superficial and deep and the force vector, magnitude and direction, to conclude that the death was no accident. He had been strangled before the minor car accident that was intended to cover up the act. The child's father was imprisoned for nineteen years. But between you and me, after concluding the process on the boy, I went out back and cried my heart out.'

Penn wasn't surprised to learn that.

'Tell your boss that and I'll tell her you passed out.'

Penn had no intention of telling his boss anything. He knew better than to get in between the sparring of these two.

'Take a minute to go to your happy place. It helps to keep it real.'

Where exactly was his happy place these days? Penn wondered. Once upon a time it had been spending time in the kitchen with Jasper, trying new recipes and enjoying the sheer joy on his brother's face when a new idea worked or the laughter when it didn't. Those times were growing less frequent as his teenage brother powered through life allowing nothing, not even Down's syndrome, to stop him.

Where the hell was his own happy place now? When was the last time he'd laughed with another adult?

Impulsively, he took out his phone and sent a quick text message.

'Ahhh...' Keats said as he stood back for a minute.

Penn put his phone away. He had learned that that one syllable non-word was a signal from Keats to himself. It meant something, but if questioned too soon, Keats would not answer.

'Hmm...'

Now that was unusual. He hadn't known an 'ahhh' followed by a 'hmm' before.

'Keats?'

'Did you say your boss wanted to be informed of even the smallest development here?' the pathologist asked.

'I did.'

'Then I think it might be a good idea to give her a call.'

SIXTEEN

As Bryant parked the car, Kim turned in her seat. The journey had been spent with her consciously preventing herself from calling Woody for an update on Symes. Given his instructions, she suspected she would have been strongly advised to focus on the case at hand, which is what she was trying to do.

'Leanne, you can stay here.'

So far today she'd been quite successful in ditching her protection.

'Yeah, cos I'm going to let you enter an open site swarming with hundreds of people who have unrestricted access in and out the building.'

'The morgue ain't usually that busy,' Kim said, hoping their destination was going to put her off.

'You've got to get there first.'

It didn't.

Kim groaned as she got out the car.

Her phone rang as Leanne fell into step behind her. It was a number she didn't recognise.

'Stone.'

'Detective Inspector, it's Gavin. Gavin Daynes. Zach's husband. You came to—'

'I know who you are,' she said with a brief smile.

'Rachel's just been on the phone. They're both struggling. May I come and do what you asked? Maybe it'll help them; acceptance, closure, I'm not sure, but I need to try and do something to help them both.'

'Of course. I understand. We'll make the necessary arrangements,' Kim answered.

By the time she'd finished giving him directions, the three of them had reached the outer doors to the morgue.

'Look, still alive,' she said to Leanne as the doors were opened.

Leanne offered no response but stepped aside for both Kim and Bryant to enter first.

'Hey, Keats, meet my new friend properly. Her name is Leanne, and you'll like her a lot,' Kim said, entering the morgue anteroom where Keats was washing his hands. Through the glass panel she could see a sheet-covered figure on a gurney beside the metal dish. Penn stood by the second metal dish, checking something on his phone. He waved an acknowledgement.

'Stone, we all know you have no friends,' Keats said, turning to Leanne. 'Do you find her just as insufferable as the rest of us?'

Kim saw the first signs of a smile on Leanne's face.

So did Keats, who offered his hand. 'Enough said. Pleased to meet you, and for whatever has transpired to force you into her company you have my deepest condolences.'

Bryant chuckled, and Kim wondered if there was anyone who was on her side.

'Keats, you haven't got time for this. We have a family member en route to identify the bodies.'

'Are you joking?'

'What's your gut say?'

His gut and her expression gave him the answer.

'All of them?'

Kim nodded. Yes, it would be a gruelling task indeed.

Keats immediately switched to organisation mode. It was usually preferable to have the victims identified prior to post-mortem, but circumstances often dictated that a level of urgency prompted the process to begin immediately.

'Okay, well, Mrs Daynes hasn't been touched yet so we'll work our magic and start with her, then Mr Daynes followed by Lewis and then Rosalind last, which will give me the chance to complete her.'

Kim waited. All eyes in the room were on Keats.

'Oh yes, of course. I called you here, didn't I? There's been a development I think you should be aware of.' He paused. 'Rosalind Daynes was approximately four months pregnant.'

SEVENTEEN

'Do you think she knew?' Bryant asked as Keats disappeared to prepare the bodies for identification.

'Rozzie or Helen?' Penn asked.

'Helen, of course,' Bryant said, 'I'm assuming Rozzie knew what was going on in her own body.'

'Not always the case,' Penn continued. 'There are hundreds of occasions where women have been taken by surprise when the contractions have started.'

'But isn't there a psychological condition that—'

'Guys, it doesn't make a difference if Rozzie knew or not. She didn't kill herself,' Kim said, wondering how she'd missed this sniping between them. 'It doesn't even make much difference if Helen knew about the baby.'

'Come on, guv,' Bryant protested. 'That's her grandchild. She'd have to be totally deranged to—'

'And you don't think she'd have to be to shoot her husband and two youngest children? If Helen Daynes had been in any rational state of mind at the time, she'd never have been holding a loaded gun in the first place.'

'Did someone say gun?' Mitch asked from the doorway. As

the head forensic techie he had a small office down the hallway, backed up with all the technical resources at Ridgepoint House in Birmingham.

'The gun, a 16-gauge Holland & Holland, was held on a shotgun licence. Perfectly legal with a 24-inch minimum length overall and a non-removable magazine that held no more than two rounds. Just had the ballistics report back. Everything is a match. That gun definitely fired those shells. Obviously the GSR test is a formality, and the results will be back tomorrow. In the meantime, Nigel Adams is over at the house now investigating the cause and damage of the fire. Oh, hello,' he said to Leanne as an afterthought.

'Thanks, Mitch,' Kim said as her phone rang. 'He's here, guys.'

She'd told Gavin to buzz her phone when he was outside so she could escort him into the viewing room.

'Can one of you let Keats know we're up.'

Keats had rushed off to make the viewing of Helen Daynes as trauma free as he could.

Bryant nodded as Leanne followed her.

'Don't worry, I'll wait outside,' she said as Kim stepped into the hallway.

Gavin looked red eyed and pale.

'Thank you for doing this. It's not going to be easy,' Kim said honestly. The man had four dead bodies to view.

'Easier on me than Zach or Rachel.'

Kim nodded as she guided Gavin back into the corridor.

'In here,' she said, opening the door to the viewing room.

Leanne took up a sentry position as Kim closed the door behind them.

'Not the cheeriest of rooms, I'm afraid.'

'Would it matter if it was?' he asked, rubbing his hands.

He took a few deep breaths in quick succession. Kim guessed he was eager to get this over and done with.

'I think they'll be bringing Helen through first. I have to warn you that it will be a difficult sight to see. Keats will do his best but...'

He took another breath. 'Will I be able to recognise her?'

Kim thought of the scene that had greeted her. The words 'just about' hovered on the tip of her tongue.

'Yes.'

Kim heard the telltale sound of wheels on the concrete floor.

She placed a reassuring hand on Gavin's arm as the double doors opened.

She both felt and heard his sharp intake of breath as the sheet-covered trolley came into the room with Keats at its helm. It was indeed an eerie sight, one that she had become inured to over the years.

Keats waited just a moment before looking to her for a signal.

She nodded.

Keats moved to the side and pulled the sheet back to the neck.

There was no way to hide the fact that the left half of her face was missing, but Keats had managed to remove most of the blood and had placed a gauze so that it ran close to the edge of her nose, leaving the right side of the face looking reasonably normal.

There were times that this man aggravated the life out of her. And then there were times that he didn't.

A soft cry escaped Gavin's lips.

She gripped his arm, and his other hand covered hers for support.

She watched as his eyes filled with emotion and reddened.

'Wh-What exactly do I have to do?'

'Just confirm to us that this is Helen Daynes, your mother-in-law.'

'It is,' he said, fighting back the tears.

He looked to her, his eyes filled with grief. 'May I?'

She looked to Keats who nodded.

Gavin took two steps forward. His right hand rose and touched a lock of hair resting on the right side of her forehead.

The tears ran unchecked over his face, and his voice was a grief-stricken whisper.

'Oh, Helen, what the hell did you do?'

EIGHTEEN

Symes watched as the bitch entered the hospital walking ahead of her colleague and her girlfriend. The Fiat Panda he'd taken from the old lady's drive wasn't exactly a status symbol, but it was the kind of car that got ignored and that suited him fine. He'd been enjoying following her from place to place, knowing he wasn't far away. He knew better than to get too close, but there was a pleasure building within him at the fact that she had no idea he was there.

The heady mix of anger and excitement surged through him, and he could feel the rage growing at her blasé attitude to his escape. A woman and a few cameras? Was that how seriously she took the threat of his freedom? Part of the fun was in making her suffer as much as possible before the final act.

He'd only felt rage like this once before.

Symes had always felt that he wouldn't be allowed to grow old in the army, though his intention after he signed up was to stay put for as long as he could. It was the first place he'd ever felt he belonged. His tours of Afghanistan had been the best years of his life. He'd left all the hearts and minds bollocks to the pansies and the cowards. If they wanted to go into villages and try to win over the locals, fine. He was first in line to go in and shoot the place up when a strategically placed IED exploded in their faces. You didn't win wars with flowers and chocolates.

He'd seen many sights that would have been enough to keep him in counselling with PTSD for a few lifetimes, but counselling was for lightweights as well. He'd always marvelled at the psychological frailty of some of his comrades. What the hell had they expected to see when they'd signed up? Had they imagined a life of building bridges and training exercises? Had they thought Afghanistan was a tourist destination getting a bad rap in the press? No, it was a war zone, had been for decades. There was noise, blood, limbs, explosions, mistrust and death. Lots of death. And he hadn't minded it one little bit.

Army life had suited him. He knew when to get up, eat, exercise, train, go to bed. He hadn't minded the authority as long as he got told when to fight. He had relinquished his own autonomy in exchange for being able to inflict violence and call it a job.

But that had all been taken away from him by people who had decided he was past his sell-by date. Corporal Harris had fought to keep him, but the annual pruning across all age groups had removed him from the one place he'd ever felt he belonged.

If he hadn't been retired from the army, he would have been by Harris's side and would have stopped that IED that tore off three of his limbs and pretty much decapitated him. A bloody good soldier had been lost, and he hadn't even been there.

He welcomed this feeling of injustice inside him. It ate away at his insides like neat bleach. There was only one way to exorcise it, he thought, cracking his knuckles.

Every ounce of his rage for everything he'd ever lost was directed at one single person, and he was about to do something that would rock her world.

NINETEEN

It was after five when Kim walked Gavin Daynes out of the mortuary doors. It had been a harrowing experience, and she had seen him grow paler with each viewing.

At one point she'd considered asking him about Rozzie's pregnancy but had decided against it for two reasons. He honestly looked as though he could take no more and, secondly, Rosalind was far more likely to have shared that information with a blood relative, perhaps her sister.

'Okay, Keats, anything more to note?' she asked, walking into the morgue. Bryant and Leanne had remained outside the viewing room, and Penn had continued to observe the post-mortems.

'Just working on Helen and there's little out of the ordinary. All organs appear to be healthy and functioning normally. Wear and tear on a couple of joints but nothing that was going to cause any major issues.'

That destroyed any notion she might have had that some kind of terminal illness had prompted a psychotic episode.

'Height and weight all in normal parameters, and her last meal was some kind of pasta dish.'

'Little,' she said, fixing her gaze onto the pathologist. 'You don't use the wrong words or misspeak. You said there was little out of the ordinary. You didn't say nothing.'

Keats smiled that secret smile that meant he was playing games with her. Luckily, she'd been on the pitch for the same number of years as him.

'Yes, Inspector, you are correct and this may be nothing but...'

'I'll be the judge of that,' she said, moving closer to the metal dish.

Keats lifted the sheet and brought out Helen's right arm. He offered no explanation and allowed her to see for herself.

'Is that a bruise?' she asked, looking at the discoloured skin around the wrist.

He nodded as he placed the arm back beneath the sheet.

'She may have knocked it, hit it during a fall or bruised it for any number of reasons. The colouring tells me it's no older than a day or two at the most.'

'Okay, Keats, thanks,' she said, heading for the door. She paused for just one second. If Keats had any bombshells to drop, he normally waited until she was halfway out the door.

There was nothing.

She continued into the corridor.

'Okay, I think we've got just enough time to go take one last look at the house before we announce the incident at the six o'clock press conference.'

'You can't do it,' Leanne said from behind.

Bryant jumped as though even he had forgotten she was there.

'Why the hell not?'

'Because you can't.'

'Oh, okay.'

'Really?' Leanne asked.

'Hell no. Are you out of your mind?' Kim asked as they exited the building as a threesome. 'I bloody hate press conferences but they're part of my job. We're getting hammered with press requests, and I'm not going to be told what I can and can't do by you.'

'Feel better now?' Leanne asked calmly.

'Much,' she said, smiling at Bryant.

'Is that your final word?'

'Yep,' Kim said, feeling empowered. Who knew she could get her own way by just being firm with the woman?

Leanne took out her phone and pressed a button.

She put it on loudspeaker and Kim was surprised to hear her boss's voice.

She stopped walking.

'DCI Woodward, we have a problem,' Leanne said.

'And it took this long?' he asked. 'I was way off in the sweepstake.'

'Sir,' Kim protested.

'She wants to return to the station to do a press conference,' Leanne offered in the vein of a head girl telling the teacher another kid had been running in the corridors.

Woody was silent for a good ten seconds.

'Stone, you can't do it,' he said eventually.

'For fu—'

'For a number of reasons,' he continued. 'Firstly, we need you to stay away from the station as much as—'

'Sir, how can I do my job?'

'Not altogether, Stone, but as much as possible. You're harder to find if you keep moving.'

'Who's on the run, me or him? Okay, never mind. I can do the press conference away from—'

'Impossible. I need Leanne to be right by you at all times, and she can't be on camera. You know what her job is.'

'Yeah, ruining my life.'

'A bit dramatic, even for you, Stone. I'll take care of the press conference.'

The line went dead, giving her no more opportunity to argue.

Leanne put the phone back in her pocket.

'And you can take that look off your face, Leanne,' she said, storming towards the car.

Calling her boss was pretty low.

'I'm gonna bet you told tales at school. You do know that snitches get stitches, don't you?'

'Was that a threat, Inspector?' Leanne asked, getting into the back seat of the car.

She could see the amusement dancing in Bryant's eyes.

'And you can shut up.'

He chuckled as he put the key in the ignition.

'One minute,' she said, taking out her phone.

Stacey answered on the second ring. Kim hit loudspeaker.

'Hey, boss, been waiting for you to come back.'

'Yeah, apparently I'm under car arrest. What've you got?'

'Err... not sure what that is but wanted to confirm that the family has absolutely no financial problems, and that the medical records show that Helen has been on medication for depression and anxiety for many years.'

Kim made a signal with her hand for Bryant to start the car and get rolling, before continuing her conversation with Stacey.

'From what the neighbours said, she had some kind of breakdown twenty years ago. Possibly linked to the loss of a child. The anniversary of that event is next week.'

Rachel's words were still in the back of her mind. Yes, it was a traumatic event to face, but she'd faced it nineteen other times without shooting her family.

'Do the records detail her mental-health issues?' Kim asked.

'Not so much. Her surgery was a one-man practice until seventeen years ago. Not a lot of detail prior to that except for prescription register, but the loss of the child wasn't the cause of her problems. Her first prescription for antidepressants was in '93.'

'Thanks, Stace. Now get off home,' Kim said, ending the call.

Helen had been struggling with her mental health for twenty-nine years.

So what the hell had caused the problem in the first place?

TWENTY

The house in Pedmore was still alive with activity, and Kim struggled to believe it had been only twenty-four hours since their first visit.

The emergency service vehicles had gone, but squad cars and forensic vehicles remained. A small Nissan on the far side of the drive told her that Nigel Adams, Fire Investigator, was still in attendance.

'What's the plan, guv?' Bryant asked.

'Talk to Nigel and then do a walk through,' she said, entering the house and turning left, away from the stairs.

Two rooms later, she reached the kitchen and was completely underwhelmed.

'That was the fire?' Kim asked, making Nigel jump out of his skin.

'Evening, Inspector. And yes, it was hardly the towering inferno.'

The fire appears to have originated from the kitchen bin directly beneath a small window that was open.

'I'm assuming the bin didn't catch fire by itself?'

'You assume correctly. No accelerant, no fuel, just a good old lighter.'

She moved closer and peered into the bin. 'Books?'

'Looks like journals or diaries to me. Fire didn't destroy them as much as the zealousness of the fire service I should imagine.'

'Bryant, get a techie to bag them up,' Kim instructed. She knew Ridgepoint had different methods for preserving paper evidence. Sometimes they air dried it, other times they freeze dried it depending on the level of damage. It would be useful if they could find out if there was something Helen had been trying to hide.

Kim held out her hand towards Bryant. Their years together told him she wanted a pen.

She used his biro to move the pile of books just over to the side.

'This isn't burned,' she said, moving around a paper bag with a fast-food logo on it. It was wet but not even singed.

Nigel stepped towards her. 'Fire didn't burn that long. Beneath the books were the leftovers of some kind of tomato and pasta dish. It was wet so the fire couldn't spread further down the bin. The plastic coating on some of the books prevented it from properly taking hold. Could have been a lot worse.'

'How long would the fire have burned?' Kim asked.

'No more than fifteen minutes – smouldered for another five or ten at most.'

'And the only place the smoke was escaping was through that window?'

Nigel nodded.

'Thanks,' she said, heading back out the kitchen with a couple of questions in her mind.

What had Helen been trying to hide if she was planning to kill herself anyway? If she didn't care enough not to kill her two youngest children, why did she care what her two eldest learned after she'd gone?

She stood silently at the kitchen door, lost in thought.

'All the doors and other windows were locked, guv,' Bryant reminded her, as though sensing the direction of her thoughts.

'I know that,' she snapped. They all knew there was no evidence of outside involvement. The pathologist was sure, she was sure, her boss was sure enough that he was planning in twenty minutes to announce to the world that Helen Daynes had murdered most of her family.

'Okay, we believe that Helen set her books on fire in the bin?' Kim asked.

'Correct,' Bryant answered.

She walked towards the stairs.

'Let's assume she already had the gun. She walked upstairs. She looked in the rooms of both of her children and made the conscious choice of shooting Lewis first because Rozzie was wearing headphones.'

Bryant walked behind her nodding, and Leanne was close behind him offering nothing at all.

Kim crossed the hall.

'There was a pause between shot two and three while she reloaded the gun. William heard the shots and was getting out of bed. She was standing around here, and her husband was on the right side of the bed.'

'Yep,' Bryant agreed.

'She shot him, and then used the last bullet on herself.'

'Exactly as Della Porter said,' Bryant added. 'Shot one, shot two, pause, shot three, pause, shot four.'

Yes, it was exactly as Della Porter had said.

She closed her eyes for a second and then glanced around the room with fresh eyes.

She had viewed the scene yesterday with the presumption

of events. What they'd been told matched everything they'd suspected. Everything had been locked and deadbolted.

'Bryant, we have a couple of problems.'

'Of course we do.'

'If Helen lit the fire before she got the gun, why did Della hear shots around three? Her son saw the smoke while out running at 7 a.m., but we know it only burned for a total of half an hour.'

'Maybe Della got confused.'

'That's not all,' Kim said, stepping further into the room. She could still remember every detail of the bodies as if they were still lying there. 'Helen was wearing her nightdress. She was ready for bed. Her denture is still in a glass on the bedside cabinet. Is that normal behaviour for someone who's about to shoot their family?'

'That entire sentence is a contradiction. What is normal behaviour if you're planning to do such a thing?' he argued. 'The word normal doesn't enter into it. Helen may have gone to bed as normal. Fallen asleep then woke up later and had the compulsion for whatever reason to do what she did.'

She searched her memory again as a feeling formed in the pit of her stomach.

'Slippers and pockets.'

'Guv, what the hell...?'

She looked at her watch. It was four minutes to six.

'I'll explain in a minute but first get Woody on the phone. Now.'

TWENTY-ONE

This was the golden hour for more reasons than one, Symes thought as he pulled into the car park. During his period of supposed rehabilitation while married to Gloria, he'd attended a prison photography course. He'd learned that the golden hour occurred before sunset when the daylight is redder and softer than when the sun is higher in the sky.

It was also the time that parents were squeezing the last few moments out of the local park before the sun disappeared completely. It had been a mild, pleasant March day and there were two cars left in the car park. Two women and two children. One woman stood and called out. The little boy came running, took his mother's hand and headed to the car. Within minutes he was buckled in and the car was pulling away.

One woman and one child. A girl.

Perfect.

He got out of the car right before the woman called over to her child. He dangled the piece of rope with a loop on the end.

'Bruno,' he called out, looking around and paying no attention to the woman approaching her car.

'Bruno,' he called more urgently.

The woman eyed him suspiciously but continued towards her vehicle.

'You haven't seen a poodle on your travels, have you?' he called out.

She shook her head as he moved a bit closer, looking beyond her all the time. His eyes searching for Bruno.

'Wife got to choose the dog; I got to choose the name,' he said, rolling his eyes.

The wariness hadn't quite left her eyes but there was the hint of a smile. The mention of a wife and type of dog had lessened the perceived threat.

'Little bugger slipped his lead. I thought he'd come back to the car but...' His words trailed away. He had kept her attention long enough that he was now just six feet away.

'I'm sorry, I haven't seen him,' she said, fumbling in her bag for her car keys. The kid had the sense to eye him suspiciously from beneath her tawny fringe.

'Oh well, I suppose you'll have to do then,' he said, moving forward quickly, widening the noose and slipping it over her head.

The shock rendered her numb for just a second, which gave him the chance to start pulling her towards the car. He grabbed the child and put a hand over her mouth as the mother tried to make noises.

'If you scream I'm going to kill your mummy, understand?' he said to the little girl. Her eyes filled with tears as she watched her mother struggling for breath and trying to claw at the rope.

The woman's legs buckled as she tried to fight him. He lowered his arm and continued to drag her across the ground, prompting retching and coughing noises to come out of her mouth. Her heels were gathering gravel as he pulled her along.

He opened the back door of the car and pulled the woman to her feet.

'Keep quiet and I'll let you go. Make a sound and you're both dead.'

He could see from the fight in her eyes the second he let go of the rope, she was going to scream for all she was worth.

He gave her a left hook to the side of the head. Her eyes rolled, and he folded her into the back seat.

'Mummy... Mummy!' the girl cried.

He pushed the child in after her mother and slammed the door shut. The priority was to get away from here and get onto the back lanes like he'd planned.

He threw himself into the car, started it up and tore out the car park at speed. The park had been chosen because it lay at the outer edge of a small estate in Wollaston. Right opposite was a lane that wound past a couple of properties and then disappeared into a maze of single-track roads that ran along the east side of the Bridgnorth road. He crossed the main road onto the first winding lane and let out a sigh of relief. They were now out of view.

The child was still crying for her mother to wake up. She sat up and tried to grab at him through the gap in the seats.

Looks like he had a spirited one.

He backhanded her, and she fell back onto the crumpled heap of her mother.

The crying intensified, and Symes heard a low groan from the mother.

'Mummy, Mummy, wake up.'

'It's o... okay, Em. It'll b... be... fine. I'm h... here. We're together. No one is going to h... hurt you.'

Symes smiled. None of her words were true, but she didn't know that yet.

He heard movement in the back.

'Stay down,' he barked, which made the little girl cry more.

Darkness was descending even quicker along the country lane with no street lights.

He knew he had to act quickly before the fog in the mother's head cleared and she tried something stupid. She knew she was fighting for her own life as well as her child.

He drove quickly as he heard more movement amongst the crying. He pushed his foot down on the brake hard, sending them both crashing about on the rear seat, then drove forward at speed, bouncing them around like ragdolls. The spot he wanted was right in the middle of this three-mile lane. He stopped sharply on a bend. By the time he was finished, she wouldn't have a chance to get his licence plate.

He stopped the car.

The crying intensified.

He walked around to the rear passenger door and pulled at the rope still around the woman's neck.

'Get out,' he shouted.

She wrapped her arms tighter around her child as a protective barrier.

'Let her go or I will kill you both.'

He pulled her again.

'No, don't take her. Take me. Let her go,' she cried, trying to hang on to the screaming child.

He yanked the woman towards him. 'No trade. I don't want you. Now let her go or I'll cut both your fucking throats right here.'

'No, no, no,' the little girl cried, trying to hang on.

'Oh, for fuck's sake,' he said, reaching in and placing a meaty hand around her little fingers. He squeezed hard and then yanked again.

The child cried out in pain, and the woman became free.

'Please, I'm begging you. Don't—'

He slammed the door shut and pushed the woman forcefully into the brambles and put his foot on her neck.

'Listen carefully or you'll never see your daughter again.

The detective you want is DI Stone and give her a message from me. One down, one to go.'

He removed his foot, jumped back into the car and drove away, travelling further into the night.

TWENTY-TWO

'Care to explain to us why you've just told Woody to delay the press conference?' Bryant asked once she'd ended the call.

There hadn't been a chance to give him the details, but she'd stopped the announcement in time and that was all that mattered.

'Well, I'm not sure Leanne gives a shit but I'm happy to tell you.'

'Go on then.'

'Muscle memory for starters,' she said, moving to the left side of the bed.

She pointed to a pair of moccasin slippers positioned neatly just in front of the bedside cabinet.

'If you're a slipper wearer it's automatic. Your legs sweep over the bed and your feet go straight into them. It's an unconscious act. If you're planning on traipsing around your house loading guns and starting fires you might not want to do it barefoot.'

Bryant opened his mouth as he searched his memory bank for an angle to argue. He closed it again.

'Agreed?'

'Let's just say I see your point. That's the slippers. What about the pockets?'

'Did you see any in Helen's nightdress?'

'Do nightdresses normally have pockets?' he asked, turning to Leanne.

She shrugged. 'Dunno. I sleep commando.'

'Urgh, not on my sofa you don't,' Kim said. 'Tonight, you take the spare bed and you put some clothes on.'

'Pockets,' Bryant reminded her.

'We know Helen could find her way around a gun. She must have known how many shells the gun held and that she would need to reload at least once. She had no pockets, so you're telling me she carried the spare shells in one of her hands when she needed both hands to aim the gun. Think about it. In either hand it's going to be a hurdle,' she said as she heard footsteps coming up the stairs.

'Just in time, Mitch,' she said as the techie came into view.

'Heard you were sniffing around again, Inspector.'

'Err... I'm the police and it's a crime scene, Mitch.'

'I know that. Three dead folks and one shooter gave it away.'

'Leave the smart-arse comments to your colleague,' she advised. 'And find out how a fifth party got in and out.'

He shook his head. 'Didn't happen. Everything was checked yesterday. The fire service broke the deadbolts on both the front door and the kitchen door. Every window in the place was checked and found to be either locked or closed properly, except for that small kitchen window that wouldn't even accommodate a medium-sized dog.'

'Check again, Mitch. With every minute that passes, I grow more convinced that someone else was here.'

'Insp—'

'Mitch, I'm not backing down.'

He shook his head in defeat and headed back down the stairs.

'We're now looking for motive,' Kim said, stepping back into the hallway. 'And this is where I want to start,' she said, heading back towards Rozzie's room.

'We know that she was pregnant. We don't know by whom or even who knew.'

As she spoke, both she and Bryant were opening drawers and taking a quick look inside.

'Helen was a diary keeper so...'

'We're assuming those are Helen's diaries in the bin cos we thought she started the fire, but they could be Rozzie's,' Bryant offered.

'Too many. Few teenagers keep a journal or diary religiously. There were at least ten books in the bin.'

Kim wondered if teenagers put deep and meaningful stuff on their phones or iPad these days, both of which were long gone to Ridgepoint.

Kim dropped to her knees.

'You know, sometimes the most obvious places... What the fuck?' she cried, reaching under the bed.

She grabbed a foot and pulled; a leg followed, and another, and then a torso.

'What the...?'

Bryant stopped speaking as Leanne barged him to get Kim out the way.

'For fuck's sake,' Kim snarled, looking over Leanne's shoulder. 'Why would Symes be here?'

Leanne said nothing until Bryant hauled the guy onto his feet.

'Who the hell are you?' Bryant asked as Leanne let her pass.

'And how the fuck did you get in here?' she added.

'I'm sorry. I'm sorry,' he said, holding up his hands and backing away.

'Stay where you are, fella,' Bryant advised.

'Answer the question,' Kim demanded.

'Which one?' he asked, genuinely confused.

'Who are you?' Kim barked.

'I'm... I'm Reece. I live next door. I'm sorry. I never should have... I just... I'm sorry.'

He had tufts of dirty blonde hair sticking out from under his baseball cap, and his complexion was tanned and healthy. Kim guessed him to be early thirties.

'Do you have any idea how many things I could fucking charge you with right now?' Kim screamed.

'I didn't mean any harm.'

'You've contaminated a crime scene. What the hell were you thinking?'

He was shrinking before her eyes, but she didn't care.

'How the hell did you get in?'

'Copper on the door was called to the garage. I didn't think I'd get inside. I could hear voices but...'

'You knew exactly where you were going?'

He nodded.

'To Rozzie's bedroom?'

'Yes.'

'Is there something wrong with you? What exactly did you want to see?'

He blushed.

'I just wanted to make sure. I mean I didn't really believe they were all gone. I just wanted to see for myself.'

There was a shiftiness to his eyes that told Kim he was hiding something.

'Did you know Rozzie well?'

He nodded then shook his head.

'I worked here. I did stuff for Mr and Mrs Daynes. Just shit they didn't want to do. Am I under arrest?'

'Not yet but keep talking and you might be. What the hell were you thinking?'

'I wasn't... I just... I'm sorry.'

Kim exhaled, not sure how many more times she could shout at a man who said sorry every other sentence.

'Did you take anything?' she asked, eyeing him suspiciously.

He shook his head vehemently. 'No, I swear. You can search me.'

'Oh we will, you can count on that.'

Kim looked to her colleague. 'Bryant, have a word, eh?' she said, nodding towards the stairs. Leaving the guard post of a crime scene was going to cost someone their job. She just wanted to make sure it didn't happen again. 'And bring Mitch back with you.'

'On it, guv,' he said, leaving the room.

She turned back to Reece. 'Wasn't it you that raised the alarm yesterday morning?'

He nodded. 'I saw the smoke. I was on my morning run. Every morning at 6.30. Have done for years. It keeps me—'

'Okay, Reece, got it,' she said, holding up her hands. 'Did you see or hear anything else unusual?'

He shook his head. 'Nothing. I didn't hear a thing. I'd tell you if I heard anything or knew anything. I swear.'

Kim regarded him silently for a minute. He was agitated. Too agitated.

Bryant appeared with a harassed-looking Mitch in tow.

'Sonny Jim here was hiding under the bed. Get one of your guys to bag his clothing, give him a blue suit and escort him back to his house.' She turned back to Reece. 'Where you will stay until you report to Halesowen police station at 8 a.m. tomorrow.'

'What for?' he asked, losing what little colour he had left.

'To make a formal statement. Now go with Mitch and then go home,' she said, putting him out of his misery.

'Is that it?' Bryant asked as Reece followed Mitch out of the room.

'What do you suggest I do?'

'He knows something.'

'You think he's gonna tell us the state he's in right now? And I left my "absolute truth" extractor back at the station.'

He rolled his eyes at her sarcasm.

Whatever he knew, they'd focus on getting it out of him tomorrow. She could definitely see why some of the Daynes family called the neighbours the weirdos.

'He's been handed over to Geoff,' Mitch said, reappearing. 'Who also said to tell you that everything has been checked again, and he can confirm that I was right and no one left this house after the incident.'

Kim regarded Mitch for a full minute. 'Did Geoff really say all that?'

'No, but I wanted someone else to be responsible for giving you the answer you didn't want.'

'Okay,' she said, heading for the top of the stairs.

She wasn't sure what he'd expected her to do but he let out a sigh of relief.

'You're not right so don't celebrate just yet. I'm just figuring out how I'm going to prove you wrong.'

She came to a halt in the upper hallway.

'Right, let's play this through. We don't know if the dead-bolts were on all the doors when he came in. Not as important. More important is how he left the house to be sure it looked locked up tight.'

'He?' Bryant questioned.

'An assumption for the purpose of the exercise,' she said as her mind started racing ahead. 'He gets the gun, loads it as he's walking. He shoots Lewis and then Rozzie,' she said, moving from room to room.

She closed her eyes as she visualised the scene. 'He pauses

to reload the gun. Both Helen and William are getting out of bed. He shoots William. Helen keeps coming at him. He grabs her wrist and forces her to the ground. He shoots her under the chin and wipes his prints off the gun. He wraps Helen's hand around the handle and allows the gun to fall from her grip. He goes looking for what he came for. Takes him a while to find the diaries. He takes them downstairs and puts them in the bin. He sets fire to them and then he... then he...'

Kim narrowed her eyes and charged across the hallway and down the stairs. At least four officers moved aside as she stormed to the kitchen.

She opened the door to a store cupboard that held a vacuum and a couple of mops. Everything had been pushed to one side.

'He lights the books on fire by the open window and waits for someone to raise the alarm. He stays perfectly still until the fire service have put out the fire and go searching for victims. He lets himself out of the cupboard, slips out of the back door and vanishes silently into the night.'

The three people who had followed her regarded her silently until Mitch broke the spell.

'Aww, shit and for once I thought I was right.'

TWENTY-THREE

It was almost eight when Bryant pulled up outside her house on what had been another thirteen-hour day.

She'd spent most of the trip back from Pedmore on the phone to Woody who, understandably, wanted to see her first thing in the morning. Neither he nor the press office were pleased with her last-minute press conference cancellation. She was pretty sure they'd be even less pleased if she'd allowed Woody to declare to the world that Helen Daynes had murdered three people, only to rock up the next day to say 'Oops, sorry, no she didn't'. She had no idea how many heads would roll on that one.

'Have a good night,' Bryant said with a twitching lip as she and Leanne got out of the car.

Kim managed to offer her colleague a withering look before he pulled away with a smile on his face.

Kim walked up the driveway.

Her heart leaped into her mouth as a shadow appeared to her left.

'What the—?'

For the second time in as many hours she felt herself being

pushed to the side as Leanne knocked the lurking figure to the ground.

Kim looked down at the tangle of female limbs on the ground. A familiar voice sounded from underneath Leanne.

'Get this bloody woman off me.'

Kim stood back and folded her arms. 'Frost, what the hell are you doing here?'

For a second, she couldn't help the amusement she felt at the sight of Leanne sprawled all over the reporter, pulling Frost's arm up her back.

'What the fuck is going on here?' Frost asked as Leanne got off her and offered a hand to pull her up.

Frost offered her a filthy look before pushing herself up from the ground.

'A bloody reporter knows where you live?' Leanne asked.

'It's a long story. Go inside, I'll—'

'Err... no. I think we'll all go inside,' Leanne said, looking around as Kim unlocked the door.

'What the fuck is going on?' Frost asked, closing the door behind her. Leanne had already started her sweep of the house.

'And where's Barney?' she asked, looking around.

'On holiday. Now what the hell are you doing skulking around my house at night? You do realise that's crossing a line?'

Frost shrugged. 'I want my question. Press conference was cancelled, and I want my bloody question.'

Kim allowed the relief to wash over her that the lurker had been no one any more dangerous than Tracy bloody Frost.

'You really think I'm going to answer any question about the case? And you just lost the privilege anyway by turning up at my home uninvited.'

Frost was unperturbed as she followed Kim to the kitchen.

Kim turned. 'You do know I'm going to physically throw you out in a minute, right?'

Frost took a seat on one of the stools at the breakfast bar. 'Yeah, whatever. So I'd like to take my question now please.'

Kim was struck by the irony that her own home was currently filled with women she didn't like. Although at least over the years Frost had earned a modicum of respect from her.

'I'm not going to answer anything.'

'It's not about the case. I mean it was about the case but not anymore. Now I have a different question.'

Kim sighed. 'Go on.'

'Who is she?' Frost asked as Leanne swept through the kitchen and headed towards the door leading to the garage.

'My girlfriend.'

Frost laughed, and Leanne paused and raised an eyebrow.

'My sister.'

'You don't have one.'

'My second cousin twice removed. Come on, surely I have one of those somewhere.'

'You know I'll just make shit up if you don't—'

'Isn't that how you normally write your articles?' Kim asked.

'Stone.'

'Okay, but once I've told you, you've never seen her and she becomes invisible to you.'

'This ain't a movie, and I'm not sure you have spell-casting capabilities. On top of that I'm not a bottomless pit of favours; nor do I work for West Midlands Police.'

'No, you're sitting in my kitchen and one step away from a phone call to your editor to lodge a formal complaint.'

'Got any snacks?' she asked, looking around.

'Out,' Kim snapped, moving around the breakfast bar. 'Out of my house now.'

'Okay, I'm going,' Frost said, hopping off the bar stool.

'No you're not,' Leanne said, coming back into the kitchen from the garage.

'What?' Frost and Kim said together.

'Not before you tell her the truth,' Leanne said, filling the percolator jug.

Frost showed the surprise that Kim felt at Leanne's familiarity around her home. Although if Frost hadn't distracted her, she would already have done it herself.

'You're kidding?' Kim asked.

Leanne shook her head. 'No. She already knows too much. We have to silence her somehow. She's a reporter of all things.'

Frost's mouth started to fall open at the gravity in Leanne's voice.

'Silence me how?' she asked, looking from one to the other.

'But surely if we tell her, we'll then have to...'

'Yes, kill her,' Leanne finished.

'Are you two out of your fucking minds?' Frost snapped.

'Seriously, Stone, you're gonna have to tell her,' Leanne said, turning her attention back to the coffee.

'Okay, Frost. You know how you always felt I wasn't quite human. You were right. Apparently I was shot to earth in a giant egg from the planet Storga and every laboratory in town wants to capture me for experimentation. Leanne is a mutant ninja turtle sent to protect—'

'You're not funny,' Frost said even though Kim could swear she heard a chuckle from Leanne.

Oh but it was light relief poking fun at Frost after a long, hard day.

She glanced at Leanne who nodded subtly.

'Wait a minute,' Frost said before she had a chance to speak. The reporter looked from one to the other. 'This is about Symes, isn't it?'

'And the penny finally drops,' Kim said, folding her arms.

'She's your protection in case he comes looking for you?'

'Along with more security hardware than the Bank of England,' Kim offered.

Frost's forehead puckered. 'Do they really think he's that stupid?'

'No, they absolutely know he is. He's made no secret that I'm the only loose end he wants to tie up before he dies. It's a suicide mission for him.'

'Wasn't he going to beat those little girls to death?'

Kim swallowed. 'Yes.'

'And she's gonna stop him doing the same to you?' Frost asked with disbelief in her voice.

'She got you to the ground easy enough,' Kim defended.

'A slightly different prospect really. Against Symes I'm not too sure...'

Leanne turned to face Frost. 'Let me worry about Symes while you worry about you. From the point at which you leave this house, you should try not to be alone. Stay where it's busy and even stay over at a friend's house for the night.'

'Not here,' Kim interjected.

'Try to make sure that someone knows where you're going at all times, and check in with colleagues and friends regularly. Got it?'

Frost nodded.

'If you repeat this to anyone, your editor will be told you endangered lives. Not one word...'

'Stone, can you tell Rambo here that I retain information quite easily and I don't need to be told when something is important.'

Kim looked at Leanne, who nodded her understanding.

'Fair enough. Now you can go,' Leanne said.

'Hey,' Kim said. 'Only I get to throw Frost out of my house.' She turned to the reporter. 'Now piss off.'

'Gladly,' Frost said, heading for the hallway.

Kim followed her and opened the door. Frost was two steps out of the house.

'Oi,' Kim shouted.

Frost turned.

'Do what she said.'

'Yeah, you too,' Frost said, before turning away and heading out of the gate.

Kim closed the door and felt a weariness wash over her.

After a day like today she'd normally spend a few hours on the bike, talking to and fussing Barney before taking him for a long walk before bed. Barney was having a whale of a time, judging by the photos of him running on the beach sent to her phone by Charlie.

Leanne was no replacement for her best friend, she thought as the woman entered the kitchen doing something on her phone.

'Who's delivering your meal tonight, the SAS?' Kim asked.

'Nope, Just Eat. Want anything?'

Kim shook her head. She wasn't hungry. All she wanted was a bit of time on her own.

Leanne's phone tinged receipt of a message.

'Food order?' Kim asked.

Leanne shook her head as she approached the alarm panel.

'No, it's a reminder that we've been in the house for fifteen minutes and the alarm hasn't been rearmed.'

'For fuck's sake. This is worse than prison. Am I under curfew now?'

'Jesus, your boss was right about the drama. The system is doing exactly what we asked it to.'

'Well I might accidentally just switch the bloody thing off just for my own amusement as soon as your back is turned,' Kim said, feeling her irritation at the constraints boil over.

'Go ahead, but you won't much care for the security team that breaks down your door.'

'What bloody team?'

'It's not a standalone alarm with just an audible siren. Nobody even listens to them anymore. The system is linked to an alarm receiving company who will dispatch manpower if we don't stick to the protocols we've set. The external cameras are now being monitored by them.'

'That's why you didn't go to bed,' Kim observed. 'And now I can't even go outside my own home without appearing on someone's monitoring screen. You know, Leanne, I sure am glad you came.'

'You're welcome.'

Kim could think of few people who infuriated her more than this woman, and being stuck with her twenty-four hours a day was really starting to get on her tits.

She couldn't even go outside for a breather without setting off some kind of tripwire or motion sensor.

'I'm going for a bath or a shower or maybe both. I'm going to be in the bathroom some time and I don't need your protection in there.'

Her dramatic exit was interrupted by a knock at the door.

Her heart jumped for the second time as she looked to Leanne, who quickly accessed the app on her phone.

The frown disappeared and was replaced with puzzlement.

'Open it. It's fine.'

Kim unlocked every bolt she'd just locked and pulled the door open.

She was completely unprepared to see the person who was standing on the other side.

TWENTY-FOUR

How hard would it be? Symes wondered, keeping watch on the ground-floor flat in Dudley. It hadn't been difficult to find out where the young detective lived. He'd guessed that all the bitch's colleagues had been given instruction, so he hadn't been surprised when she'd exited the station with her curly haired workmate.

The child was where he wanted her. She was bound and gagged and alone. Hopefully neither she nor he would have to wait too long, and she too would help him torture the bitch.

He wondered if he should have taken more time to cover his tracks, but it was like being at an all-you-can-eat buffet without using a napkin. He didn't care what he left behind of himself. He'd have happily left a signed confession if he'd had the time. So what if they knew it was him. He had no intention of being charged with any crime. He had no intention of ever going back to prison. He would complete his missions and then run until they put a bullet in him.

And one of those missions was to cause the bitch as much pain as he could, so after leaving the cottage, he had simply pulled up at the edge of a trading estate which had given him a decent view of the station.

He had slipped in two cars behind and followed Wood and her colleague through Old Hill and Netherton, taking care to park the second the driver had started to slow. He'd watched as Wood exited the vehicle, took out her keys and entered the property. Due to the open blinds and a powerful light, he'd even seen the passionate kiss she'd exchanged with her partner.

The detective removed her jacket while the other one appeared to be serving up a meal. There were smiles, laughter, a bottle of wine taken from the fridge. They carried plates and glasses out of view before the light went off.

A snapshot. Normality. Coming home from work, enjoying a nice meal and a glass of wine. Relaxing on the sofa half watching the television while exchanging the events of the day. Such simple pleasures and so fucking nauseating. How fragile was this simple existence? Just five minutes with Detective Constable Stacey Wood and that peaceful, idyllic picture would be blown to smithereens.

There was a reason he'd decided to target Wood. He'd kept a keen eye on the bitch's activities since being inside. He knew that Wood had been kidnapped by a gang of racists and that the bitch had saved her life. Shit like that bonded you to a person. His tours of Afghanistan had taught him that. It was a connection that never went away. The loss of any of her team would hit her hard but probably this one most of all.

He was about to pull away when the kitchen light illuminated the space once more. By the time he'd moved the car closer, they appeared to be in some kind of heated discussion. The body language of hands on hips, shaking heads and shrugs told him this wasn't a normal end-of-day conversation.

He watched with interest as the detective's partner appeared to be rushing around the kitchen. She grabbed a bag and some keys and shrugged herself into a bomber jacket while Wood continued to talk.

They stood and stared at each other for a couple of seconds before the partner brushed past Wood and out of the room. The kitchen once again descended into darkness.

The partner came out of the house and headed for the car. She started the engine and then paused as though considering whether or not she should go back inside.

In his excitement, he'd forgotten to swallow, and a trail of saliva travelled over his chin.

His prayers had been answered.

Stacey Wood was about to be left alone.

TWENTY-FIVE

'Sir, what are you doing here?' she asked DCI Woodward as she stepped aside for him to enter.

Immediately he looked out of place in her home. Oh no, this wasn't right at all. There was a good chance once this was all over that she might sell the house and buy a tent and pitch it on some waste ground somewhere. She'd discuss it with Barney upon his return.

Woody nodded towards Leanne as he took a seat on the sofa. He didn't remove his jacket or the scarf from around his neck.

'Symes has kidnapped a little girl.'

'Wh-What?' she asked, dropping to the sofa opposite her boss.

'Around 6 p.m. this evening he abducted a seven-year-old girl named Emma Bunting from a park in Wollaston. Initially he took the child's mother but threw her out of the car a couple of miles away from the site. He mentioned you by name, so he wanted you to know what he'd done as soon as possible.'

'Did he hurt her?' Kim asked.

'Mother or child?'

'Both.'

'Mrs Bunting was pretty banged up and has a mild concussion and, according to her, he struck her daughter a couple of times to keep her quiet.'

The rage inside her began to bubble.

She stood up and reached for her phone.

Leanne hadn't moved from her position at the breakfast bar. Kim wasn't sure if it was the same coffee in her hand or a refill. She was going to have to swill it down. They had work to do.

'What are you doing?' Woody asked.

'Assembling the team. We're already four hours behind the snatch time. We need to mobilise—'

'Put the phone down,' Woody said gravely.

Suspicion began to rise when she counted back the hours.

'Why am I only hearing about this now?'

'Because you're not going anywhere near it.'

'Sir, you have to let me run this case. I know how he thinks,' she protested hotly.

'And he knows how you think. That's the problem. His only aim with that taunt was to draw you out. To lure you. He knows how you'll react. One of you has to act against type, and it's going to be you.'

'Give me twelve hours and I'll have Emma back—'

'Not happening. A team has been assembled working out of Dudley. You are strictly forbidden from involving yourself in any way with the abduction case. Go anywhere near it and there will be consequences. I'm talking severe repercussions.'

'He's going to kill her,' Kim protested. 'He feels he's owed two lives. If you don't get her back, she could be dead by the morning. There could even be another—'

'Calm down, Stone. Let's not get ahead of—'

'Sir, I swear, if you let me work with the search team, I'll find her—'

'There is nothing you can do or say that will sway me so

stop wasting your breath. Symes is playing with you. He's after maximum suffering. He's also trying to get in your head. Divert your focus. Do not let that happen.'

He stood. 'If you try and get involved in the investigation, you'll be a distraction to the team running the case. You have to let them do their job or you may be putting Emma's life in danger.'

She followed him to the door, still reeling from what she'd been told.

'How severe, sir?' she asked as she pulled back the locks.

'Sorry?' he said, putting one foot out the door.

'You said the repercussions of my involvement in the abduction case would be severe.'

'And I meant it. It's a direct order.'

'So, how severe?'

'Now is not the time to test my limits, Stone.'

'How severe?' she repeated.

He thought for a moment. 'It's safe to say that if you go anywhere near the team running the abduction case, it will be the last thing you do for West Midlands Police. I promise you.'

He said nothing further as he turned and headed down her path.

It was only once he was out of sight that she realised he hadn't told her exactly what it was that Symes had said.

TWENTY-SIX

Penn held the two napkins and wondered where they were supposed to go. Did they go underneath the cutlery or to the side of it? He thought about his last restaurant dining experience and personally he hated having to move his cutlery to gain access to his napkin. He placed it to the side of the cutlery.

He took a breath as the clock struck nine. She would be here any minute.

Lynne had responded to his text message invitation almost immediately when he was at the morgue. He'd felt the smile form on his face the moment he'd seen the bobbed-out-tongue emoji. He could imagine her taking a quick, sneaky look at her phone when no one else was looking or while Travis was giving one of his long, laborious briefings.

Keats had asked him to find his happy place, and Penn had realised that he was rarely happier than when he was with Lynne. He hadn't realised it when they'd worked together, but he'd missed everything about her once he'd transferred back to West Mids. She'd still been engaged when he'd left, and even when that relationship ended, he hadn't wanted to rock the boat of their friendship.

But now it was a boat worth rocking because the very thought of her meeting someone else and talking to him about it like they were just buddies filled him with a rage he wasn't used to feeling. It also brought a little bile to the back of his throat.

On cue, three light taps sounded on the glass panel of the front door.

She always did that, and it made him smile.

'Come on in,' he said, opening the door.

Her short brown hair had been freshly blow-dried, and her elfin features had been shown the make-up brush. It didn't bother him in the slightest. He'd seen her covered in mud and sweat after a brutal foot chase, but it pleased him that she'd made the effort. For him.

'Blimey, Penn, what's all this?' she asked as a smile pulled her lips upwards. 'I thought we were doing pizza and beer like we normally do.'

Despite her protestations, he could tell she was delighted.

'Doesn't hurt to be civilised now and again,' he said, pulling out her chair.

'Why, thank you kindly,' she said, removing her jacket first.

He quietly admired her sequinned top, which was not a beer-and-pizza kind of top.

'Wine?' he asked.

'On a school night?'

He would never presume that she was not going home. 'Uber?' he asked, with the bottle poised above her glass.

She nodded and he poured.

'What smells delicious and how much did you have to pay Jasper to prepare it for you?' she asked, sitting back in her seat.

God, how he loved that playful sparkle in her eye when she was winding him up.

'An Xbox game and cinema tickets for him and Billy.'

Lynne threw back her head and laughed. The sound washed away every stress of the day.

'Just kidding. It's lasagne and I made it myself.'

'Oh.'

He rounded on her, laughing. 'Hey, I can cook you know.'

'Jasper,' she called towards the stairs. 'We need you.'

'He's not going to hear you. He's at Billy's tonight.'

'All night?' she asked.

He nodded as he took the lasagne from the oven. A simple green salad had already been prepared.

He placed both dishes in the centre of the table, lit the candles and turned out the lights.

The darkness blocked out the rest of the kitchen, illuminating only the dining table and creating immediate intimacy.

'Hmmm...' Lynne said appreciatively.

He wasn't sure if she was responding to the food or the scene he'd created.

'Oooh, forgot the spatula,' he said before he sat down.

Lynne burst out laughing. 'Not even in my top ten of things you might say next,' she said once her giggles had subsided. 'But a man should never be without his spatula.'

Penn laughed along with her. He knew there were times that his social cues were not fully functioning, that he could easily misread subtleties and say inappropriate things, but Lynne had never made him feel uncomfortable or stupid or inadequate.

Lynne put her elbows on the table and rested her chin on her folded hands. His breath caught. Never had she looked more beautiful.

'Nice job, Penn,' she breathed.

Her hand reached across the table towards his. She took the spatula from his grip.

'I'm bloody starving. Let's dish up some food.'

He laughed as she dug in to the pasta and ferried a decent piece across to her plate. Humour had always played a huge part in their relationship, but he knew that something else was growing between them.

He was about to ask how her day had been when a knock sounded at the door, surprising them both.

'Jasper?' Lynne asked.

'He has a key,' Penn said, pushing back his chair.

It wasn't the dead of night, but it was past the acceptable time for unannounced visitors.

The door knocked again.

'Stacey?' he said, surprised to see his colleague standing there.

'Sorry, Penn. Devon was called in to work and we're not supposed to be alone, so I'm trying to follow the rules, but I couldn't go to my parents cos if Symes sees me do that... They're old and I can't put them in...' Her words trailed away as she saw Lynne and the table behind him.

'Oh shit. Oh sorry. Oh my goodness.'

'Come in, Stace,' he said, unable to leave her on the doorstep.

He closed the door.

'Everything okay?' Lynne asked as they entered the kitchen.

'Yeah, sorry if I've interrupted something. Just needed a quick chat with Penn.'

'I heard you say something about not being alone and trying to follow the rules. What's going on?'

'It's umm... err...' Penn stuttered.

'Can't say,' Stacey offered weakly.

Lynne looked from one to the other. 'I think I'm gonna go.'

'No,' Penn and Stacey said together.

Lynne hesitated as though waiting for Stacey to offer to leave. He could see the discomfort on his colleague's face. She couldn't offer to leave, and he wouldn't have let her go.

Lynne gave a small nod as she pushed her chair back from the table.

'Thanks for the thought, Penn,' she said, handing her napkin to him as she passed. 'It really was lovely.'

Penn felt something drop inside him as he followed her to the door.

'Lynne, let's do this another—'

'Penn, we're good mates. We'll always be good mates. Let's not try and take this anywhere else. It doesn't work.'

He opened his mouth to argue but she shook her head.

They were done.

TWENTY-SEVEN

'Okay, guys,' Kim said, after her first swig of coffee, 'it's official. It's murder. Helen Daynes did not kill her family.'

'Shiiit,' Stacey said.

'Bloody hell,' Penn agreed.

'With that in mind, it's back to the drawing board. Go over every statement, check all CCTV in the area for the night before and up until 10 a.m. the next morning.'

'But weren't the shots heard around 3 a.m.?' Stacey asked.

'We think our guy hid in the house and slipped out when the fire service broke the door down.'

'Clever but risky,' Penn said.

Yes, it was clever, Kim conceded. One single fact of there being no clear way of exiting the building had been enough to rule out other inconsistencies. Almost but not quite.

'We found something else back at the house last night,' Kim said, swigging more of her coffee. 'We found Reece Porter hiding under Rozzie's bed.'

'For what reason?' Penn asked.

'That's what you're going to find out. His clothes were bagged, and he was escorted home with his ears ringing, and he'll be here for interview at 8 a.m. Sticking with you, Penn, Mitch will be getting the diaries and fire remains over here later. See what you can piece together.'

Stacey frowned. 'So was the fire to destroy the diaries or to raise the alarm?'

'That is a very good question,' Kim answered. It was one of the things that had been on her mind all night. But it wasn't what had kept her awake. That award went to the visions of what Symes was doing to a seven-year-old girl. She knew she had to trust in her fellow police officers at Dudley. They would want to recover Emma Bunting as quickly and as safely as possible. She just hoped they knew what kind of psychopath they were dealing with.

Woody couldn't have been clearer in his instruction to stay away, and she had to respect that. She could understand that the team working the case would treat it like any other missing child. Every process would be followed diligently. Any intrusion from her was just going to consume their time and energy, which was better spent trying to find the little girl. Being told to stay away from it didn't stop her asking about it. His response to her 6 a.m. call had been short and terse, with the news that the little girl hadn't yet been found and that if that should change, he would let her know. Short of camping out in front of his office door, she was going to have to beg for scraps of information as and when she could get them.

She forced her attention back to what was now a quadruple murder investigation. She was pleased to see that the boards had been updated to include the bruise to Helen's wrist and Rozzie's pregnancy.

'Usual for you, Stace,' Kim continued. 'Phone records, social media, background, gossip.'

'Yummy,' she said, rubbing her hands.

'In other news, Woody paid me a late-night visit to inform

me that yesterday Symes abducted a seven-year-old girl from a park on the edge of Wollaston.'

Stacey and Penn looked at each other in horror. Bryant had already been briefed in the car.

Penn's back straightened, and Stacey reached for her pen. She was sure they were both wondering why this was 'other news' instead of the main headline.

'No involvement from us,' she said with a sigh.

'How can we not be involved?' Penn asked.

'We know him,' Stacey agreed.

'Which was raised with Woody last night, but he wouldn't hear of it. Apparently Symes named me specifically when he beat the girl's mother and threw her out of the car.'

Stacey closed her eyes and shook her head, and Penn's fist clenched.

'It's a goad,' Leanne added.

'It's a missing bloody child is what it is,' Kim snapped. 'No one seems to get that I don't give a shit about the games and the power play he thinks is going on. I couldn't care less about whether or not he triumphs in rattling me or pissing me off or if he's trying to force me out of the woodwork to beat me to death. What I care about is that there's a seven-year-old girl now in the clutches of a madman and there's fuck all I can do about it.'

TWENTY-EIGHT

The image she'd seen of Emma Bunting on the news was still on her mind when Bryant pulled up outside the home of Rachel and Daryl Hewitt. Bryant was under strict instructions to keep the police radio on for any news. Every muscle in her body ached to go after Symes and bring that little girl back alive, but Woody didn't threaten her lightly, and she'd been ordered to keep her attention on the murder of the Daynes family.

She'd asked Zach and Gavin to meet them there and was pleased to see their car in the driveway.

'You okay, guv?' Bryant asked as he turned the engine off. The journey from the station had been made in silence.

'Yeah, I'm fine,' she said, getting out of the car.

'Now I know you're lying,' he said. 'Normally any concerns as to your well-being would be met with a short, hostile response containing a curse or two.'

'Bryant, fuck off.'

'Better but too late,' he said as they walked up the drive. As usual, Leanne wasn't too far behind.

'Don't speak,' she instructed Leanne after knocking the door.

That wouldn't be too hard, Kim realised. They'd been joined at the hip for around thirty hours now, and the number of sentences uttered by the protection officer had barely reached double figures.

The door was opened by Daryl Hewitt, already dressed in a shirt, tie and suit trousers. He was clearly planning on getting off to work as quickly as possible.

'Thank you for accommodating our request, Mr Hewitt,' she said, stepping inside.

His gaze narrowed towards Leanne.

'Don't mind her,' Kim offered. 'She's observing to see if she wants to be an actual police officer.'

Leanne cleared her throat, showing Kim she'd understood the jibe.

Kim stepped into the formal lounge as she had the day before.

Gavin and Zach sat side by side on the three-seater sofa she and Bryant had occupied.

She nodded in their direction, surprised to see how much they looked like visitors.

She'd seen siblings in each other's homes before, where they had free movement, familiarity, comfort and ease borne of frequent visits. The two men sat as though they were the new neighbours who'd been invited for a cup of tea and really didn't want to stay.

'Is Rachel here?' Kim asked.

'She's sleeping in the baby's room. She often drops off in there after one of the feeds. Do you need me to wake her?'

'Absolutely,' Kim said, taking the single chair.

Rachel definitely needed to hear what she had to say, and Kim was not going to do the woman out of the opportunity to say I told you so after her vocal and resolute protestations about her mother's innocence.

'Is this connected to the cancelled press conference yesterday?' Zach asked, reaching for Gavin's hand.

'It is, but I'd like everyone to hear it at the same time,' she said as Daryl came back into the room.

'Okay, she's awake and... on her way down.'

Kim followed his gaze. The break in his words had come when he'd seen the two men holding hands.

'Thank you, Mr Hewitt. I was just going to thank Gavin for assisting us yesterday. I know how hard that must have been.'

'Yes, Gavin, thank you for that,' Rachel said, entering the room. 'However would we manage without you?'

Gavin coloured and Zach shot daggers at his sister.

Rachel took a seat on the other single chair. Daryl stood behind his wife, as far away from the two Mr Dayneses as he could get, as though they were carrying something contagious.

Bryant was in the doorway, and Leanne had remained in the hall.

'If she's a liaison officer, I don't want her,' Rachel said, nodding towards the door. Leanne had stayed in the car the previous day.

Despite the circumstances, Kim had to hide her amusement at the unlikelihood of that ever happening. Just the thought of Leanne having to raise a smile, offer understanding, patience and sympathy was a picture that just wouldn't form in her mind.

'Understood, Mrs Hewitt.'

'Rachel,' she corrected.

'Of course,' Kim said, realising that only Daryl Hewitt had not offered the use of his first name.

She could feel the tension crackling in the air between the two couples. Although not a part of her remit, she did wonder at the family dynamics at play here.

'I'm afraid I have some disturbing news to share with you

all. After careful consideration of the evidence, we now believe that your mother' – she paused, looking from Rachel to Zach – 'was not responsible for the murders of your father or siblings; nor did she take her own life.'

'I bloody knew it,' Rachel said, jumping up from her seat. 'I knew Mum would never do such a thing. I told you that.'

Kim nodded her acceptance of that fact as Rachel rounded on her brother.

Her face contorted in disgust. 'And you just accepted that our own mother would do such a horrific thing. You could actually see your own mother shooting a hole into Lewis and Rozzie. I'm ashamed to call you my brother,' she spat, raising her hand.

Zach's arm sprang out and he gripped her around the wrist. 'Don't even think about it.'

'Rachel,' Daryl snapped as Gavin removed Zach's hand.

'Back off, Rache,' Gavin whispered.

Her eyes held the gaze of her brother-in-law for just a second before she retook her seat. Daryl placed a hand on her shoulder, and Kim wondered if that was for reassurance or to keep her pinned down.

'Didn't someone say the doors and windows were locked?' Zach asked.

'We believe he hid in the pantry in the kitchen and snuck out once the fire service had extinguished the fire. It wasn't a big fire, so the fire officers continued through the house to check on the occupants.'

'Bloody brave,' Daryl observed, shaking his head.

'He?' Rachel asked.

'Or she,' Kim clarified. 'We haven't ruled out either.'

Rachel appeared satisfied.

'Given that we now know that one or more members of the household were targets, can you think of anyone who might want to hurt them?'

'Officer, I'm sure you must hear it a lot but they were good people,' Gavin offered. 'They weren't loud or flashy or arrogant. They didn't advertise their wealth, they donated to various charities and kept themselves to themselves.'

'No neighbour issues or disgruntled employees?' she asked, turning to Daryl.

'Capable of murder?' he asked incredulously. 'We employ over three hundred people and I'd like to think not one of them is capable of doing something like this.'

'Even so, Mr Hewitt, I'd appreciate you taking a minute at work to look over recent dismissals, complaints or grievances. You never know how someone might react if they get desperate.'

He opened his mouth as if to argue but closed it again.

'If you could all give it some thought and let us know if you can think of anything at all, however small.'

'I'll have a think,' Daryl said, pushing himself up from the arm of the chair. He looked to his wife. 'Darling, I really must...'

'Are you taking the piss?' Rachel snarled. 'You're heading off to work, barely five minutes late, after what we've just been told?'

He coloured slightly. 'The detective has asked me to look for—'

'I don't think she meant in the next ten minutes but go – just go.'

He hesitated for just a minute before grabbing his suit jacket from the back of the chair.

He leaned in to kiss his wife on the cheek. She turned her face away.

As he left the room, Kim exchanged a look with Bryant.

He coughed, then coughed again, and again.

'Sorry, Mrs Hewitt, may I trouble you for...'

'Oh my goodness. I'm sorry. Where are the manners my mum taught me? May I offer you a drink, officers?'

'Water please,' Bryant said.

'Coffee, black, no sugar,' Kim said, rising from her chair.

She offered her colleague a light smile in appreciation of his acting abilities.

'Rachel, I'll just come and give you a hand.'

TWENTY-NINE

Penn headed down to the interview room with his folder.

He'd seen a male in his late twenties approach the building and chain-smoke two cigarettes before stepping through the doors. From the boss's description, he was guessing it was Reece Porter.

He wasn't surprised to see the man sitting behind the desk of interview room one, tapping a disposable lighter against the edge.

Penn offered his hand and immediately understood why the boss had asked him to take this statement. Penn knew that both his appearance and demeanour were non-threatening. His unruly blonde hair tended to defy any kind of restraint. The curls flopped around his face, and his inability to wear any suit smartly gave the impression he wasn't really a police officer – not a serious one anyway. And that worked well. He intimidated no one. Meaning people normally relaxed in his presence.

Lynne had been very relaxed in his presence the previous evening before Stacey had turned up. He wanted to call her but had no idea what to say. He pushed the thoughts away.

'Thanks for coming in, Reece,' he said. First names

promoted intimacy and ease. 'If we could just talk generally for a bit about your knowledge of the family and then I'll take your statement about Saturday night, Sunday morning. Sorry, this is a no-smoking building, but any time you wanna nip out for a smoke just let me know.'

Penn saw the man visibly relax. There was nothing more threatening to a smoker than being told you couldn't.

'How well did you know the Daynes family?'

'Not all that well. They always kept themselves to themselves. They didn't really mix with any of the neighbours. I mean it's not like *Corrie* or anything like that but the odd party or barbecue on the lane. They never came.'

'None of them?'

'Not once.'

Sociable lot, he thought.

'Was there any bad feeling between them and any of the neighbours?'

'Nah,' he said, sitting back in his seat. 'No issues I know of. Folks just thought they were a bit up themselves.'

'Understandable,' Penn said quietly, playing into the mood of the conversation.

'I mean, some folks had nicknames for them, you know, like Mr and Mrs Snooty Pants but nothing nasty,' he said as though remembering they were dead.

'My DI said something about you doing odd jobs for the family. How did that come about?'

'Mr Daynes put an advert in the local shop. Old school, like details on a card, asking for a bit of labouring, cutting lawns, mending fences, that sort of thing. It was just a phone number. I didn't even know who I was ringing. I was surprised it was Mr Daynes, and he told me to pop round.'

'And when was this?'

He thought for a second. 'Probably about a year ago. He'd just had a hip operation and it was taking longer to heal.'

'Go on,' Penn urged.

'Started off a couple of days a week. They've got eleven acres, you see, that they don't really know what to do with. The area is spread across three fields. They don't keep any animals or grow anything, but the land needs tending – trees pruning, fences mending, moles trappin', that kind of thing.'

'The moles were a problem?' Penn asked.

'Oh yeah, but not so much as the rabbits – them little bastards chew through anything. Kept eating the missus's flower beds, tried everything to keep 'em out, but she wouldn't hear of trapping. Okay for the ugly moles but not for the pretty bunnies,' he said ruefully. 'The mister wanted all the land kept spick and span. It was the look of it, you see. Well, for the most part anyway.'

'What do you mean?'

'Well, there was one area that the mister wasn't all that fussed about.'

The man before him was fully relaxed now, just as he'd intended. Reece obviously thought he was never going to be asked about being found inside a crime scene hiding under a teenager's bed. Timing was everything.

'What area?'

'At the very edge of the property, east side. Told me to dump all the cuttings and grass along that edge. I wasn't happy about it. I mean, legally you gotta keep the area accessible. You don't have to put out a welcome mat, but you can't obstruct it either.

'The stile had been knackered for years, but folks had made a gap in the hedge to the right of it, and he kept trying to block it up. Kept waiting for the complaints to come, but the mister wasn't bothered a bit about the Ramblers Association or—'

'Hang on,' Penn said, 'are you telling me that there's a public footpath that crosses the Dayneses' property?'

Reece nodded. 'Been there about two hundred years. Ain't nothing he could do about it.'

'So just about anyone can come off the pavement on the main road and find themselves within feet of the Dayneses' home.'

'Well, I suppose so, yeah, if they want to.'

'Shit,' Penn said, realising what this meant for their case.

Reece shrugged, not understanding the enormity of what he'd just said. 'So can I go and have my smoke now?'

THIRTY

'Does he really need water and are you going to drink the coffee I make?' Rachel asked, turning to face her in the kitchen.

Kim shook her head as she stepped into a kitchen extension that had trapped every ounce of light available from a sheet of glass that led to the patio and a lantern roof above.

Kim felt an instant airiness at the open plan, uncluttered area that looked out onto a rolling lawn that led towards open fields beyond.

'Not bad, is it?' Rachel asked, following her gaze.

A single chair was placed in the far-right corner of the space.

'For the sunset,' Rachel explained.

Kim hadn't really had Rachel pegged as a sunset kind of girl.

'Ask away,' she said, resting against the granite work surface. She hadn't even bothered to put the kettle on.

Kim had followed her for one single reason, but there were other things she wanted to know first.

'You and Zach. You're twins?'

Rachel frowned. 'Is that relevant?'

'There seems to be a lot of animosity between you.'

She shrugged. 'We have our moments. Shit started quite young for us, but you don't want to hear—'

'Yes, I do,' Kim said. Rarely had she met twins so far apart. Her own experience of being a twin couldn't have been more different.

Mikey had been the other half of her, the better half, the softer, sweeter part. Even now she missed him every day. The picture of her mother lying on a bed tore into her mind again. She pushed it away. Patty wasn't allowed to come to work with her.

'I don't even know how to explain it. We were close when we were small, but as we grew older, we began to blame each other for our mother's lack of attentiveness. That sounds awful, doesn't it? On the face of it we had a great childhood. We weren't spoiled but we didn't have to worry. We knew we were loved, but there was something missing from our mother, and I think we blamed each other for that.'

'Missing?' Kim queried.

'Yeah. It's like we knew she loved us, but it never felt all-encompassing. Do you have children?'

Kim shook her head.

'From the second I had Mia, my whole life perspective changed. I'd grown fond of her while I was growing her, but nothing prepared me for that breathtaking realisation that I would give up my life to stop anyone hurting a hair on her head. I hold her, I kiss her head and tell her how much I love her every chance I get. Her well-being and happiness consumes me. There's a fire. Do you ever hug people?'

Kim shook her head.

'Jeez, you're a tricky one to explain to.'

'I have a dog.'

'You love him?'

'Oh yeah.'

'When you see him after a long day at work, what do you do?'

Kim felt the longing to see her buddy. 'I get down on the floor, pet him and then give him a big squeeze.'

'Why the squeeze?'

'Dunno. Just happy to see him, excited.'

'From our mother, we never had the squeeze if you know what I mean. We had ninety per cent of her, which is better than what a lot of kids get, but it's almost like we were nieces and nephews. She loved us but at a slight distance.'

Kim appreciated the loyalty to her mum but also heard the sadness behind her words.

'It was much later that Zach and I learned that she had become ill while pregnant with us. I think we began to blame each other so the odds were stacked against us before...'

'Before what?'

'Never mind. We just had a big falling-out a few years ago that we've never quite recovered from.'

'Do you want to...?'

'No,' she said in a voice that brooked no argument.

Kim would also have liked to touch on the dynamics between her and her husband but thought that might be a bigger push, and she didn't want to get thrown out of the house before she'd asked the most important question. They were a young couple with a new baby. Why wouldn't there be tension?

'Were you closer to Rozzie than you were to Zach?'

'Nice transition there, Inspector. I like your style. There was twelve years between us so it's not like we had lots in common. We did share our experience of our mum, and we chatted generally a couple of times a week, why?'

'Did Rozzie tell you she was pregnant?'

'Wh-What?' she asked, reaching for the side to stabilise herself.

'Approximately four months,' Kim said. 'Hardly showing at all.'

'I only saw her last weekend. I didn't suspect a...' Her words trailed away as she thought of something.

'What is it?'

'Actually, I did notice that she was a bit quiet. She wasn't poring over her phone like normal. Most times Mum would tell her off and she'd blow a raspberry, complete with a dramatic eye-roll, but not last week. I even mentioned it to Daryl on the way home. He said it was probably teenage hormones or something. I agreed and didn't give it another thought.'

Tears filled her eyes. 'Shit, I should have just called.'

'You think she knew?'

Rachel dabbed at her reddened eyes and nodded.

'From the way she was acting I'd say so.' She paused. 'Another life lost. Five victims.'

'Rachel, do you think your parents knew?' she asked gently. The woman was having to process a lot right now.

Rachel shook her head. 'One of the things that drew my attention to Rozzie was that my mum seemed to be eyeing her with concern as well.'

'Do you know of any recent boyfriends?'

Rachel shook her head. 'I'm ashamed to say that I didn't have a clue about her love life.'

Kim watched as a shadow of regret passed over her face. Missed opportunities that she'd never get the chance to take now.

Bryant appeared in the doorway. 'Guv, sorry to interrupt, but there's a little one upstairs that sounds like she needs something.'

'On my way,' Rachel said, heading out of the kitchen. She stopped in the doorway and turned. 'You're going to get them, aren't you?'

'We won't rest until we do,' Kim offered as Rachel disappeared up the stairs.

She suspected that Mia was going to get an extra special squeeze when Rachel held her.

Kim had not been able to ask her final question – had Rachel had any clue as to the identity of the baby's father? But it was clear to Kim that Rachel didn't have the slightest idea.

THIRTY-ONE

'Happy to continue?' Penn asked Reece as he came back into the room.

'Yeah, man,' he said, appearing relaxed after his nicotine break.

Penn had taken the time to print off an aerial view of the Dayneses' property. He'd drawn a pink line around what he thought was the border.

He pushed the single piece of paper across the table. 'Have I got the border right?'

Reece looked at it for a moment before nodding.

Penn pushed a green felt-tip across the table. 'Can you mark up the footpath for me?'

Reece took the top off the pen and drew a tidy line along the most easterly point of the property. It snaked the far edge of two fields before disappearing through the hedgerow.

'It comes directly off the road down here and travels diagonally across that big field over there.'

'You know a lot about the path, eh?'

'I use it for running. You don't wanna piss off the local landowners by running somewhere you're not supposed to.'

'Ever happened to you?' Penn asked.

'Just once. I'd taken a wrong turn and ended up jogging past a couple in their outdoor swimming pool. Awkward.'

Penn took the sheet back and glanced at the line. On paper it looked as though that green line travelled close to the property, but in reality it was a good hundred metres away from the outbuildings with a fence and hedging in between.

'So you take a wrong turn into the house last night?'

Reece took the lighter from his pocket and started tapping it on the table.

'You knew we were gonna have to talk about that so best to just come clean. Why were you there?'

He considered his words carefully. 'I just couldn't believe it. I heard the whispers around that they were all dead and I just needed to see it for myself.'

'Why?'

'Morbid curiosity I suppose.'

'But you weren't particularly close to any of the family, were you?'

He shook his head.

'Why Rozzie's room?'

He coloured.

'Did you like her?'

'Yes, of course... no... I mean...'

'It wasn't a trick question. I only asked if you liked her.'

'I wasn't sure what kind of liked you meant.'

'Was she nice to you when you worked at the house?' Penn asked.

'I didn't see her very often. She wasn't the outdoorsy type.'

'But you must have seen her,' Penn pushed, ignoring his evasiveness.

'Now and again I suppose. She always smiled. She wasn't like some of those bitchy girls. She didn't have a permanent sneer or anything. She smiled but it wasn't always genuine. She did it to be polite, but she often looked preoccupied, pensive, as though there was something she was working through in her mind.'

'That's a lot of presumption when you say that you rarely saw her.'

'I... I... can just tell these things.'

'So why were you under her bed?' Penn asked, taking another look at the aerial view of the property.

'It was stupid of me, I know. I heard the voices and I just dived under there. I knew I shouldn't be there, and I thought I could just sneak out.'

'Have you repeated anything you heard?' Penn asked.

He shook his head vehemently. 'No chance. Your boss is fucking scary, mate. I reckon she'd have my guts for garters.'

He wasn't wrong, Penn thought as he pulled the piece of paper closer. A question was forming in his mind. 'You raised the alarm early on Sunday morning?'

'Yeah, yeah, I did,' he said, as though eager to be on to something else.

Penn said nothing. Nervous people filled silences.

'I always run the same route. Three or four times a week.' He tapped his wrist. 'I time myself. I'm always trying to knock a few seconds off my personal best. The Dayneses know I run that way. They don't... didn't mind.'

'Always the same time?'

'Roughly, maybe five or ten minutes either way.'

'Still darkish around 7 a.m. at the minute, isn't it?'

'Oh yeah. You have to watch out for the occasional dog shit on the public footpath. Folks don't clean up after themselves and there ain't no street lights.'

'Just the hint of the sun coming up?'

'That's right. Some mornings it's just a last little bit of moonlight.'

'But not Sunday?'

'No, Sunday was pretty dark. I remember thinking it was likely to be a grey sort of day.'

'Hmm... that does cause me a bit of a problem,' Penn said, frowning.

'Why's that?'

'Well, you jogged the track, as normal, there was very little light and the kitchen is on the other side of the house, at the furthest point away. The fire itself was small and hardly a bonfire, so how did you see the smoke from such a distance in the dark?'

'I... err... It was... umm...'

His words trailed away.

Penn waited.

And waited.

'I think I've had enough,' he finally said, unable to meet Penn's gaze. 'I think it's time for me to leave.'

THIRTY-TWO

'Okay, Penn, thanks for the update,' Kim said as Bryant pulled into the car park for Dudley Social Work and Safeguarding Services on Corbyn Road.

She had spent the entire journey from Rachel's house being updated on the explanation and behaviour from Reece Porter.

'Does Penn think he's good for it?' Bryant asked.

'Depends if he thinks he's in the same American cop show as you. If you're asking if he thinks he's capable of the murder, the answer is no, but he is sure that the guy is hiding something.'

'DNA test?' Bryant asked, following her own suspicion that Reece knew Rozzie much better than he was admitting to. Something was off and she intended to find out what it was.

'What floor are we heading for?' Kim asked as the three of them got out the car. She'd made the appointment with Jonathan's care worker after getting just a couple of details from Rachel.

Zach and Gavin had left Rachel's house at the same time as she had, after being assured by Kim that if she needed them she'd be in touch. Clearly the twins were not going to share their grief.

'Ground floor,' he said as they entered the building.

A receptionist behind a glass screen insisted on seeing identification from all three of them before signing them into the visitor's book. They were then told to take a seat.

Beyond the reception she could see what looked like a small army of people at tiny desks separated by cubicle boards.

Kim tried to imagine spending your whole working day sitting in what was little more than a corner. She could see the attempts made to personalise the small, cramped spaces with photographs, uplifting postcards and humorous memes printed from the internet.

Five minutes into their wait a woman in a pink shirt and black trousers came through the keycoded doors and beckoned them forward into a small meeting room on the left. She held the door and then closed it once they were all in.

Kim and Bryant again took out their identification. She glanced at Leanne who did the same.

'Didn't realise they gave you people one of those,' Kim muttered as Leanne walked around the table to take the seat at the furthest point away.

'Daphne Adams,' the woman said, offering her hand.

Bryant shook it while Kim appraised the civil servant, who appeared to be mid-fifties with brown eyes and auburn hair with a sprinkling of grey. Dangling from her ears were two tiny silver horses, and around her neck was a chain holding a delicate pile of books. It was as though the woman wore something to signify everything she loved in life.

'Shocking news about the Daynes family,' she said, resting her hands on a brown folder. 'Fire, wasn't it?'

'The details of the incident haven't yet been released, Ms Adams.'

The press conference was still a couple of hours away.

'If we can just get some background on the Dayneses' involvement with Jonathan Pike.'

She opened the folder but read nothing from it.

'Jonathan Pike is seven years old and has been in care for almost five of those years. He doesn't really know any other way of life, as he was very young when his family gave him up.'

'Under what circumstances?' Kim asked.

'Jonathan was the youngest of five children born into a poverty-stricken family. Not our place to judge and we were already involved with the family, who were just about surviving. Unfortunately, Jonathan was a handful – very advanced for his age but also quite violent. He has since been diagnosed with ADHD. It wasn't an easy decision for the family, however all parties agreed it was the safest course of action for all involved.'

'Safest?' Bryant asked.

'He is a very angry, misunderstood little boy who needs a great deal of love, patience and attention.'

'And you felt that the Dayneses could offer that level of security?' Kim asked.

'They fell in love with the boy.'

And you couldn't look a gift horse in the mouth, Kim couldn't help thinking, probably unfairly.

Daphne caught her expression. 'Jonathan's family is now out of the picture completely. They've since moved away and have relinquished all parental rights. Placing a young boy like Jonathan is problematic for any family with young children, and the possibility of him growing up totally institutionalised is very real. Statistics show that children in care—'

'You knew of Mrs Daynes's health problems?' Kim asked. She didn't need to hear statistics of children in care.

'We knew she had suffered with depression, but if we ruled such sufferers out, we'd have no foster register left. We look for reasons why people are suitable, not why they aren't.'

'Is Jonathan exactly what the Dayneses came looking for? Did they particularly want a troubled little boy?' Kim wondered, thinking of the January sales – where customers are presented with mountains of bargains which are basically items that just haven't sold.

'They wanted to care for a child that might not have had the best start in life.'

'And you proposed Jonathan to them?'

'We had an open day. It's where—'

'I know what an open day is,' Kim interrupted. During her years at Fairview they'd called it the meat market.

A selection of kids were chosen to be dressed up, taken to the main hall and paraded before couples who got to choose which child they'd like to have a chat with.

It was at one such market day that Kim had met Erica and Keith. She'd been ten years old and had already been in three foster homes. She'd glared hatefully at anyone who had glanced in her direction.

It had been Keith who had noticed her first. When she'd spotted his salt-and-pepper beard and unruly hair, she'd been reminded of a photo she'd seen of Albert Einstein, though he wasn't as old.

She had been taken aback when he had glared back instead of just looking away and moving along.

Every so often he'd turn around and glare at her again and then smile. She only knew because she didn't stop watching him from the moment he'd met her gaze.

Eventually, when most of the shoppers had gone and Kim was waiting for the signal to leave the hall, he approached her, holding the hand of his wife.

'Hey there, I'm Keith and this is my wife, Erica. She reckons I'm unbeatable in a scowl-off. Wanna prove her right?'

She shook her head and gave him her filthiest look.

'Ah, you're scared. No problem, I can...'

She sat up straight on the chair and put a fist beneath her chin in a direct challenge.

No one called her scared, and she had known she could out scowl anyone.

Keith sat opposite.

Erica stood behind him with a warm expression on her face.

Never one to shy away from a challenge, she donned her best angry face and looked him right in the eye.

He met her gaze with his own scowl.

The room emptied around them. After what seemed like hours, her facial muscles began to tire. Her lower jaw started trembling with the effort of maintaining her set expression. Her eyes were watering because she refused to blink.

'Aah, aah, atchoo,' Keith cried, putting his hand to his nose. 'Okay, you win,' he said, and she finally relaxed her face. The muscles in her cheeks felt like jelly.

'Well done, sweetie,' the lady said to her with a wink. 'I'm glad someone finally beat him, and I love your fighting spirit.'

Kim said nothing.

'Maybe a rematch sometime?' Keith asked.

She shrugged and left the room.

Within a week she was living in their home, about to begin the best three years of her life.

It was only later that she realised in that initial meeting she never opened her mouth once.

She couldn't help wondering where Jonathan Pike would go now. Getting a good foster family had changed her life. Sadly for her, Keith and Erica had been killed in a car accident on their way back from a solicitor, seeking advice on adoption. At thirteen she was back in the system and on the conveyor belt for her next foster family.

'Did the Dayneses want anything more long-term?' Kim asked, thinking about the child they'd lost.

'Oh no, that would never have been allowed because of their past...' She stopped speaking as the colour flooded her cheeks. She had clearly said something she shouldn't have done.

'You'd already had dealings with the Daynes family?'

'I can say nothing more about the past, Inspector. I'm afraid those records are sealed.'

THIRTY-THREE

'Penn, have I told you how sorry I am about last night?' Stacey asked.

'Only about forty-seven times now.' He checked his watch. 'And it's not even lunchtime.'

'Can we talk about it?' she asked, wishing he'd show some kind of irritation with her. Yes, he was the usual affable, good-natured, a little bit off-the-wall Penn, but he had to be feeling some kind of way about what she'd ruined last night.

She'd felt awful when Devon had picked her up at midnight after not being needed on the call-out. She and Penn had watched a bit of television for an hour in an uncomfortable silence during which Penn had checked his phone a dozen times. It hadn't tinged once.

'I messed it up for you, didn't I?' she asked miserably.

She knew how long he'd been waiting for this first real date between him and Lynne, and he'd gone to a tremendous effort to make it a good one.

'What else were you supposed to do?' he asked, not answering the question she'd asked.

'Stay at home and pull on my big-girl panties,' she said, wishing that was exactly what she'd done.

'You did what you were told and I'm glad you chose to come to me.'

'Really?' she asked hopefully.

'Nope, but I also don't want you feeling shit about it. It's not your fault.'

'I don't think there's been any time in my life that I've been a cock block.'

Penn burst out laughing. 'Stace, stop apologising. If we're meant to get over it, we will; if not, you're helping me with my Tinder profile.'

'Deal,' she said, happy she'd made him laugh.

'Now talk to me about the damn case.'

'Well, it doesn't appear that Rozzie's doctor knew anything about her pregnancy,' Stacey said, closing the teenager's medical record. No appointment, no blood test. 'She may not have known herself.'

'Okay,' Penn said, frowning. 'I'm a guy, humour me. I know it can happen but how is that even possible? Surely there are physical changes.'

'Some women can go months without a period because of contraception, stress, anxiety, illness.'

'Okay, enough about that but—'

'How can you gleefully attend post-mortems, digest and ruminate over every part of that process but not have a conversation about periods?' Stacey asked. Her colleague sure did pick his times to get sensitive.

'Yeah, we'll skate over that one. What I'm saying is how is it possible to have a human being growing inside you and for you to not know the little critter is there?'

Stacey shrugged. It wasn't something she'd had experience of.

'Anything interesting on social media?' Penn asked.

'I'll let you know,' Stacey answered. 'Of the four of them, Rozzie was the only one with a substantial online presence. I don't think Lewis had really discovered social media yet, and Helen and William weren't present at all.'

Penn grunted before returning to his own work.

A Google search for Rozzie Daynes had brought over a thousand results. She was present on all social-media forums. She appeared to be what Stacey called a bleeder on social media, where she appeared to use different platforms for different purposes, but there was a bleed of certain posts across all forums. She had her own YouTube channel, where she appeared to be a budding influencer. She wasn't a particularly remarkable girl, but there was something appealing about her round, pleasant face and self-deprecating manner. Her first video had been a humorous observation of living with naturally curly hair. There were snippets of her showing the tight curls after showering, the problems with different headbands, tie backs and clips. Each post had received more likes until her last post, advertising a certain type of conditioner, had amassed her a subscription total of half a million followers. A couple of her suggestions about hair products had been shared on her Face-book page, but that had mainly covered her social life, with only a couple hundred friends and high privacy settings.

She rarely used Twitter, and her Instagram was a mishmash of everything: videos, photos, live streams. TikTok held just a few videos of her messing about with friends.

One thing Stacey noticed on all forums was a reduction in posts. Rozzie had still been active, right up until the day she died, but the posts had definitely lessened in number.

What had happened six months ago that had prompted a change in the girl?

One of the things the boss had asked her to look into was any male that Rozzie was close to. Identifying the father of Rozzie's baby was a priority.

She'd pored over the last couple of years' worth of posts, making a shortlist of boys in photos, interaction and post tagging. She'd ruled out obvious friends and ones who appeared to be in relationships with other people for now.

She now had a short, short list of two, but her gut kept reacting to Warren Cox, a boy one year older who had been in couples photos on and off for the last three years. There wasn't anyone as serious as Warren Cox anywhere else on her social-media feed.

Due to his poor privacy settings and his frequent posting, Stacey had a good idea where he'd be. She sent a text to the boss and returned her attention to the computer.

She wasn't done with Rozzie yet.

THIRTY-FOUR

Symes rubbed witch hazel onto his knuckles. It helped bring out the bruise and reduce the swelling. Lucky for him, he relished the pain in his hands. It travelled directly to his nerves and helped calm him down. It was like that satisfying ache in the muscles after a good workout. It was pain, but it was good pain.

After the disappointment of the previous night, he knew he was going to have to shelve his plans for decimating the bitch's team. His euphoria had quickly been quashed when Wood had joined her partner in the car before they'd driven off together. He'd considered following them, but it was clear they'd been given instructions on staying safe. His side plan of causing as much pain as he could through her team could become a distraction. It was taking unnecessary risk which could jeopardise his real mission.

He knew it wouldn't be long until his face was plastered all over the national news in connection with the abduction. He was going to have to be more careful and move around in the shadows, but the first part of the plan was complete, and the kid was tucked away nicely.

'Shut up,' he shouted as the elderly figure in the middle of the room groaned.

In all honesty he'd been surprised she'd still been alive when he'd returned earlier.

In a way he was relieved that she was. The smell of a dead body might raise the alarm quicker than he'd like.

'Damn it,' he said when the whimpering stopped.

He went to the sink and filled a beaker with water. He hated being responsible for another thing. It was why he'd never had a pet.

'Here,' he said, repeating the process he'd used before he'd left.

He put his foot over her frail bony toes and applied a small amount of pressure. One move and he'd be able to break every toe.

He lowered the gag and tipped water into her mouth.

She began to choke so he pulled it away.

'That's enough,' he said, refixing the gag.

He had no idea if it was enough to sustain her, but he was more bothered about the smell. He couldn't stand her stench a second longer.

He returned to the sink and refilled the cup almost to the top, then looked underneath the sink until he found what he was looking for. He poured a generous measure from the bottle of disinfectant into the mug before approaching the pathetic figure from behind and throwing the liquid so it drenched the back of her head and soaked the back of her nightdress.

Immediately the aroma of pine began to fill the air.

She cried out before continuing the whimpering, and he rolled his eyes. He'd given her a shower and still she wasn't happy.

He left the living room and went back to the kitchen. The aroma of spaghetti bolognese filled the air. He had plummed so lucky in finding someone who had delicious ready meals delivered to her door weekly.

He took a couple of slices of bread from the bread bin and plonked himself at the small table in front of the patio window. Not that he could see anything – the curtains were still closed.

He hadn't realised how hungry he was or how he'd become acclimatised to the shit, tasteless slop they called food in prison.

Once finished, he expelled a humungous belch that filled the room then laughed out loud. Fuck, he loved freedom, and if he didn't hate the bitch with every fibre of his being, he might have considered trying to disappear long-term and having a good old time of it, but he couldn't do that.

He couldn't properly enjoy another minute of his life while there was breath still circulating around her body.

THIRTY-FIVE

Kim was still wondering why a social services case involving Helen Daynes had been sealed almost thirty years ago when they drove into the multistorey car park at Merry Hill shopping centre.

'Around the time she was first diagnosed with depression,' Bryant had noted as they'd left the building.

She agreed that the two had to be linked to each other, but were they linked to her murder? Much as she wanted to keep digging on Helen, she had to focus on other members of the family.

'I don't like this,' Leanne said, looking around the car park as Bryant headed towards the car wash. Shoppers were busily going in and out of the shopping complex.

'Get over it,' Kim said, glancing at the camera that was focussed on the valeting business.

Kim immediately spied the young man matching the photo she'd been sent by Stacey.

His good-looking face was formed in concentration as he buffed the bonnet of a Ford Kuga with a giant orange mitten on his hand.

He glanced their way as they got out of the car and headed towards him.

'Warren Cox?' she asked, holding up her ID.

He nodded as he looked from her to the two people standing behind her. 'Is this about Rozzie?'

'Yes. Is there somewhere we can talk?'

He looked around and then back at the car. 'Wanna get in?'

It wasn't the weirdest place she'd interviewed someone.

She opened the front passenger door.

'Guys, really?' she asked as Bryant and Leanne opened the rear doors. The idea of the two of them sitting behind her in an enclosed space while she asked a teenage boy a few questions was quite frankly ludicrous.

They closed the back doors and stepped aside.

Instantly she was overcome by the citrus aroma from the cleaning spray with a whiff of pine from the tree hanging on the mirror.

'I understand you knew Rozzie quite well.'

He nodded.

'How long?' she prompted.

'Since junior school.'

Kim hadn't realised they went back quite that far.

'You knew the family well?'

He shrugged. 'I suppose.'

Rozzie hadn't hung around with him for his conversational skills. Blood and stone came to mind. Open questions were not going to work with him.

'Did you get on with her family?'

'Is she really dead?' he asked, surprising her.

'Yes,' Kim answered.

'Shot?'

'Mr Cox, can you answer the—'

'Yeah, we got on okay when I saw them. We didn't go to Rozzie's all that much.'

'In all the years you knew her?'

He shrugged. 'She preferred to be out.'

'Were they close?'

Again with the shrug. 'Seemed okay. They didn't beat her or anything.'

Was that the current yardstick on good parenting? Kim wondered.

If there was anything amiss between Rozzie and her family, he hadn't seen it. She could only focus on the relationship between the two of them.

'So were you two together?'

'At times.'

'And was now one of those times?'

There was a slight hesitation before he shook his head.

She filed that away for later.

'I've moved on,' he clarified, wiping a piece of lint from one of the heating vents.

'You have a new girlfriend?'

'Yeah, about six months.'

Either he felt no emotion or he was holding it in.

'Why the split?'

'Rozzie didn't really know what she wanted. Sometimes she wanted to be in a relationship and other times she wanted to be free to do whatever she wanted, and she didn't seem able to understand that she couldn't have both.'

Kim waited a few seconds to see if he would continue. It was the most words he'd offered in one go.

He didn't.

'She wanted to be with you but mess around with other guys?'

'Yeah, and I ain't into that kind of shit. If I wanted to be a fuckboy, I wouldn't have a girlfriend.'

'Did her work stuff get in the way?' Kim asked. Stacey had updated her on Rozzie's growing social-media presence.

'Sometimes. It was good when it started. It gave her a lot of confidence, but it turned into an addiction. Everywhere we went, everything we did, she photographed and posted. I remember once asking if she wanted to go for a walk up Clent. She told me she'd already posted from up there. Everything became about likes and hearts, followers, and contacts.'

'She became obsessed?'

'Yeah, it was all the time. I'm just not into it on that level. If I needed to know what my mates were having for tea, I'd text them and ask them or bum an invite.'

Kim hid her smile. She didn't spend much time on social media, and this was one of the reasons why.

'I mean, she tried to calm it down. A few months ago, she backed away from it a bit, but I was already over it.'

'Did she do that because you asked her to?'

'I doubt it. I'd asked so many times. She'd gone a bit quiet, a bit moody, but like I said, I'd moved on. I'd already met Sasha.'

Had Rozzie's withdrawal from social media and into herself come at the same time as finding out she was pregnant? Kim wondered.

'Warren, you seem like a man that appreciates directness. When did you last sleep with Rozzie?'

He coloured instantly. 'Err... I'm not... I... About seven months ago.'

Kim had seen him do the calculation in his head. She suspected it was to coincide with the beginning of his new relationship. Had there been a crossover?

'Did you know Rozzie was pregnant?' Kim asked. She was getting a clearer emotional response firing questions at him.

His jaw dropped open. 'No... no... I didn't know.'

'Would you be prepared to submit a DNA sample so you could be ruled out as the father?'

His response was immediate and definite. 'No, Officer, I'm sorry but I'm not prepared to do that at all.'

THIRTY-SIX

'Penn, any clue when Percy is getting here?' Stacey asked.

'Dunno – give him a call.'

Percy was a techie from Ridgepoint who sometimes got lumbered with transporting evidence. He hated driving and was never pleasant if you tried to chase him.

'You ring him. Last time I called he ripped my head off about the traffic on Hagley Road.'

'Why, you got something urgent?' Penn asked.

'Just a timeline I wanna follow. Boss just said Rozzie withdrew a bit six months ago, which I'd already noticed on her social media, but I've just been trawling through her YouTube channel and found a few negative remarks around that time, all from someone named Martey.'

'Like what?' Penn asked, sitting back.

'On a video for headbands, which incidentally, you could do with watching, he tells her that she's cheapening herself with mindless promotion. On another he says she's wasting her brains and being lazy; on another he calls her a marketing whore. It's like he's been getting more aggressive.'

'Has she responded?'

'No, and I'm wondering if that's the reason for his escalation. Has he been trolling her posts for some kind of reaction or acknowledgement? Has he contacted her directly on other platforms?'

'May not be a he,' Penn offered. 'Plenty of women can become fixated with who they perceive as minor celebrities too.'

'Agreed,' she sighed, minimising the screens she had open. She felt like she was on a roll with this line of enquiry, but she needed Rozzie's devices to go deeper, and they were probably stuck in traffic somewhere between here and Ridgepoint.

For now she'd have to turn her attention to checking out family members.

She typed Daryl Hewitt's name into the PNC system. The Police National Computer held every detail of offenders: name, address, date of birth, characteristics and offences.

She expected no hits but was surprised when his image popped up on screen.

Her eyes widened as she read further down the page.

My, my, Daryl Hewitt you have been a naughty boy, she thought as she reached for the phone.

THIRTY-SEVEN

Daynes Furniture was located at the end of Hagley High Street. The building was made up of two halves – a three-storey block that housed a sizeable showroom on the lower level and two floors of offices above. The rest of the property was single storey, approximately the size of a football pitch, accessed by a double roller shutter.

The cars parked in front of each part of the building appeared to be symbolic: Jags and Mercedes to the left and Fords and Citroens to the right. She wondered if the divide was as obvious inside the building.

'Fell on his feet here, didn't he?' Bryant asked as they all got out of the car.

Kim's thoughts exactly, especially given the information they'd just received from Stacey.

She opened the door into the furniture showroom and the eyes of three assistants huddled together fell upon her.

Two more sales staff appeared from the left-hand side of a space that was even bigger than she'd originally thought.

The area was divided into room mock-ups as far as the eye could see. Every space was tastefully staged to be aspirational.

Kim could imagine customers walking in to purchase one item and leaving after placing an order worth thousands.

The middle-aged woman who had appeared from the left approached with her hands clasped together. All staff wore a uniform of black trousers and T-shirt with the company name on the left chest area.

'May I help you?'

Kim held up her identification. 'Mr Hewitt please.'

'One moment.'

She retreated to the desk as more assistants congregated, made a quick call and then motioned for them to follow.

Kim travelled through mock-ups of kitchens, lounges, bedrooms and offices, all filled with exquisite furniture.

She noted that the items did not bear price tags and was reminded of the saying 'if you have to ask, you can't afford it'.

The woman pushed open a 'staff only' door that led to a set of stairs and a lift.

She pressed the call button and the lift doors opened immediately.

'Third floor and Mr Hewitt will be waiting,' she said as the doors began to close.

Bryant hit the number three and the lift elevated them smoothly to the third floor.

The doors opened on Daryl Hewitt waiting for them. His jacket had been discarded, his tie loosened and his wrist cuffs unbuttoned and turned over.

The reception area into which she'd stepped was furnished with pieces similar to what she'd seen downstairs.

'Thank you for seeing us, Mr Hewitt,' Bryant said as they stepped out of the lift.

'Not at all. If there's anything I can do to help, just ask,' he said, guiding them along a well-lit corridor. He opened a door with a sliding plate bearing his name.

The office itself was bigger than the entire footprint of the downstairs of her house, with a desk as big as her kitchen and an entire wall lined with bookcases and other furniture. It appeared that the showroom wasn't only downstairs.

'Impressive space,' Kim acknowledged as Bryant whistled.

Light shone in from the two windows that formed the corner of the room. Vertical blinds were pulled to the edge.

'I'm so busy I hardly notice,' he said, somewhat disingenuously. One couldn't help but be impressed by such a workspace, and she suspected he was still pretty pleased with himself no matter how many times he entered it.

Almost miraculous given where he'd been ten years ago.

'Please take a seat,' he said, straightening up papers on the boardroom-sized meeting table positioned at the farthest point from the distraction of the windows. 'Rota changes are always a chore,' he said, forming a single pile.

'Changes?' she asked, taking a seat.

'The introduction of a night shift and full-day working on Saturday.'

'Popular?' she asked.

'Necessary,' he answered. 'Our products are in high demand. There was a time when customers were happy to wait three months for a bespoke piece of furniture, but retail now demands a faster turnaround. If we don't adapt, we won't stay in business for very long.'

'And Mr Daynes approved these changes?' she asked, just because she sensed it would annoy him, and from his mildly tightened jaw she could tell she'd hit her target. She wasn't keen on his proprietary manner on a family business into which he'd married.

'William handed over the day-to-day running of the business months ago. He was no longer informed of such changes.'

Kim wondered if he'd still have had something to say about such a drastic alteration to work patterns. But she wasn't here to discuss rotas and working practices.

'Lucky that Rachel married someone so willing to help out the family business,' she said. 'Was the intention for you to care-take it until one of his children was ready to take the reins?'

Colour flooded his cheeks. 'Like whom, Inspector? Lewis was a child who couldn't see beyond the end of a game controller. Rozzie was a self-absorbed YouTuber obsessed with followers and approval, Rachel has no interest and Zach only wants things that belong to other people.'

'Hmm...'

'Sorry,' he said. 'But I've put my heart and soul into this business.'

'Good to know how you really feel about the family, Mr Hewitt,' she said, and she could see the regret in his face. He was wishing he hadn't been quite so honest. 'But I'm interested as to how you got into the business. Were you in this line of work when you met Rachel?'

He shook his head, and Kim suspected he was still looking for a way to backtrack and rephrase the harsh things he'd said about the Daynes family, most of whom were now dead.

'No, I wasn't working when I met Rachel.' He smiled. 'We literally bumped into each other in Stourbridge. She was backing out of a coffee shop, and I was walking in, distracted on my phone. We both fell over, felt indignant and burst out laughing at the exact same second. I offered to replace her spilled coffee, which she accepted. She offered to replace my broken phone screen, which I refused, but I did ask if I could take her number instead.'

'Smooth.'

'Didn't feel like it at the time. It felt clumsy and awkward but, cheesy as it sounds, I knew she was the one for me.'

'Love at first sight?'

'For one of us. Rachel was a little slower, as she was nursing a bruised heart, but luckily she fell for me too eventually.'

'And did Rachel recommend you to her father?'

He looked affronted. 'No, Inspector, I did that all on my own.'

'How, Mr Hewitt? I am both intrigued and eager to know how you reached the dizzying heights of managing director in a relatively short space of time.'

'I had been offered two jobs at middle-management level – one for a national car-hire company and another at a meat wholesaler. I asked his advice on which one to—'

'You showed him the job offers?'

'I can't quite remember if it was the actual letters or the adverts but, either way, he told me he had a similar position at "the shop" as he called it and asked me to consider taking it. I started here in the buying office and worked my way up.'

'Fortuitous,' Kim observed, trying to keep the disbelief out of her voice. There was something not ringing quite true about this whole situation.

'For both of us.'

'Of course. And your rise to senior management?'

'I think William saw something in me. I fell in love with this business. I made it my mission to find out everything I could about the manufacturing processes, advertising, shipping, everything. I was the first person here each morning and the last to leave. William saw how committed I was to the family business. He trusted me.'

Kim couldn't help but wonder if Daryl Hewitt had married Rachel Daynes or her father.

'The other staff didn't mind?'

He shrugged. 'Does it matter?'

Not to you, Kim realised, not liking the taste in her mouth.

'Didn't it concern you that you had your whole personal and professional life all tied up in one family?'

'Why? Neither of us is planning on going anywhere.'

After witnessing the obvious tension and distance between them, Kim wouldn't have bet her next meal on that, but she'd got enough background and there was one question to which she really wanted an answer.

'When making all these important decisions on trust and faith and ability, did William know of the three years you spent in prison for fraud?'

All colour drained from his face. He was genuinely shocked.

'Mr Hewitt, you had to know we'd uncover your criminal history?'

'I didn't even realise you would look,' he admitted.

'I'm guessing that the answer to my question is no, you didn't share that information with him. Did you tell Rachel?'

'It was an accident, I mean—'

'What, you fell over and deposited over half a million pounds into your bank account over a period of two years?'

'I was ill, Inspector,' he said, loosening his collar further. 'I'd been suffering from depression and—'

'Did you buy the holiday cottage and the Porsche to cheer yourself up?' she asked pointedly.

That last barb hit the mark and his face darkened.

'I served my time,' he said frostily.

'I know that, but you don't think you should have mentioned your past to William?'

'I learned my lesson, Inspector, and I would never take anything from William.'

'Our forensic accountants will support that, I'm sure, once you furnish them with the annual accounts of the last five years.'

'Of course,' he said, knowing he had no legal right to withhold them.

'Did William also not know of your earlier, shorter stretch in prison for assault?'

'Good grief. That was twenty years ago. I was seventeen and it was a drunken brawl.'

'Mr Hewitt, you don't get a nine-month sentence for a ruck on a night out. You get it for a prolonged and unprovoked attack on someone that jumped the queue in the chip shop and was left with permanent injuries.'

A muscle jumped in his cheek. 'I don't see how that has any bearing on current events, but no I chose not to share that with Rachel or her family.'

It may not mean much to him, but it showed her that the man had form for violence and theft and that he had no compunction in sharing only the truth that suited him.

She sat back in her chair.

'Mr Hewitt, for whatever reason, you didn't have the best start in life. You left school with no qualifications and a bad attitude. Whatever you thought the world owed you appears to have landed in your lap. You have a beautiful family, you had a ready-made, extended family and a thriving instant business to run that, although not your own, is not without its perks,' she said, looking around.

He appeared affronted but she could have gone much harder and used the words that were flying around her brain: manipulative, opportunistic, advantageous, calculated.

'I have worked very hard for this family of which I am a part, and I don't appreciate—'

'The other reason for our visit,' Kim interrupted, unable to listen to his own opinion of himself any longer, 'is to ask if you'd had any further thoughts on disgruntled staff members or—'

'There aren't any of those.'

There soon would be, Kim thought, looking at the pile of new shift patterns.

'But there was one person who verbally threatened William.'

'Go on,' Kim said, sitting forward.

'A supplier, Roy Burston, used to supply all the timber for

the furniture. William realised a few months ago that he was paying more than he needed to and withdrew the contract.'

Kim couldn't help but wonder who had brought the price comparison to William's attention, but it was an interesting lead all the same.

'He made threats?' Kim asked.

'Over wood?' Bryant asked.

Daryl nodded.

'What exactly did he say?'

'He said that William would be sorry and that he should be prepared to lose everything.'

THIRTY-EIGHT

Penn smiled as Stacey wriggled her fingers at the appliances now on her desk.

'Okay, let me at it,' she said, opening the lid of the laptop, her eyes alight with the challenge.

His own package was nowhere near as impressive.

From what the boss had said, the bin had held quite a few books and diaries. He understood that both the fire and water would have caused substantial damage. He'd hoped for a little more than what he was looking at now.

Percy had explained that the drying out and separating process had been largely unsuccessful due to the sheer volume of water. The only thing remotely salvageable was a few pieces of paper from the book at the lowest point of the bin. He had seven pieces of paper all held individually in their own plastic wallets.

Like someone who had won the star prize and felt sorry for the loser, Stacey peered over.

'You gonna be able to get anything from them?'

'Not sure,' he said, taking a magnifying glass and his head-phones from the drawer.

He looked over all of them quickly to see if there was anything obvious. One of the sheets stood out from the others. Six of the seven were on lined paper but the seventh was lighter paper, white, unlined with washed-out black ink. A typed letter.

He put the others aside and focussed on the one that was different.

At the top right of the page, he could just make out a date which was one week earlier. The whole first paragraph was completely washed out, but the heading of the letter had been typed in bold and underlined. Some of the letters were legible.

He took a pencil and notepad and began playing his own form of hangman.

L t ill an T me t

He left that to the side as he held the paper in front of his desk lamp. It did nothing to highlight the text in the body of the letter, but it did show something he hadn't noticed earlier.

An icon.

He stared at it and tried to recreate on his notepad what he could see.

His pencil formed the shape of a shield, with a plant sprouting from a black line beneath it. The shield was divided into four – two sections black on white and two white on black. Two squares had a letter inside and the other two had motifs that were too small to fathom. Some kind of jewellery sat above the shield.

Plants, a shield and jewellery. What the hell?

'Stace?' he said, holding up the piece of paper.

'Sex,' she shouted out.

'What?' he asked, looking at what he'd held up. Where had that come from?

'Isn't that what crazy folks shout out when being shown those weird pictures?'

'No idea, but what do you see?'

'A big fat waste of your time if you want the— Ooh, hang on a sec,' she said, frowning.

As ever, he watched in awe as her fingers flew over the keyboard.

She turned her computer screen.

He looked at the emblem on the screen and back at his pad before holding the paper back up to the light.

The black line was a scroll.

The letters were capital initials.

The pictures were a gavel and scales.

The jewellery was a crown.

'Pass it every day on the bus in Dudley Town,' Stacey said.

It was a firm of high-priced solicitors, and the long line of text at the top said the subject of the letter was: *Last Will and Testament.*

What exactly had the Dayneses been trying to change?

THIRTY-NINE

Despite the vast, almost empty space of the warehouse on Bromley Lane in Lye, Kim could still smell the rich earthy aroma of timber as she approached the entrance. She heard Leanne's tut of annoyance that she'd walked from the car at speed. She didn't have the time to wait for the woman to carry out a full visual appraisal of everywhere they went. Bryant was used to catching up with her when the speed of her thoughts became directly linked to the speed of her feet.

Leanne had covered the ground well and was right behind her when a guy in his early sixties, wearing a high-visibility vest, jumped off a stacker truck and headed her way.

He started speaking before she'd even opened her mouth. 'I've been waiting for you and no, I didn't mean it.'

Kim still produced her ID, which he barely looked at.

'Roy Burston?' she clarified.

'That's me,' he said, rubbing a meaty hand over his bald head.

'You made a threat to William Daynes?'

'I did. I was angry, and I know exactly who pointed you my way.'

A second male approached, a younger version of the man they'd already met.

'My son, Davey.'

Davey nodded and put his hands in his pockets.

'Can you tell me what you said?' Kim asked.

'I can't remember, but I was pretty pissed off. It's been a busy few months,' he added sarcastically.

'Apparently you were going to make him pay and that he should be prepared to lose everything.'

He thought for a moment and then nodded. 'Sounds about right, and if that's what his little weasel said then I'm sure it's true.'

'Dad,' Davey warned.

'I ain't lying to coppers, son. I said what I said and that's it. It was an empty threat, but I still said it.'

'Empty?'

'Yeah, I meant legally, officer. I fully intended to take him to the cleaners legally, but turns out I didn't have a leg to stand on.'

'Go on,' Kim urged, appreciating the man's honesty.

'I've known William for many years. Started my business not long before he did. We both did okay and grew pretty quickly. William wasn't my only customer, but he was my best. I did everything to keep him happy, but I did have other clients. We kinda struck a verbal deal that I would supply only to him, and that's what I did until dipshit wannabe bigshot convinced him to take his business elsewhere for a saving of two hundred quid a month.'

He motioned around him. 'Put me out of business. I had no customers left cos I'd thrown all the eggs and the bloody chicken into one basket, and I got shafted. No income, no business, nothing to hand down to my own kid. Just because some donkey brain wanted to save a few quid.'

'Did William know the effect it was going to have on you?'

'Yeah, I told him it would do us in, but it was just business,' he said, shrugging, but he couldn't hide the hurt that flitted across his face. Clearly, he'd thought they were better friends. She glanced briefly at his son, but it wasn't hurt that shaped Davey's features – it was good old solid rage.

'We've sold off the last few tonnes for peanuts just to give our suppliers something, but tomorrow we close the doors for good after thirty-eight years.'

Kim felt a wave of sadness for a man who had lost everything because he was too trusting.

'But I didn't hurt 'em,' he said.

'Dad,' Davey warned again.

'I wanted to hurt him, not his wife and kids, but I ain't that stupid, and you'll find no trace of me in that house. Now the little pretender of a shitbag is another story. I could quite cheerfully put my hands around his—'

'Dad.'

'Mr Burston.'

She and his son had spoken together. She continued. 'Don't say something you might regret later.'

'You think I'd say it in front of three coppers if I was serious?'

Kim almost said two and a half.

'Still, best not to threaten people right in front of us,' Bryant advised.

Kim thanked the man for his time and headed back to the car.

'If you really wanna find out what happened, you might want to start looking a bit closer to home.'

By the time Kim turned, Roy Burston had walked away.

It was Davey Burston who had called out.

She held his gaze for a good few seconds before he turned and followed his dad.

FORTY

'Every single bloody platform,' Stacey said, throwing down her pen.

'Huh?'

'Martey was harassing her all over the place. Messaging her on Facebook, Twitter, Insta. I can sure see why she cooled the social media.'

'Didn't she block him?' Penn asked, putting down his magnifying glass.

'Repeatedly but he'd just set up another account and change the number. On Insta he was up to Martey27. He's a real nasty piece of work. Calling her all kinds of names, insulting her appearance, her weight, everything.'

'Shit, sounds pretty determined. Could he be just another keyboard fruitcake?'

Stacey shook her head. 'I don't think so. Every account he's set up is for the sole intention of harassing Rozzie. There are no other posts, comments or interaction. It's all about her, and it could be literally anyone that's doing it.'

'No way to trace it?' Penn asked.

'You know how these platforms protect the data of their

customers. All I've got is online abuse. They're not going to give anything up on the back of that. The other problem I've got is that these accounts are leaving no footprint anywhere else. The profiles are set up and they literally do nothing but troll Rozzie. There are no friends, no photos, no likes, no followers, just a name that changes every few days.'

'Could they have done all this to just get to Rozzie?' Penn asked doubtfully.

'I don't know, Penn. I honestly don't know.'

FORTY-ONE

It was almost two when Kim called the rest of her team on loudspeaker. She, Bryant and Leanne had silently consumed a meal deal and a hot drink after leaving the lumber yard.

The silence had given her an opportunity to check her messages from Charlie. Barney was being spoiled rotten by both Charlie's best friend and his sister, with early morning beach walks and lots of treats. Kim suspected she was missing him way more than he was missing her.

Damn that bastard Symes for parting her from her buddy and giving her Leanne King instead. Shit deal. She hated the fact that his continued freedom was also forcing her to stay away from the station when she needed to communicate with her team. She pushed away the questions in her head about how the search was being conducted. With the brick wall that was Woody standing between her and the investigating team, the thoughts did her no good.

'Hey, Stace,' Kim said as the constable answered the phone.

'Hiya, boss, I think Penn wants to go first.'

Kim's silence gave him permission.

'Boss, I think the Dayneses were in the process of changing

their will. There was a recent letter in with the books but there's very little to go on. I've requested a meeting with the lawyer handling it, but he's not available until the end of the week. He's in court, but I'm trying to get an appointment with the family's accountant, who'd also have to know what was going on.'

'Anything else?'

'Still trying to put together some words from the diary entries. There's not a lot left.'

'Okay, get cracking on the warrant for Warren Cox. Not sure why he's refusing to give us a DNA sample but we're gonna get one.'

'Go it, boss.'

'Stace, you there?'

'Here, boss. Looks like Rozzie had herself a real-life stalker. Pretty aggressive and potentially violent. There's nothing behind any of the accounts except hatred towards Rozzie. I've contacted the platforms to see if I can get any details of the account holder.'

Kim already knew that was going to be tricky. All the platform providers guarded personal details closely and they were unlikely to get anything without a court order.

'I just wanna do a bit more digging on how easy she was to find off the internet.'

'Okay, guys, keep at it, and if you need anything, just shout,' she said, ending the call.

'What about us, guv? We taking the rest of the day off?'

'You wish, Bryant,' she said, turning something over in her mind.

'We're doing everything we should be, right? We're chasing every lead, every possibility, every family member, every secret. Everything is covered and we're not missing anything?'

'Err... yeah. That's our job, but why do I feel a big but coming?'

'Why her, Bryant?'

'Huh?'

'Why target Helen? Why make it look as though she'd slaughtered her family? Why not William, even Rozzie? Why Helen?'

'Easiest?' he asked.

'Whoever did this wasn't interested in easy. There were easier ways. I think we need to step back and refocus our attention on the mother, except there's just one place I want to go first.'

FORTY-TWO

Symes pulled into the church car park at the end of Colley Lane, the road which held Colley Lane Junior School.

He had just a couple of minutes before hitting the perfect time to carry out the next part of his plan.

He jumped out of the car with the screwdriver already in his hand, went to the front of the car and unscrewed the number plate, then went to the back and did the same before throwing them both in the rear seat. He paused and decided to add one last obstacle to the identification process – he used the tip of the screwdriver to prise off the silver metal emblems and the make and model of the car.

A witness claiming they saw a small cream car wouldn't exactly give the police a lot to go on. And witnesses were certainly going to see the car, he thought, getting back in and closing the door.

He'd given great thought to how he was going to get the second girl. Most parents would be extra vigilant after hearing the news that little Emma Bunting had been snatched, so trying to do the same again wasn't going to work. Parents would be bundling their kids into their cars and homes as quickly as possible once they left the school grounds. As soon as they were no longer safe in large numbers, their radar for anything unusual would be on high alert.

He moved the car slowly to the church car park exit, poked the bonnet out and looked up the lane towards the school.

Perfect.

The road was in school collection chaos.

Parents were rushing on foot with other kids in tow and pushing prams. Cars were pulling in and pulling out all over the place, and small huddles of parents stood together while their kids played close by.

As he approached, he shook his head. There were lots of mums discussing the recent abduction while chattering away to each other but not actually watching their kids.

One little girl in particular caught his eye. She was a bit younger than he'd wanted, but her curly blonde hair reminded him of the one he'd lost. Her jacket was falling off her shoulder, and a painting was clutched in her little hand while she chased another girl around in circles.

He stopped the car in the middle of the road, jumped out and opened both doors. Then he grabbed the girl by the back of the neck and hauled her towards the car. Her scream attracted the attention of everyone around.

Their collective shock rendered them numb for just a second, which was long enough for him to throw her in the car.

'Chloe... Chloe... Chloe...' he heard amongst the cacophony of calls that all sounded at the same time. A petite woman was speeding towards him, screaming. She reached the door as it slammed shut.

Her fist beat on the windows as she continued to shout her daughter's name.

'Mummy... Mummy...' the child cried.

Symes hit the accelerator and mounted the pavement opposite to avoid the traffic. Parents were pulling their children in all directions to get out of the way of the speeding car.

Using the pavement helped him to avoid the speed bumps that led all the way to the main road. The traffic lights at the crossroads were on his side, holding the traffic, enabling him to cross straight over into the Tanhouse Estate, which would take him to Oldnall Lane and then Wynall Lane and the country roads where he'd barely meet a soul.

Adrenaline was shooting through his body. Even the squealing and crying from the back seat wasn't affecting him. He was pumped.

'Mummy... Mummy... Mummy,' the child cried between sobs.

'Shut it or you'll never see her again,' he hissed.

He was sure there were people looking curiously through the window at the hysterical little girl crying in the back, but he didn't care.

By the time the police attended the school, got details and put together any other reports, he would be long gone.

His stomach turned with excitement.

He finally had his two little girls.

FORTY-THREE

Kim was surprised to hear a baby crying as she knocked on the door of Zach and Gavin's flat.

'You know Leanne's probably putting a call into the boss right now, eh, guv?' Bryant asked.

Kim shrugged. 'There's barely room for us two in there, never mind—'

She stopped speaking as Gavin answered the door. He smiled and stepped aside.

'You two started a family since the last time we were here?' she asked.

'Niece sitting for Rachel. She needed to get out of the house for a bit.'

Kim marvelled at the dynamics of the twins; one minute they were acting as though they hated each other, the next Rachel was leaving Zach in charge of the thing she valued most in the world.

'Everything okay with Rachel?' she asked.

'Yeah, she just needed some space for a few hours – to process everything that's happened. It's how she deals with stuff.'

Kim followed him into the lounge that had shrunk since their last visit due to the Moses basket and baby holdall now in the room.

Mia was fidgeting on Zach's lap.

'Hello, officers. Gavin, I think she's, err...'

He lifted the child up and held her forward for Gavin to take. His nose wrinkled with distaste.

'I swear, Zach, you'd better not be this precious when we have our own,' he said, calmly taking the baby from his husband's arms.

The top of the sideboard had been cleared and turned into a baby changing space.

'Just move the nappy bag and take a seat,' Zach said as Gavin lay Mia on the changing mat. Her fussing had changed to a low gurgling noise.

Gavin used one hand to squeeze a squeaky teddy in front of her face and the other to open the all-in-one suit.

'Nicely done,' Kim observed.

'Lots of siblings growing up,' he said, undoing a nappy with one hand.

Zach was watching him with a smile on his face too.

'So you and Rachel made up after this morning?'

She had pretty much screamed all kinds of loser in his face.

He looked genuinely confused. 'Oh, that was nothing. You should see us when we really get going. There's fur flying all over the place, though it doesn't last long. She gets a bit uppity being the firstborn – oldest child and all that by about eight and a half minutes – but who's counting? I've beaten her at everything else since, and besides, Rachel always comes around by the time she wants something.'

'She didn't ask her husband to come home so she could take some time out?'

'I think she might have been planning on calling him to

meet her for a coffee. A bit of time alone,' he said, nodding towards Mia.

'She certainly needs his support right now. You're very lucky,' she said, nodding towards Gavin, who was fastening up Mia's all-in-one suit.

'Luck has nothing to do with it,' Zach said with a strange smile. The closest name she could give it was satisfaction with a hint of smug secrecy.

'He's very passionate about the business, isn't he? Daryl?' Kim asked.

'Someone in the family has to be,' Zach answered. 'Bookcases and sideboards just don't do it for me – or for Rachel either.'

From what she'd seen, the business was far more than that, and it was probably hurtful for William that neither of his adult children had any interest in the business that had supported them their whole lives. She couldn't help wondering what Zach's actual passion was.

'May we talk about your mother, Zach?' Kim asked.

He eyed her suspiciously. 'I thought you said she had nothing to do with it.'

'That hasn't changed. Your mother didn't kill anyone, but we'd like to understand the nature of her emotional troubles.'

'If you find out, let me know. I remember her going away for a rest when she lost the baby. I didn't know what that meant at the time. I remember her taking Rachel and I out in the car at 2 a.m. one morning to get ice cream. Obviously there was no one open, but it was fun and kinda weird at the same time. To us it was an adventure, but Mum seemed genuinely surprised that there was nowhere open. That was a couple of weeks before Dad found her wandering the grounds with the pushchair. Later we understood what having a rest entailed and where she'd been, and eventually she came back and things returned to normal.'

Kim wondered if Helen had ever returned to normal or just appeared to do so.

Gavin cooed softly at Mia, who was giggling and gurgling again.

'Do you recall anything before that?' Kim asked, unsure how much Zach knew.

He shook his head. 'Why would I? That was when it all started, when the baby died.'

Or she just hid it better, Kim thought.

Whatever the reason, Helen had been struggling around the time when she was pregnant with the twins. It had been a secret shared only with her husband and social services by the looks of it.

'Why all the interest in my mother?' Zach asked, narrowing his eyes. 'You haven't asked one question about my father. Surely you can't think either one of them did anything to provoke this?'

'We're going where the evidence takes us, Zach, but rest assured that we will find the person who murdered your family.'

Kim had wanted to ask him about the therapist Helen had been seeing for so many years, but she didn't want to unnerve him anymore. He seemed sensitive about excess attention on his mother.

'Okay, thanks. We'll be in touch when— Oh, actually there was one more thing. You've been reasonably kind about your brother-in-law, but he didn't extend you the same level of courtesy and hinted that you like to take whatever you want.'

Zach and Gavin exchanged a look.

'He means me,' Gavin said, placing a sleeping Mia in her Moses basket.

She waited for further explanation.

'Rachel and I were together first,' he said, taking a seat beside his husband. 'Only for a few months, until I met Zach.

Hit me like a tonne of bricks. Obviously, it was difficult for a while, but there's no one for me but him.'

It explained so much; Rachel's barely hidden expressions of tenderness when she looked at Gavin, her brief flashes of animosity towards her brother.

'We're all good now,' Gavin said. 'Now she's just like my own sister.'

Kim didn't think Rachel's feelings for Gavin were remotely sisterly.

'Again, thank you for your time,' she said, heading for the door.

She'd learned little more about Helen but a great deal more about Zach.

She'd learned that when Zach saw something he wanted, he didn't care who he had to hurt to get it.

FORTY-FOUR

'It's not beyond the realms of possibility you know,' Stacey said, bringing him back into the room.

The usual easy silence had fallen between them as they'd worked for the last couple of hours, interrupted only by the boss calling to request the address of Helen Daynes's therapist.

'What, that you're gonna leave that last cookie in the tub?' he asked, nodding towards the Tupperware bowl.

'Yeah, get real,' she said, leaning across and plucking it out.

He'd been about to suggest they split it, but the ship had sailed on that one, he thought as she took a good bite.

'I'm talking about finding Rozzie's address. This Martey person could have tracked her down. There are posts where she's checked into different places, liked local businesses, not to mention the photos giving away enough pieces of the puzzle to fit together. Up until Martey started harassing her, you could have written her daily itinerary from the information shared across all forums.'

'I think the boss is focussing more on Helen being at the centre of it,' he said.

'I get that, but this Martey is vicious. I mean, short of

deleting her social-media accounts completely she was at a loss. She tried to shrug him off. She blocked him countless times, didn't respond or react to his threats, which appeared to piss him off even more.'

'But if she kept blocking him, how did new messages from non-friends get through?'

'They sit in message requests. Facebook, for example, holds all your messages from non-friends in a separate file. You only see them if you go looking.'

'Did she go looking?'

Stacey nodded.

'So what's the point of blocking?'

'It's a need to know,' Stacey said. 'You're still compelled to read the messages, not least to see if they give you a clue. In the last one he did mention a café that she'd been to with friends.'

'You think he could have followed her?'

'Absolutely. I think Rozzie had herself a real-life dangerous stalker.'

'You think her parents knew?'

'No, she was seventeen years old. There's no police report, and I think her parents would have insisted. Looks to me like Rozzie kept all this to herself.'

That was a lot for a seventeen-year-old to deal with alone, Penn thought.

'Maybe she thought her mum had enough problems.'

'But what exactly was Helen dealing with? We know she suffered from depression, like millions of others. She had a difficult anniversary to face, but let's be honest, it wasn't like she had a rush of new problems to deal with,' Penn asked.

'Maybe they weren't that close, and Rozzie struggled to share things with either of her parents,' Stacey proposed. 'There's no mention of her mum or dad on her social media.' Stacey paused. 'So that's me. What have you got?'

Penn pulled one of the diary sheets towards him.

'Listen to this. "I never stop wondering where you are. I loved you so much. I let you down. My grief consumes me."'

'Bloody hell. That must be her outpourings for the child that died. She really didn't ever get over it, did she?'

'The clippings I've got have no date, but there's one thing I don't understand.'

'Go on,' Stacey said.

'If you've lost something so precious, don't you overcompensate and go extreme on what you've got left? At the time Helen lost that middle child, she already had twins, and following the loss, she had two more children. According to the boss, she doesn't appear to have had a close bond with any of her children.'

'What are you trying to say?'

'Gotta be honest, Stace, I haven't got a bloody clue, but something doesn't smell right between Helen and her kids.'

FORTY-FIVE

Doctor Raymond Cutler kept a surgery in the building of the West Midlands private hospital in Colley Gate.

The call ahead had won them a twenty-minute window he had at 4.40 p.m. Kim wasn't sure if he had another client at 5 p.m. or if he was a real stickler for leaving on time. And she had a minute to spare when they were buzzed into the waiting area.

'Go ahead,' Leanne said, taking a seat in the reception. It was an area where she could monitor anyone coming into the building.

After Kim showed her ID, the receptionist pointed to a hallway that curled around the greeting desk.

'Feeling a bit like a trio that just lost their least favourite friend, guv,' Bryant said once they were out of sight.

'Speak for yourself,' she said, following the sign to Doctor Cutler's office.

'Bit different to Russells Hall, eh?' Bryant continued.

She'd always found that with private hospitals everything was calmer, less frantic, as though the right amount of appointments had been made for the right amount of doctors. There was no panic, no angst of people being forced to wait hours after already waiting months. If it was *The Hunger Games*, it was definitely the difference between the Capitol and District 12.

A nurse smiled in their direction as she paused at the coffee-making station.

The door to the third office on the left opened as they approached it, and a man in his late sixties stepped into the corridor holding a coffee mug. It was emblazoned with the caption 'Built for Comfort Not Speed'.

'Doctor Cutler?' Kim asked, taking in his chocolate-coloured corduroy trousers and open-necked shirt. His hair was completely grey, tidily cut, and a pair of spectacles hung around his neck.

'DI Stone?' he said, nodding towards the door. 'Please go in while I grab a refill.'

She did as he'd asked and was surprised at the lack of personalisation in the space. The desk and bookshelves were made of light pine-coloured wood and looked generic. Two leather armchairs faced each other on the opposite side of the room.

The space was bright but uninspiring, and she guessed that maybe some patients preferred it that way. She suddenly thought of her own visits to Ted Morgan as a child. He had tried many different settings to encourage her to open up. Sometimes they'd been in his study, surrounded by books and keepsakes, other times in the sitting room with comfy sofas and fluffy cushions. Other times they'd been in the garden sitting beside his small fish pond. She had opened up in none of them, but she did remember the peace she'd felt in each place, some of the things he'd said to her that had lodged in her mind. She wasn't sure she'd have recalled anything from an impersonal space such as this, but it had certainly suited Helen Daynes given how long she'd been in therapy with the psychiatrist.

'Sorry about that,' Doctor Cutler said, closing the door behind him. 'It's my only vice, and my wife buys only decaf. Now, how can I help you?'

'As I mentioned on the phone, we'd like to talk about Helen Daynes.'

'What would you like to know?' he asked as a genuine wave of sadness passed over his face.

'Everything,' she answered simply.

He shifted in his seat. 'It may be better if you ask me some questions.'

Kim felt a little tension seep into her jaw. He was hedging.

'You treated Helen Daynes for a very long time.'

'That's not a question, but I'll answer your statement. I treated Helen for twenty-nine years. She was one of my first patients, and she will now also be one of my last. I retire fully next month.'

'Can you tell us the nature of her illness?'

'Clinical depression and general anxiety disorder.'

'For all these years?'

'Yes. There were times that she needed more help than others, but not everyone is able to put mental illness in their past.'

'What brought it on?'

'Really, Inspector, I think you understand the futility of that question.'

'But she had no medical history of depression before you saw her twenty-nine years ago, did she?'

'I can only speak from when I began treating her.'

'And why was that?' Kim asked, trying to get her answer from the back door.

'Because her GP thought she would benefit from the help.'

'Was she pregnant?'

'Yes, I believe she was.'

'And she was prescribed a cocktail of medication?'

'Yes, she was.'

Kim waited.

'My priority, Inspector, is the person standing before me. If the condition warrants pharmaceutical intervention then—'

'But the babies?' Kim queried.

'May never have been born if she hadn't had the help.'

'Was Helen Daynes suicidal when she was pregnant with the twins?'

'I'm not going to answer that. I've made myself clear that my patient was prescribed what was deemed necessary for her own well-being at the time she was referred to me.'

Kim paused for a moment. It was clear that he was avoiding something.

'Doctor Cutler, are you aware of a sealed social services case involving Helen Daynes?'

'That is not my department.'

'I'm going to take that as a yes.'

He didn't argue.

'Is that the reason Helen needed help?'

'The timing would work.'

'You're not going to make this easy for us, are you?'

'Helen was my patient.'

'And we're investigating her murder, which was committed by someone who decided to try and make it look like she'd been responsible for murdering her own children. Now would you like to help?'

'I've helped as much as I think I can.'

'You know that we're going to come back with a court order for her records?'

'Absolutely, but to my knowledge, Helen committed no crime, she didn't hurt anyone, so I'll await the court's instruction.'

'And yet something happened twenty-nine years ago that scarred her for life.'

The doctor said nothing.

'Why are you so insistent on not telling us what happened?'

'Helen was my patient. Guarding her secret is what she'd expect me to do, and in this case, it's what she'd want me to do.'

FORTY-SIX

Rachel Hewitt sipped her second double-shot latte, making the most of her temporary freedom.

Maternal guilt instantly clutched at her stomach. It wasn't that she wanted to be away from Mia – she never wanted to be away from Mia, but she did want an hour or two on her own. It was a paradox that she now understood.

She was intellectually aware that she had lost most of her family and that her life would never be the same again. Her brain understood that her younger sister had been pregnant and hadn't told her. Her logical mind accepted that she would never again see Lewis roll his eyes when she tweaked his ear. She understood, and yet she hadn't cried once.

The place she'd chosen to come wouldn't have been everyone's idea of getting away. She had taken an outside table at a small coffee shop at the busy end of Brierley Hill High Street. Buses, cars and lorries thundered past, trying to catch the lights before they changed back. Shoppers were bustling around in and out, weighing themselves down with bargain after bargain. Groups of kids were passing her by with that end-of-day euphoria, uniform in varying stages of disarray. She remained unnoticed as she lit her second secret cigarette and delighted just for a second at the action. She had given up the minute she'd even suspected she might be pregnant, and nine months nicotine free had cemented her decision not to start again, but recent events had destroyed that resolve.

As she took a long satisfying draw on the cigarette, she marvelled at how people continued to function when their world was falling apart. You didn't wear tragedy on your everyday face. You continued to smile at the cashier as she asked for your order. You continued to thank the person that held the door open for you or nod an acknowledgement at the person sitting at the next table. Nothing in your manner or actions would lead anyone to the true knowledge of events in your life.

Her thoughts continued to wander away from the feelings and questions that she had come here to face. Was the woman carrying bags of toys spoiling her kids even though it was nowhere near Christmas? Did the elderly man carrying one small bag of shopping have anyone to go home to? Was he just buying all he could afford on a daily basis? Everyone had a story, a life, problems, tragedies. She had the sudden urge to stand up and shout, 'My whole family was just murdered,' and begin some kind of impromptu group counselling session.

The smile that she felt rest on her lips was another indication that her brain had not yet fully accepted the news. It wasn't something she'd been forced to face yet. Gavin had absorbed that pain for all of them. Good old Gavin, the reason she'd been able to get away for an hour at all. She loved her brother, but she didn't trust him with her child. She knew full well that it would be her brother-in-law making sure her instructions were followed. It would be Gavin changing Mia's nappy, Gavin giving her a bottle and Gavin making cooey noises at her.

She pushed away the melancholy feeling that often accompanied thoughts of Gavin, especially in relation to her child.

There had been a time when she'd thought that any child of hers would contain his DNA too. But fate had had other ideas and so had her covetous brother. It was her default defence mechanism to blame Zach, and he had made it clear from day one that he wanted Gavin, but the realistic part of her knew that Gavin must have been ripe for the taking and hadn't been as invested in the relationship as she had been. He had been open about his fluid sexuality, as he liked to call it, from their second date. She hadn't given it a thought. If they were meant to be together it didn't matter what the sexuality was of the person trying to steal him. He'd been good at making her laugh, good at making her feel special. She just wished he hadn't been so damn good at making her fall in love with him.

It was a testament to her own husband that he'd listened to the whole sorry tale for their entire first date. She had drunk and talked, drunk more, talked more and then sobbed into his jacket, claiming, 'I wasn't enough for him.'

'I think you mean you weren't man enough for him,' Daryl had said, getting her attention.

She had shared her heartbreak of losing the love of her life to her brother, and he'd patiently listened and supplied her with Kleenex.

She had been shocked when he'd asked her for a second date.

'What? We never got to my story of a break-up when I was fourteen years old and that's one you've got to hear.'

She had laughed and agreed.

What she hadn't told Daryl then, or since, was that sense of not being enough was not new to her. Gavin's treatment of her had only solidified the feeling she'd had from her mother as far back as she could remember.

The honest acknowledgement of that fact was accompanied with a side order of guilt. She had been neglected in no way, shape or form. By anyone's standards, her mother had been a fantastic parent to them all. Despite her emotional problems, they had always been well clothed, well fed and hadn't lacked emotional nurture or interaction. She had attended, cheered and congratulated every win or minor triumph. She had commiserated every loss and disappointment. She had been the first mum in line at every parents' evening and the one shouting loudest at every sports day.

It was the moments of distraction. The numerous times she would catch her mother staring off into space with a faraway look in her eyes, almost a longing for something more. One of Rachel's earliest memories was of feeling panicked at not seeing her mother waiting at the school gates of the junior school. Zach had continued to kick a football around, unconcerned about their absent parent, but she'd spotted her mother at the other school entrance, the one for the older kids, her eyes eagerly searching the crowds of teenagers surging past her. It had taken Rachel three calls to get her attention. She'd hurried to the correct gate and laughed off her own confusion. Rachel had waited for her mum to recount the event that night at dinner to her dad, but the story had never come. Funny how she'd always remembered that.

She reached for her cup surprised at two things: her drink was now cold, and tears were running over her cheeks. She would miss every member of her family, but she would also miss the opportunity to ask her mother the one question that had been in her head all of her life.

Why hadn't she been enough?

Finally, she could feel the emotion: hovering, waiting, stalking her like an avalanche waiting to fall. It was there. It was threatening. It was imminent.

She had to get back to Mia.

She stood as the tears began to blur her vision. The chair leg got caught on the metal table and she stumbled but righted herself as the noise drew the attention of passers-by.

She moved away quickly, eager to be out of their gaze.

She wiped the tears away as she headed to the edge of the pavement to avoid a man walking two Labradors.

She didn't see that the traffic lights had changed to green. She didn't see the lorry that was thundering towards the junction. And she didn't see the hand that pushed her into the road.

FORTY-SEVEN

'What the hell was Helen Daynes trying to hide?' Kim asked as they headed towards the home of Reece Porter.

Penn had told them earlier that the man had refused to provide a DNA sample, and now Kim was curious to know why. The warrant had already been issued enabling them to request a DNA sample from their other refuser of the day, Warren, because there they had a tangible link. They wouldn't get one for Reece Porter. Being a neighbour and occasional handyman did not give them the right to twirl a swab around his mouth. With parameters that loose, they'd have been able to test half the country.

The fact that Reece Porter had refused made her want his DNA all the more. Given his sheer audacity in accessing a crime scene, she was surprised the man wasn't previously known to them, but a name check had revealed nothing.

'I mean, her therapist said she'd never hurt anyone so it's not like she killed somebody.'

'Death isn't always the worst thing you can do,' Leanne said from behind.

'Jesus, a warning next time,' Kim said. The woman hadn't spoken voluntarily in two days.

Kim waited.

Silence.

'Want to elaborate?'

'No.'

'Oh, come on. Try the police officer role on for a change.'

'No and fuck you.'

Bryant turned his guffaw into a cough the right side of getting a transfer.

'How is death not the worst?' Kim asked.

'Death is the worst crime punishable by law but not by conscience.'

'Fuck me, Leanne. It's probably good you don't speak much. We'd get nothing else done but decipher—'

'Okay, let me simplify.'

'Yeah, let me come back there and smack that condescending tone out of—'

'Guv,' Bryant warned.

Kim took a breath.

Leanne continued. 'You're thinking like a police officer.'

'Not one of your problems, is it?' she quipped.

'Killing is not always the worst thing you can do. For example, mercy killing. There's no anger, hate, frenzy. You're assisting someone to die. It's merciful. It doesn't prolong suffering. That's all I'm saying.'

Bryant crossed the last island towards Pedmore looking thoughtful 'You know, Leanne, that reminds me of a girl I dated at college.'

'Oh, jeez, Bryant, not one of your bygone-days stories. Cheers, Leanne.'

'You're welcome.'

'Hang on, hear me out,' he insisted as the memory seemed to clear for him. 'Her name was Becca.'

'Unnecessary.'

'She was studying sociology and—'

'Even more unnecessary,' Kim said, losing the will to live.

'She'd turned vegetarian at the age of eight. Any meat on her plate and she'd scream the house down.'

'Yes, killing animals is a contentious—'

'It wasn't the death that bothered her,' Bryant continued. 'She said her objection came from a family holiday to Wales, and for much of the journey they were behind a truck carrying sheep. She knew where they were going, and she swore she could see fear in the animals' eyes. That was what she couldn't be a party to: being responsible for demanding something that led to that much fear. It wasn't the death.'

'My point exactly,' Leanne said as Bryant pulled onto the driveway of the Porter home.

'No way did you two just say the exact same thing, but okay, I take your point.'

Bryant stopped the car and glanced in his rear-view mirror. If a silent high five was possible, they'd just done it.

She groaned and got out of the car.

The door to the property was open before she reached it.

Della Porter stood with her hands clasped. She wore a knee-length skirt, a white shirt and a pink cardigan draped over her shoulders in a manner Kim had never understood. Either wear it or don't was her motto.

'You're not coming in, Inspector,' she said frostily.

'May I ask why...?'

'Harassing our boy when he's done nothing wrong. We've told you everything we know, and you now accuse Reece of having—'

'Wait one minute, Mrs Porter,' Kim interrupted. 'No one has accused Reece of anything, and if we did, it would be of tampering with a crime scene.'

Della's mouth fell slack.

'He didn't tell you where we found him?'

Della said nothing but didn't move aside either. Fine, if she wanted this conversation on the doorstep, that was okay with her.

'He was found hiding under the bed of Rosalind Daynes when it was still an active crime scene. He hasn't yet been charged with any offence relating to—'

'He's done nothing wrong,' she said, ignoring what Kim had said.

'He also seemed to know Rozzie quite well, not to mention that he couldn't possibly have seen the fire from where he told us, Mrs Porter, so right now he's lucky we're only asking for a DNA sample to rule him out.'

And that was only because she wasn't sure he had the IQ to pull off the murder.

'You lot will try and pin this on anyone. Maybe he did like Rosalind, but that doesn't mean—'

'You're admitting he had feelings for her?' Kim asked.

Della Porter coloured, realising what she'd said. 'No, I mean... of course if he did have feelings for her doesn't mean it went anywhere.'

'Which is exactly why we'd like to rule him out, and given what you've just told us, I think we can find a judge who will—'

'He's innocent.'

Kim could tell the word judge had spooked her. Now she was on the rails.

'Nine a.m. tomorrow, Mrs Porter, or we'll be back with a warrant,' she said as her phone began to ring. It was Stacey.

Her finger hovered over the button.

'Well, I hope you're looking just as closely at that son of hers.'

She let the call ring.

'And why would I do that, Mrs Porter?' she asked.

'Because he was clearly upset with his parents about something.'

'And how would you know that?'

For neighbours who didn't speak, she sure knew a lot of the Dayneses' business.

'Because he almost ran me off the lane as he left on Saturday afternoon. Driving like a bloody madman he was.'

'What time?'

She shrugged. 'Mid-afternoon.'

Approximately twelve hours before the murder took place.

Kim nodded her acknowledgement as she turned and walked back towards the car.

Her phone rang again.

'Go ahead, Stace.'

Kim listened closely as Stacey spoke hurriedly.

'Oh shit,' she said, ending the call.

She turned to her colleague. 'Bryant, we need to get to Russells Hall now.'

FORTY-EIGHT

'Ah, bless,' Symes said at the sight of his little prisoners. They didn't know each other but they had huddled together either for warmth or comfort. He wasn't sure which.

Upon seeing him, the younger girl burst into tears and hid her face in Emma's arm.

After bringing Chloe earlier, he had tied her wrists and ankles together and thrown her into the same room as Emma, before locking the doors and leaving again.

He'd driven back towards town and parked a quarter mile away from a village shop, before walking the rest of the way to make a couple of small purchases.

He'd been gone for no more than two hours and the two of them were already firm friends.

He smiled in the face of their terror.

Perfect.

It was time to tighten the screws on the bitch just a little more.

He took out the pay-and-go phone he'd bought at Tesco with money from Edna's purse. Oh, Edna, the gift that just kept on giving. He'd known his image would be caught on CCTV somewhere around the store, but he had made his purchase quickly and efficiently, drawing no attention to himself. He had been in and out in less than five minutes.

The £10 SIM card had already been inserted and, although phones had come a long way during his time inside, he only needed it to do two things.

He readied the phone and he readied himself.

'Okay, girls, I know you're scared and you're right to be. You're never gonna see any of your parents again.'

Both girls burst into tears.

Press record.

'I want my mummy.'

Scream.

'Mummy... Mummy... Mummy.'

Sobs.

'P-P-Please let us go.'

Sobs.

'I'm scared.'

Oh this was so much better than he'd expected.

Wordlessly, he raised his foot and hovered it over the smaller girl's knee. She watched it with terror shining in her eyes. He touched the side of her leg with the toe of his foot.

She screamed. 'Don't hurt me. Don't hurt me.'

He captured another few seconds of fear-fuelled crying and pleas from the two of them.

'Please let us go home,' said the older girl.

He pressed the end button.

'Thanks, girls. That was quite the performance.'

That should do very nicely indeed.

FORTY-NINE

Kim tore into the A&E department of Russells Hall Hospital not caring who was shadowing her in. If Symes had jumped up right in front of her, she felt sure she could have just tossed him out the way.

A quick glance over the walking wounded in the waiting area confirmed that no member of the Daynes family was present.

Shit, that wasn't good.

'Rachel Daynes... Hewitt,' Kim corrected herself as she held up her ID.

The woman began tapping into a computer.

'Recent hit and run,' Kim clarified, drumming her fingers on the desk.

'I'm not... Hang on... the system...'

'Where's her family?' Kim asked.

'I'm sorry... I'm not sure...'

'Never mind,' Kim said, realising she wasn't giving the woman a chance to answer.

She headed through the double doors into the corridor that led to the cubicles. A nurse approached her.

'Rachel Hewitt?' she said, holding up the ID that was still in her hand.

The nurse glanced at the whiteboard and extrapolated information at lightning speed.

'Come with me.'

Kim followed her beyond the curtained cubicles to a door marked 'Private'.

She opened the door and three pairs of eyes looked Kim's way expectantly.

The nurse shook her head and closed the door behind Bryant. Kim wasn't sure exactly where they'd lost Leanne and she didn't much care.

'How is she?' Kim asked as Zach dropped his head back into his hands. Gavin returned his gaze to the window.

Daryl turned vacant, tired eyes on her. 'She's in surgery. They're trying to stop the bleeding.'

'What happened?' she asked, taking a seat beside him.

He shrugged. 'I'm still trying to make sense of it. I got a call from the police to say she'd been involved in an accident, and she was on her way here. I called Zach, who said they'd tried to call her a couple of times. They dropped Mia off at my mum's and came straight here. She was already in surgery, and then the police came, but that's a good thing, isn't it? That they got her into surgery so quickly? I mean, she'll be fine, won't she?'

'Your wife seems like a very strong woman,' Kim said, touching him lightly on the arm. She didn't like the man, but he was clearly shell-shocked.

'And what did the police say?' Kim asked.

'They asked if she'd been drinking. Onlookers said she was stumbling all over the place.' He frowned as though that was what he couldn't make sense of. 'She never drank. She didn't even like the taste of alcohol. Not even when cooking.'

Kim saw Gavin's almost imperceptible nod of agreement.

'Café owner only served her two lattes.'

'Does she ever use drugs?' Kim asked.

'Never,' Daryl said. 'She smoked up until her pregnancy with Mia. She's secretly having the odd one now and again without me knowing,' he said, allowing a fond smile to form on his face. The second he realised it was there, it disappeared.

'I should have met her. She called me...'

His words trailed away as both Zach and Gavin looked at him.

So she'd wanted some peace and quiet, but she'd also wanted some time with her husband.

'I couldn't get out... I was working...'

'The bloody business,' Zach spat. 'You were too busy to meet her because you were working at the family fucking business.'

Kim heard the sneer in the last three words.

So did Gavin, who tried to catch his husband's eye.

'It's not even your fucking family.'

'Zach,' Gavin warned.

Kim saw the hurt cross Daryl's face before it set hard.

'Doesn't matter how hard you try, you're never going to be as much a part of this family as you want to be. You're not blood, and if you want the truth, my parents only tolerated you because—'

'Zach,' Gavin warned stonily, seemingly the only person to have remembered that the man's wife was fighting for her life on the operating table.

'Well, it's true,' Zach mumbled, determined to have the last word.

Daryl's thunderous expression said he wasn't going to allow that.

'Maybe if you had been a bit more interested in the business, your father wouldn't have had to—'

'Didn't really have the chance, did I? You were sniffing

around it before you'd even walked Rachel down the aisle. She must have seemed like a real attractive prospect.'

'How dare you!' Daryl exploded, colouring.

Gavin had accepted defeat and had returned his gaze to the window.

'Please,' Kim said, holding up her hand. 'I'm sure Rachel needs you to be strong for her right now. Not to mention little Mia.'

Both men shot each other a hateful look. There was much more that they wanted to say to one another, but thankfully they heeded her words for now.

Kim knew there was little else she could do. Right now, it was a waiting game.

Following her chat with Della Porter, she had questions for Zach, but now was not the time.

'Zach, may we pop and see you first thing in the morning? Just a question or two.'

'About what?' he asked, frowning.

'Just about the last time you saw your parents before they died.'

'Feel free to ask, Inspector.'

'It's fine. We'll drop by in the morning.'

'Please, ask away. The sooner you catch the monster, the better we'll all sleep.'

'We understand that you visited your parents on the after-noon before they—'

'You were there that day?' Gavin asked as his head whipped round from the window.

He hadn't told his husband where he was going. Not unusual, but why hadn't he mentioned it since? Either to Gavin or to them?

Daryl wasn't even watching. His eyes were fixed firmly on the door.

'Would you mind telling us why you were visiting that day?'

His eyes darted around the room. 'Err... maybe we should have this conversation tomorrow. I'm unable to focus right now.'

She exchanged a look with Bryant at his sudden turn-around, but she couldn't push it, given the circumstances.

'Okay, we'll see you first...' Her words trailed away as the door opened.

A surgeon, still in scrubs, with a mask pushed up onto his head, entered the room. He closed the door behind him and removed the mask completely.

His grave expression told the story before he even opened his mouth.

'I'm sorry but there was nothing we could do. We lost Rachel fifteen minutes ago. I'm so sorry.'

Stunned silence filled the room. It was as though this possible outcome had not occurred to any one of them.

She looked to Bryant, who nodded in response. They should go.

They weren't family. There was nothing they could offer to help these people feel better. Her immediate thoughts were for Mia. A little girl who would never know her mother.

She felt her phone vibrate in her back pocket as a sob sounded from Daryl. Gavin had already taken Zach into his arms.

'We'll give you some privacy,' Bryant said, moving towards the door.

They stepped from the silence of the room into the melee of activity back in the A&E department.

She took out her phone and frowned.

'Sir?' she answered, covering her free ear to contain the sound.

'Where are you, Stone?' Woody asked.

She rolled her eyes. Had Leanne been telling tales again?

'Russells Hall, and the reason I told—'

'Get somewhere quieter.'

She held the phone to her ear as she negotiated the waiting area and exited the building.

'Go ahead,' she said as Bryant stood close by. She could see Leanne thirty feet away and, more importantly, Leanne could see her. She offered the woman a filthy look for snitching to her boss.

She heard his intake of breath before he spoke. 'Is Bryant there?'

'Who do you want, him or me?'

'Both – put me on loudspeaker.'

'Done,' she said as Leanne joined them. Her puzzled expression told Kim this had nothing to do with her.

'I need to make sure you're not going to react to what I'm going to tell you.'

'Rachel Hewitt just died, sir, so the odds are not on your side.'

'You're going to find out soon anyway, but it appears that Symes has abducted another girl.'

'Are you fucking kidding me?' she exploded. 'How the hell has he managed to do that?'

'With little care and attention for being seen by approximately seventy parents as he approached the school and snatched a six-year-old in broad daylight.'

Kim shook her head and looked to both Bryant and Leanne, who were as horrified as she was.

'How is that possible when half of West Midlands CID is bloody looking for him?'

'Everything that can be done is being done, Stone.'

'Well it's not being done well enough, sir,' she spat. 'What was his direction of travel? What type of car was he driving? How urgently is the CCTV being viewed? When—'

'Stone, my original instruction stands. You are not to get involved, and I am charging your two colleagues there to ensure you don't do anything stupid.'

'It's me he wants,' she said, trying not to think of the fear those little girls were going through. 'He's doing all this for me. I have to stop him.'

'My order stands, and if you can't follow it, you will be removed from active duty.'

He ended the call, and Kim had the urge to throw the damn phone across the car park.

'He can't seriously expect me to stand by and do nothing, can he?' she asked. 'There are times when Woody gives me instructions but really means for me to—'

'Now ain't one of those times, guv,' Bryant said, shaking his head. 'There was absolutely no nuance detected in his directive.'

'Damn it,' she said, striding back to the car. They'd been listening out all day and there had been no report of the body of a child being found. She'd assumed he'd kill the first and then take the second. But now he had them both.

She knew exactly what Symes was doing and it chilled her to the bone.

He was trying to recreate the scene.

FIFTY

Edna Trevin prayed that each breath would be her last.

She didn't know how long she'd been tied to the chair. It felt like weeks but could have been hours. She only knew that the pain ripping through her arthritic joints was excruciating. The nausea kept rising in her stomach, bile burning the back of her throat, but there was nothing to come up. It felt like days since she'd eaten and almost as long since she'd drunk anything. She remembered him pulling back her head and pouring something into her mouth, but she'd gagged at the sudden force of what felt like a tidal wave being forced down her throat. She wasn't sure any liquid had made it down when she'd spluttered it all out onto her nightdress to join all the other stains, she thought shamefully.

The effort to open her eyes was too great, and she didn't want to look anyway. She knew what her body had been forced to do in the absence of a toilet, and she hated it for letting her down. She had wanted to fight back. She'd wanted to devise a plan to free herself, but from the minute she'd been forced to sit in her own faeces, her spirit had been broken and she'd known she was going to die.

From the moment she'd regained consciousness, she'd tried to understand what he'd wanted from her. She'd told him where she kept her meagre amount of house money, since Barbra had insisted she open a bank account. He'd stuffed the money into his pockets but ignored her instruction about the jewellery. She realised quickly that he wanted nothing from her except somewhere to eat and sleep, and neither of those things were dependent on her being alive.

At first, she'd focussed on staying alive until the Wednesday phone call from her daughter but, of course, Barbra wasn't going to phone. Why oh why had her only child chosen now to have a sulk because she wouldn't free up any more money for her good-for-nothing husband, who had malingered his way through the last twenty years taking 'just to get by' money from his elderly mother-in-law?

Barbra's latest request for two thousand pounds for a fortnight in Spain because Dennis needed a bit of sun had been met with a firm no. Had her daughter been on the brink of losing her home or facing some other financial hardship, she'd have given it gladly, but not just to give the lazy sloucher a holiday when he hadn't worked in two decades.

Although she'd been angry at the time, it had faded. It seemed so insignificant now. It was just money, and she had it to give. But Barbra had taken the huff and hadn't checked in on her for days.

A wave of sadness washed over her. Barbra was a good girl. She was going to feel horrible about what she'd done when her body was found. She would carry that guilt, and Edna didn't want that.

A rush of regret surged through her, and the emotion wasn't for herself.

She could feel the life ebbing out of her. Her breathing was becoming shallow. Her body wanted to give up and she could no longer fight it.

As the darkness approached, she had one final plea from her mind straight to God.

Please don't let me be found by my daughter.

FIFTY-ONE

DCI Woodward's cursor hovered over the link to the Zoom meeting invitation due to begin at 6.45 p.m.

After harassing his own boss for twenty minutes, he'd been allowed access to the end-of-day briefing at Brierley Hill. His request to attend in person had been refused in case his physical presence was perceived by the team as him undermining the authority of the DCI running the joint operation of Symes's capture and the double abduction.

Much like members of his own team, he resented the political play that sometimes seemed to supersede effective policing, but he liked to think that he put up with it so that his team didn't have to.

The digital clock clicked on to 6.45, and he pressed the link taking him straight into the incident room.

The monitor was placed at the top of the room, giving him a long view of the scene. The space was filled with officers and desks, and he could see the clear demarcation of the teams. The Brierley Hill team were sitting at or on desks, and the search team were gathered en masse in the far corner.

'Thank you for joining us, DCI Woodward,' offered DCI Walsh from the centre of the room. 'It's been quite a day.'

A murmur of assent swept through both camps.

'Okay, incident team first. Go ahead, Burns.'

A man wearing black trousers and a white shirt stepped forward.

'As you all know, Symes abducted six-year-old Chloe Jordan this afternoon from a school on Colley Lane. The move was chaotic and desperate – driving along pavements, stopping in the middle of the road and making no effort at stealth.'

Woody disagreed with this assessment. It had been planned. He had used the element of surprise to create the chaos that offered him the cover of escape.

'He's making mistakes to feed his urges. He's cracking, so we must be doing something that's putting pressure on him. We've come close to him, I know it.'

Woody wondered if it was only him that could hear the hope in the man's voice as opposed to conviction.

'Tomorrow we start again. Re-interview every witness we've spoken to, review all the CCTV again. We're going to use persistency to flush him out.'

A cynical man might have thought this was an action borne of not knowing where to go next.

He said nothing as a wave of anxiety rolled around his stomach. He'd hoped the operational team were going to be full of creative plans, clever ideas, initiative and passion instead of retreading footprints they'd already made.

'We suspect the first girl, Emma Bunting, is dead. We think he's done whatever he wants with her and he's not had enough. He's taken Chloe Jordan to replace her, and he's going to keep on taking girls until we catch him.'

DCI Walsh nodded his agreement. 'He's on a perverted binge.'

'He's not a pervert,' Woody interjected, frowning.

'Of course he is. He's taking little girls.'

'To beat them, to break their bones. Symes is sick in another way. He's not a paedophile.'

'Okay, thanks, DCI Woodward.'

'And how are you coordinating his activities in relation to the threat to DI Stone?' Woody asked.

'We're not sure any of his actions are connected to DI Stone. We're treating this—'

'He mentioned her by name,' Woody interrupted. 'He told Emma's mother to ask for her specifically,' Woody offered incredulously. How the hell were they treating it as a separate matter?

'We're pretty sure he's doing that just to distract us.'

'Do any of you understand this man at all?'

'Thanks for your input, DCI Woodward, but I think we'll take it from here.'

A pair of blue trousers approached the screen before it went blank.

They had thrown him out of the meeting.

He threw the mouse across the room.

And he hadn't even heard what the search team had to say. Symes was a six feet tall solid structure of a man with a bald head and a glass eye. His photo had graced every newspaper and news programme and they still appeared to have no clue where he was.

'Damn it,' he cursed as he collected his mouse from the floor.

There was a part of him that wanted to get Stone on the phone right now and retract every restrictive instruction he'd given her. As tempting as that was, his first duty of care was to her welfare. He knew he was the barrier between her and this case and that he had made his instructions clear.

Symes had two defenceless little girls at his mercy and,

quite frankly, there was no one he trusted more than Stone to find them.

He knew that if he gave the instruction, she *would* find them.

He also knew it would cost her her life.

FIFTY-TWO

It was after seven when Bryant pulled into her street and the exhaustion was weighing down every muscle.

Not one word had been uttered since they'd left the hospital. Kim's own mind had been filled with images of a young, vital, energetic, spirited woman in her prime now dead, leaving behind a husband and a young child.

There was a sadness in Kim that Mia would never remember her mother. Her only picture of her own mum would be painted from other people's memories.

Was it a coincidence that Rachel had suffered a fatal accident within days of her family being wiped out? Possibly but Kim had never cared much for coincidences. They would look at it tomorrow when her team was fresh.

Woody's call had done nothing to lighten her mood, and she'd been scouring the internet for news the whole way back.

'Normal time,' she said, getting out of the car.

Bryant nodded, knowing that meant 6.45 to arrive at the station at 7 a.m.

Kim paused as Bryant pulled away from the kerb.

Something out of the ordinary had registered in her brain even though her mind had been on Rachel and the little girl.

'Err... yeah, good idea to just stand out in the open like this,' Leanne said, moving towards the gate.

Kim took a step. Something wasn't right.

Charlie's house was in darkness, strange to see but she knew why.

She took another step.

Mrs Fowkes at the end hadn't yet brought in her bin. It was her alternate Tuesday night at her sister's. Kim would hear her drag her bin in around eleven.

She took another step.

Mrs Graham's porch light was on. She always left it on until the last of her four kids was back in the house.

'Stone, I really think—'

'Okay, okay,' she said, heading down the path.

There was nothing untoward, nothing sinister going on in her street. She was just getting easily spooked.

Her legs seemed loath to carry her into the house. She suspected it was the prospect of another fun-filled night in Leanne's scintillating company.

Leanne turned. 'I swear, I'm gonna physically grab you and—'

'The car,' Kim said as the picture came into her mind.

She'd been able to see the solar lights in front of Edna's rockery.

'The car isn't on the drive,' she repeated, heading back down the path.

'Whose car?' Leanne called out, closing Kim's front door.

'Edna's. She hasn't driven it in years. Eyesight. She keeps it on the drive, so it looks like there's someone else there.'

'She could have just got rid of it or let someone else use it.'

'Absolutely,' Kim agreed, standing at the end of Edna's path. 'No lights on,' she said, opening the gate.

'Her bin is full,' Kim said, lifting the black lid.

Kim hammered on the door. Hard.

'Edna,' she called out at the top of her voice.

'You really don't care about being liked, do you?' Leanne asked.

'Not your first priority either, is it?' Kim shot back.

She hammered and shouted some more.

Nothing.

She pushed open the letterbox in the old wooden door.

'Edna, are you... Jesus Christ,' she said as the smell of faeces reached her.

'Bloody hell,' Leanne agreed as the smell wafted through.

'This isn't right,' Kim said, taking a step back. 'We need to get in there right now.'

'Call the...' Leanne's words trailed away as she realised what she'd been about to say.

'We are the fucking police,' Kim snapped. 'Now either help me or get out of my way.'

To her credit, Leanne didn't hesitate. 'What do you want me to do?'

'On the count of three, you put your weight against the top while I take a kick at the bottom.'

'Got it. Count,' Leanne said, getting into position.

'One, two, three.'

The door crashed open on the first attempt, and they almost fell on each other in the hallway.

The smell directed them to the dining room.

For one second the two women were paralysed as their gaze fell on the frail elderly lady held to a chair by ties around her wrists and ankles, and a scarf wrapped around her stomach.

'Good God,' Leanne whispered.

'Call an ambulance,' Kim instructed, moving towards the sorrowful sight.

'I'll do it while I'm checking the house,' Leanne said, rushing from the room.

Edna Trevin had never been a formidable size, but her spirit had more than made up for it. A memory flashed through Kim's mind from not long after she'd moved in. A few local kids had thrown a couple of eggs at Edna's house. Kim had been about to intervene when Edna had turned the hosepipe and a few choice words on the lot of them.

As she searched the kitchen drawers for scissors, Kim swallowed down her guilt. She could feed it later. With scissors in hand, she ignored the smell of urine and faeces and put two fingers to the woman's neck.

'Fuck,' she cried out. Although the flesh was warm, she could detect no pulse.

Leanne appeared and took a penknife from her pocket.

Kim freed the arms and torso while Leanne worked on the ankles.

'It's okay, Edna, I've got you,' Kim said gently as she took the woman's slight weight against her and lowered her to the ground.

She tipped back Edna's head and lowered her mouth to cover Edna's nose and mouth. She gave two rescue breaths.

'What can I do?' Leanne asked as Kim started the compressions.

'Flag 'em down,' she said, pressing as hard as she dared on the fragile breastbone.

'Come on, Edna,' Kim whispered. She knew the woman had fight.

After thirty compressions, she swapped again to two breaths. She could feel the fire burn through her muscles. She pumped through it even as she heard a siren in the distance.

'I'm not stopping, Edna,' Kim promised.

She leaned down once more and paused as warm air breathed across her cheek.

Kim could hear her own heart beating wildly as she focussed on the woman's chest.

It was slight but the chest wall was definitely rising and falling on its own.

'It's okay, Edna,' Kim said, taking her hand. 'Help is coming. You're going to be okay. He won't hurt you again.'

As she said the words, two paramedics entered the room. They had no reaction to the sight or smell that greeted them.

'You got her back?' Leanne asked as both paramedics kneeled down and began to tend to Edna.

Kim moved out of the way as the male paramedic started talking to Edna as though she was fully conscious. He told her everything he was doing and why.

Kim took out her phone.

'Who are you calling?'

'Woody,' Kim said as her trembling finger scrolled the contact list. The adrenaline was leaving her body as the realisation dawned that Symes had been feet away from her home.

'Done, Stone, now take a fucking minute.'

Kim raised an eyebrow.

'Called him while waiting for the ambulance. He's contacting the Symes search team and a board-up team for the door.'

Kim knew the officers searching for Symes would have their own forensic techs to look for any clues that might help them track him down, but she ached to call Mitch; a man she trusted. If Symes had left anything behind, he would find it.

'She's stable enough to move,' the male paramedic said. 'You brought her back strong,' he added with an appreciative smile. He looked around. 'Family?'

'We'll sort it,' Kim said. She was pretty sure Edna had a daughter.

'Hey, Stone, look at this,' Leanne said, standing at the kitchen window.

Kim stood beside her and glanced to the left. Between two ornamental trees in the garden next door was a perfect view of her front door.

'He's been able to watch us the whole time?' Kim asked.

'Yes, he fucking has,' she answered through gritted teeth.

Kim guessed that Leanne was beating herself up for missing this, but for the first time since Sunday afternoon, Kim was grateful for Leanne's instruction. Barney would have been home alone most mornings before Charlie collected him. She shuddered at what the evil bastard would have done to her dog to make her suffer. If he had no issue leaving a vulnerable, elderly lady in this state, she could only imagine Barney's fate.

'Hey, wake up. Call someone,' Leanne said, standing by the door as the paramedics gently placed Edna onto the trolley.

Kim strode to the house phone on the kitchen wall and pressed redial. Whoever Edna had called last would know who she was.

'Hello.'

In that one word, Kim could hear a cool distance in the woman's voice.

'Who is this?' Kim asked.

'This is Barbra and what are you doing in my mother's house?'

The tone had changed; scared, upset, worried.

'Barbra, my name is DI Stone. I live—'

'Where is my mother? Is she okay? Put her on the phone.'

'I'm a police officer. Your mum has been hurt, but she's stable and on her way to the hospital.'

'I don't understand. Who...? What...?'

'Barbra, please. Everything will be explained later, but for now, just make your way to the hospital and be with your mum.'

FIFTY-THREE

It was after eleven when Kim finally stepped out of the shower. After calling Edna's daughter, they'd briefed the officers who would liaise with Barbra at the hospital, and then liaised with the search team.

Their first call had been to someone called Burns, which had sounded pretty heated and urgent. It had taken all her time not to follow the officer, grab the phone and ask this Burns character if he was taking his head from up his ass any time soon.

Out of respect for Woody's instructions, she had bit her tongue – hard. After that initial conversation, the officers had gone to work counting bowls, dishes, plates for timeline clues and searching every inch of the house. Despite her aching need to know everything about their investigation, she was careful not to do anything her boss might deem disruptive. Their urgency and focus didn't invite interaction.

A quick phone call to the hospital before undressing had confirmed that Edna was still alive and stable. Barbra was by her side, and for that Kim was grateful.

She pushed the mother-and-daughter thoughts away as she

headed down the stairs and into an alien sensation. The smell of food.

'What the hell is that?'

'Fish finger sandwiches and cheesy chips. Your food pantry is pretty sparse,' Leanne answered.

Somehow basic provisions seemed to materialise in her fridge every couple of weeks. She suspected Charlie liked to try and take care of her.

Leanne had one plate holding fish fingers wedged between two pieces of fresh crusty bread and a second plate of oven chips with a melted cheddar topping.

As wrong as it was, the smell was delicious.

'Hmm...' Kim said, moving closer.

'Not enough for two,' Leanne said, pulling both plates towards her.

'Hang on. You use my food in my kitchen, but I can't have any?'

'Since you put it like that,' she said, reaching for a knife and a second plate. She cut the sandwich in half and then slid half of the cheesy mess onto the side plate.

'Make yourself at home, why don't you?' Kim said, taking a seat on the visitor's side of the breakfast bar.

'Seeing as I've spent more time with you than I have my entire family in the last five years, I'll take you up on it.'

'MI5 not free to bring your supper tonight?'

'It was almost funny last night, less so tonight.'

'I'm praying to God I don't have to say it again tomorrow,' Kim said, taking a bite out of the sandwich.

'You and me both,' Leanne said, throwing a couple of cheesy chips into her mouth.

The thrown-together sandwich was delicious, so much so that she went in for another bite before she spoke again.

'You're not close with your family?' Kim asked. They were

about to spend their third night together and she felt entitled
to ask.

'It's complicated so keep eating cos you're gonna need your
strength in the next ten minutes.'

'For what?' Kim asked, taking a cheesy chip. She added
some salt to the pile before taking another.

Leanne simply shrugged and took a big bite of her
sandwich.

Kim continued to eat in silence, wondering how hard
Leanne would laugh if she asked for the recipe. She could see
the recipe right in front of her. It was a sandwich and chips, yet
in her hands it would be a sawdust-dry, gloopy, tasteless mess.
She finished the sandwich, took another couple of chips and
then ripped off a piece of kitchen roll to wipe her hands.

She took a deep breath and allowed the air to expand her
ribcage. She'd never been one to practise breathing exercises,
but a good deep breath always helped to ward off the feelings
trying to grow inside her.

'I still can't believe he was just doors away,' she said,
heading around to the correct side of the breakfast bar. They
swapped places and Leanne slid her plate across to the bar
stool.

'I just keep seeing Edna, tied to that—'

'And here it is, right on time. You didn't need the full ten
minutes,' Leanne said, wiping her own hands clean.

'What?'

'The guilt train. It's just pulled into the station and is
waiting for you to climb aboard.'

'You do know you're a total freak, right?' Kim clarified.

'Doesn't mean I'm wrong. It's right on time. I called it for
eleven thirty and it's five minutes early.'

'Emotions don't run to a clock. They can't tell the time,' Kim
snapped, adding coffee to the machine. She didn't know about
Leanne, but she wasn't going to bed any time soon.

'Actually, they kind of do. They run on succession. Guilt is an indulgent emotion, rarely accurate and serves no purpose.'

'You know, being lectured on human emotions by you is the very height of—'

'Every emotion you used tonight was beneficial. Your anger propelled you into action; your fear alerted you that something was wrong. Your stubbornness meant you didn't stop working on Edna until you brought her back. Your sympathy prompted you to hold her hand. Your empathy got her daughter to the hospital. Your tenacity ensured we stayed there until there was nothing else that could be done.'

'Why am I even still listening to this shit?'

'Since coming back into the house you've taken care of your basic physical needs. You've drunk a pot of coffee, showered and eaten a sandwich. Survival. Now comes the part you don't need, but everything else is taken care of so let's explore some useless emotions that will help no one.'

'Bloody hell, once you start, you can't stop, can you?'

'What's going through your mind?'

'Fuck off.'

'Proving me right, Stone.'

'How the hell am I not going to feel responsible for what happened to a frail old lady?'

'Err... because it wasn't your fault. Symes hurt her not you, and that's not even the whole story, is it? That's not even the whole bag of guilt. Let's go in on the girls now and really get this party started.'

'It's all because of me.'

'Conceited much, Stone? And he did it because he could. He hurt Edna because he wanted to. He didn't have to. He wanted to. He has snatched two girls because he wants to hurt them. That's on him.'

'If he hadn't been looking for me, none of this—'

'Again, not true, Stone. Symes is held together by hate. If it hadn't been you, it would have been the judge or the prosecutor or the guy in the coffee shop who forgot to give him sugar. He is a man that lives to hurt people.'

'I don't need a shrink, and you're full of shit anyway,' Kim shouted as her annoyance rose.

'No, I'm not and you know it, which is why you're getting agitated.'

'I'm getting fucking irate because you're trying to tell me how to feel.'

'Nope, it's because I won't let you wallow in the most indulgent, useless emotion that we are able to feel.'

'I'd really like you to fucking leave.'

'And miss all this fun? No way. Who exactly does your guilt help? Your neighbour, her daughter, the doctors and nurses taking care of her? The techies trying to find clues? The girls? The officers trying to find them? Who does it help, Stone? Who the hell does it help?'

'Me,' Kim shouted in her face.

'And there you have it, ladies and gentlemen. The truth. DI Stone wants a reason to feel shit, to beat herself up, to punish herself even more.'

'You finished?' Kim asked, crossing her arms as the coffee started to filter.

'Not quite. If you need to feel shit, do it because you have a bad attitude and an obtuse manner. Feel shit because seventy per cent of people who meet you don't like you. Feel even shitter about the fact that some of those people like you even less after spending' – she checked her watch – 'over fifty hours with you. I can give you many reasons for you to feel shit about yourself, but not being able to stop Symes doing what he's been planning for years isn't one of them.'

Kim burst out laughing. She had no idea why but it felt good. 'Do you provide this service for all your clients?' she asked.

'Only the ones I really can't stand. So, you gonna let the guilt train leave the—'

'Enough with the bloody train already.'

Leanne surprised her by laughing. 'Fair enough. Analogy overload. I get it and coffee's ready,' she said, nodding towards the percolator.

'You lost your legs?' Kim asked.

'I made dinner.'

Fancy word for the meal, but she did have a point, Kim thought, taking out her phone. She sent a brief text message and wasn't surprised at the quick reply. She scrolled to the number and called, having checked the detective constable was still up.

'Yeah, boss,' Stacey answered.

'Did the lorry driver's statement come back?' she asked.

'Delayed cos he insisted on having a solicitor present. I didn't hang about and—'

'No, of course not,' Kim said, interrupting the apology. She hadn't expected her to.

'Do you want me to check the system to see if it's on yet?' Stacey asked.

'Oh, Devon would love me for making you—'

'Devon's fast asleep. It's okay.'

'Nah, it's fine. We'll get to it tomorrow. Get some rest,' she instructed before ending the call.

Leanne was cradling her mug and regarding her with a half-smile.

'What?' Kim asked.

'Why not just ring and tell her you're checking on her? I mean, that is what you were doing, isn't it? Devon would just love me...' Leanne mimicked. 'You just wanted to make sure Devon was there. Is it really so hard to show your team you care?'

'Fuck off.'

'I'll take that as a yes.'

Kim was happy for her to take it however she liked. She didn't need to admit that she was concerned about the safety of them all, but probably Stacey more than the others. Stacey had been taken before and she'd managed to get her back. She wasn't going to let the same thing happen again.

'So, Leanne King, what do you do for fun when you're not protecting undesirables?' Kim asked, pouring her own coffee.

'They're not always awful, but for me to fully relax, I need your help.'

Kim passed her coffee and raised an eyebrow.

'Got any kitchen appliances you don't use?' Leanne asked.

'Take your pick,' Kim said, waving towards the double oven.

'Not quite what I had in mind – like a spare toaster or a blender.'

'I don't know what a blender is, and who has a spare toaster?'

'Never mind.'

The toaster was the only thing she did really use but she was too intrigued to stop now.

She unplugged it. 'What now?'

'Cover your dining table in newspaper or something and grab a couple of screwdrivers.'

'Are you taking the piss?' Kim asked.

'You brought it up.'

Yes, she had and she was still interested enough to see how this woman unwound.

She unlocked the door to the garage and retrieved an old sheet and two screwdrivers: a Phillips head and a flat head.

She laid the sheet over the table and placed the toaster and screwdrivers on top. 'Okay, ready.'

'Oh no, that's not all the help I need,' she said, turning her back.

'What now?'

'Take it apart.'

'Why the hell would I do that?'

'So I can put it back together, but it's no challenge if I watch you dismantle it.'

Kim looked at Leanne's back and then at the toaster.

Oh, what the hell. It was eleven thirty, she had no dog to walk and sleep was nowhere in her future.

'Okay, but the least you can do is entertain me while I do it. What's the story with your family?'

'Just never really fitted in. How about you?'

Kim said nothing.

'Weird thing about conversation is that it's a two-way thing,' Leanne said.

'I don't talk about family.'

'Neither do I normally, but as I've got my back to you, I'm actually conversing with your oven.'

Kim smiled as she removed the outer casing of the toaster. It was a bit more complicated than she'd thought.

Leanne sighed. 'Okay, I'll share first. I was adopted and I always felt that way.'

'My mother tried to kill me and my twin from the moment we were born. She finally got my brother when we were six.'

There was a moment of silence.

'For fuck's sake, Stone, you always gotta win?'

Kim laughed. For some reason it was easier to like Leanne when she wasn't having to look at her.

'You were adopted?' Kim asked.

'Yeah. As a baby, so I shouldn't have felt like I didn't belong, but I did.'

'Is it because you were told?'

'No. I didn't know until I turned twelve, but I felt it way before then. I have two older siblings, brothers. My mum couldn't have any more and she'd always wanted a girl.'

'What made you feel different?'

'You know, it was nothing big. I wasn't beaten and kept in

the cellar. I wasn't fed the scraps that my brothers didn't want. It was a subtle thing like Mum asking the boys what they wanted for tea before me. I was always third if that makes sense. It's not something where I can recite a hundred examples. It was something I just knew.'

'Did you share this with your mum when you found out?'

'Hell no, it would break her heart. I know she loves me, but I also know that it's in a slightly different way to my brothers. To them she's bonded by blood, and to me it's by a signature.'

'I don't think every—'

'I'm not speaking for every adopted child. For me the piece of paper my parents signed didn't equal conception and birth.'

Kim digested her words. Her only experience of parental love was from two strangers who had not been bonded to her either by blood or a piece of paper.

Given the solitary nature of the job Leanne did, Kim wondered if she'd ever felt part of any kind of team in her life.

'My mother is dying and I haven't told a living soul,' she blurted out. It was easier talking to the back of someone. She wasn't waiting for any kind of response. It was almost like talking to yourself.

'Why not?'

'Because they'll all tell me the exact same thing. Go see her, forgive her.'

'Why?'

Kim shrugged as she removed part of the element.

'I don't know. Apparently, forgiveness is in these days and it will help me heal.'

'It will.'

Strangely, Kim was disappointed in the response.

'So you think I should go and see her and offer forgiveness?'

'Maybe and no.'

'Good answer.'

'I think you should go and see her if you need to, but I don't think you should offer forgiveness because the time limit on the option is about to expire. The supermarkets mark down food at the end of the day, but I don't go and buy shit I don't like just cos it's about to go in the bin.'

'Jesus, you and Bryant with your weird analogies.'

'I mean, forgiveness might be healing for you but not until you actually feel it in your heart. Until then it's just words, purely for the benefit of someone else.'

'I can't give her that comfort,' Kim said honestly.

'Then don't. Only go to see her if there's something you want to say, something you need her to hear. Go because you'll regret not doing so when it's too late, but don't go because other people think they know what's right for you.'

Kim felt a small weight lift from her shoulders. She realised that was the reason she hadn't shared the news with anyone. Everyone would have an opinion with good intentions. They would want her to do something she wasn't ready to do. Ted would urge her to go. The counsellor had seen her at just about every stage of her life. He had tried everything he could to help her heal. Bryant would offer to drive her, but any forgiveness would be a lie. She wasn't there yet, and she wasn't sure she ever would be.

Kim surveyed the mess on her dining table. She didn't know how to put it back together and she was the one who had taken it apart.

'Okay, Leanne, it's all ready.'

Leanne stood and turned, surveying the mess.

'Jeez, Stone, I didn't think you'd actually do it. Great chat but I'm tired now so I'll do a final check and then I'm off to bed.'

Kim's mouth fell open as the woman headed for the garden.

She'd been punked by Leanne fucking King.

FIFTY-FOUR

'Pull off without her, Bryant. She stole my food and broke my toaster,' Kim said, getting into Bryant's car.

'You drive while I call the feds,' he quipped as Leanne got in the back. 'Not bothered about the food but I am intrigued about the toaster.'

'We'll give her the slip later and I'll tell you all about it.'

'Can't wait,' he said, pulling out of the street. 'Any issues last night?'

Kim was surprised at the question and then realised her team knew nothing about the events that had taken place once Bryant had dropped them off the night before.

'Seems Symes was under our noses the whole time. Well, four doors down to be exact.'

'What the hell? Good job, Leanne,' Bryant offered.

'Can't see through walls,' she retorted.

Kim told him in detail about the night before and just finished as Bryant pulled into the car park.

'Wanna do a quick visual before she gets out, Leanne?' Bryant asked when Kim's hand rested on the door handle.

Kim turned to her colleague. It wasn't something he'd suggested before.

'Err... not sure.'

'Get out of the car, Leanne,' Bryant said. 'And give us just a minute.'

She did as she was asked.

'Bryant, what the...?'

'Not happy with this situation, guv. He was within metres of you, and she didn't even know.'

'To be fair, she couldn't have known,' Kim said, surprising herself in defending Leanne. 'It's not her job to find him. It's her job to make sure he doesn't get near me and, so far, so good, especially given how close he was.'

'I'm just not convinced you're taking it seriously enough. He's already successfully abducted two girls. Maybe you should consider Woody's—'

'Bryant, stop worrying. I appreciate your concern but I'm not running away, and I'm doing everything I've been told, so short of Jenny making up your spare room...'

'Already done, guv,' he said, getting out the car.

She laughed. 'Thanks, but I like Jenny way too much to subject her to me.'

She appreciated her colleague's concern, but Leanne's presence was reminder enough that Symes was still out there and he was setting some kind of scene especially for her. She didn't want it on her mind every minute because then she'd do nothing else but look over her shoulder, and they were paying Leanne to do that.

As she walked, she took out her phone. She'd texted Woody first thing for an update on the investigation. So far there had been no reply.

A movement caught her attention from the left. A figure appeared. Kim caught her breath – she instantly knew who it was.

Leanne had spotted her too.

'Back off, Leanne,' Kim whispered, blocking her with her arm. 'Wait over there with Bryant,' she said, pointing to the entrance.

Kim headed towards the woman, who was pulling a light anorak tighter around her slim body. A worn satchel crossed her frame, and she held something in her hand. Her blonde hair was pulled back in a loose ponytail. Her skin was pale and her face drawn around eyes that had not rested in days.

'D-Detective Stone?' the woman asked.

Kim nodded. 'Mrs Bunt...'

'This is her,' the woman said, thrusting a photo in her face. 'This is my baby.'

'I know,' Kim said. 'I know what Emma looks like.'

'Can you find her?' she asked hopefully. 'He asked for you. He said your name. Do you know where he's taken her?'

Kim swallowed down her emotion as the tears fell from the woman's eyes.

'Please help me. Where is my daughter?' she sobbed.

'I don't know where she is,' Kim said, feeling the pain emanating from her small frame.

'But it's you, isn't it? He wants something from you?'

'Everything is being done to find Emma, I promise.'

'He's taken another one, hasn't he?'

Kim said nothing, wishing she had the power to take the woman's pain away.

'God forgive me but I don't care about anyone else. I need her back. Please help...'

'I swear that the team is doing everything they can to bring—'

'No, no, it's you. It's not about the team. It's all about you.'

Kim had the urge to turn and run, escape this woman's agony as it worked its way right into her soul.

'Can't you just give him what he wants? She's so little – look at her, look at her.'

Kim looked again at the face she already knew well. The smooth skin with a few freckles scattered over the bridge of the nose, the brown hair and the hazel eyes, the toothy smile, the joy and innocence in her face.

'I'm sorry – I have to go,' Kim said, turning away.

'Please, please, I beg you. Whatever it takes, Detective. Please bring my daughter back to me.'

The words rang in her ears as Leanne and Bryant joined her at the entrance to the station.

'Guv, you can't—'

'Leave it, Bryant,' she snapped, heading up the stairs.

Right now she was getting a bit pissed off at being told what she could and couldn't do. The woman was desperate for news of her daughter. She could only imagine the pictures that were going through her head, and after her own encounter with the man, Kim was sure she understood that mercy was not a character trait he possessed.

Kim took a deep breath before entering the squad room.

'Hey guys,' she greeted Penn and Stacey, who had clearly got in just minutes before she had.

Penn headed for the coffee machine.

'Leanne's turn today,' she said, turning to the protection officer. 'If you drink it, you gotta make it.'

Leanne shrugged off her jacket and took a bottle of water from underneath the printer to add to the percolator.

Kim took another breath and focussed her attention on the wipe boards. 'Okay, guys, quick recap from yesterday. After catching the neighbours' son hiding under the bed in an active crime scene, we know that Reece had some kind of emotional attachment to Rozzie. We also know that to spot the fire from the kitchen window, he had to have been closer to the house than the public footpath at the edge of the property. We know he's not keen on offering a DNA sample, but I feel confident he'll be here this morning to comply.'

'You think he might be the father of Rozzie's baby?' Stacey asked.

'Perhaps, but I'm also thinking he could be the elusive Martey who was making her life a misery on social media. We have no way of knowing if his attention was positive or negative. We only know that he knew an awful lot about her.'

'Maybe she spurned his advances,' Penn said.

'Why, because he was the handyman?' Bryant snapped.

'No, because he was considerably older and she seems to have preferred boys her own age,' Penn replied evenly.

Why had she not noticed these occasional terse exchanges between the two of them before Woody had handed her the microscope?

'Also coming in this morning is Rozzie's on-off boyfriend, so we may have an identity for Rozzie's baby's father soon.' She paused. 'We spoke to Roy and Davey Burston yesterday,' she said, nodding towards the board where their photos had been placed with everyone else. 'There's no doubt that both father and son are angry. They've lost their livelihood because of one business decision. I just can't help feeling they're angrier with Daryl than they are with William. Still need checking on, Stace,' Kim instructed.

'Got it, boss.'

'We know that relationships between the family members were not conventional. Rachel was with Gavin before Gavin met Zach, and I think she was still a bit in love with him, but of course we'll never know.'

'Convenient accident, guv,' Bryant offered.

'Or not. Stace, I want you to comb every bit of CCTV in

the area. I know the witness accounts claim Rachel was all over the place, but take a good look around.'

'Want me to speak to the lorry driver?' Stacey asked.

Kim shook her head. 'His statement offers nothing except self-preservation. He makes no mention of anyone other than Rachel, and he's already instructed a solicitor.'

Traffic division were investigating his actions before considering charges. Right now they weren't going to get anywhere near him.

'Focus on what we can see with our own eyes.'

'Will do, boss.'

'Penn, any luck on the papers retrieved from the fire?'

'Still working on it, boss. It's clear that Helen and William were in the process of changing their will, so there may be a motive there.'

'Keep at it. In other news, we found out yesterday that Helen is the subject of a sealed social services case, the timing of which corresponds with the beginning of her mental-health problems.'

Her gaze moved between Penn and Stacey. 'I want to know the second that court order comes through.'

Doctor Cutler wouldn't be able to argue with that piece of paper.

'And finally, we found out yesterday that Zach visited his parents just hours before their murder. According to Della, he didn't look a happy man, and it's not something he's mentioned to anyone, not even Gavin. He started to explain and then changed his mind, so we're heading there first thing.'

'Boss?' Stacey asked. That one word held a question.

She nodded. 'Yes, I know about the little girl and yes, Woody has reiterated that we're not going to help anything by getting involved. Any of us.'

If she tried to find a back door into this one, Woody would have no issue firing her team. She knew that was why he'd insisted that Bryant hear the conversation the night before. He would make sure she was reminded at every opportunity that they were all at risk.

She had been told to keep away, maintain her distance. Not once had she actually attempted to insert herself into the Symes case, and yet he'd been camping out four houses away from where she lived. The mother of one of the abducted girls had just pleaded for her daughter's life. No matter how much she tried to stay away, the case was coming to her. Every time Woody told her to stay out of it, he was bending her natural reaction, her innate need to go out and try to find those girls herself.

She wasn't sure how many more times she could bend before she broke.

FIFTY-FIVE

Symes closed and locked the door to the middle cottage behind him. The girls were silent and would remain that way until he returned. His mother had lived in this very cottage until the day the compulsory purchase order had expired. Her neighbours had left well before, having accepted generous compensation packages, but the stubborn old cow had refused to budge until police intervention had cleared the way for the sale of the land by the council to a private developer could be completed. Six months later, after countless surveys, the developer had been unable to secure insurance for building due to subsidence risks. The developer had cut his losses without even spending the money to demolish the properties. Well, the builder's loss was his gain, he mused.

The scene was set. He had everything in place. It was perfect – or as close as it could be to what had been taken away from him.

In exchange for kidnapping the two girls from the leisure centre, he had been promised their lives. He hadn't wanted a penny of the ransom. Just some time alone with the girls once it was done. And he'd almost had it until DI Stone had taken it away from him, along with the sight in one of his eyes.

This time she would not foil his plans. He would get to do what he'd always wanted, and she would have a front-row seat.

And when he had broken those two little bodies, he would turn his attention to her.

He looked back at the building. The next time he saw it he would have her with him.

He would be bringing her here to die.

And he had the final temptation that she would not be able to resist.

FIFTY-SIX

'What exactly are you hoping to find?' Bryant asked, parking the car a few spaces away from the coffee shop.

'Proof, one way or another, and a double espresso, your shout,' she said, taking a seat outside.

'Leanne?' he asked.

'Same,' she said, pulling out another chair.

'Busy,' Kim noted. It wasn't even nine, but the high street was alive with shoppers and fast-moving traffic.

'Is that...?'

Kim followed Leanne's gaze to a stain on the edge of the pavement. It had been washed but an outline remained.

Blood. Rachel's blood.

A woman appeared to clear the table next to where they'd sat.

'Excuse me, were you at work yesterday?' Kim asked.

'Got no bloody choice. It's my café,' she said, keeping her back to the road.

'Did you see the woman involved in the accident?'

'Yeah, me and the two members of staff who have called in sick today.'

If they witnessed the actual event, Kim could quite easily understand.

'Is there anything you can tell me about her demeanour?'

'Are you a reporter?' she asked, narrowing her gaze.

Kim realised just how much she relied on Bryant. She took out her identification.

The suspicion deepened. 'We all gave statements yesterday. It was an accident. She was crying, she fell over the chair when she got...'

Her words trailed away as a lorry thundered towards the traffic lights, clearly demonstrating what she'd been about to say.

'Fuckers trying to beat the lights all the time. We've reported it a dozen times but until someone—'

She stopped speaking as though realising her worst fears had come true.

'Was she upset when she came into the shop?' Kim asked as Bryant appeared with a tray.

The café owner stepped out of the way so he could lay the drinks down.

'Not at all. She was pleasant and polite, didn't seem upset, but it was like the longer she sat there, the more upset she became.'

The woman watched as another customer entered the café.

'Sorry, but I've got...'

'Thank you,' Kim said, letting her get back to her business.

'Why are we here, guv?' Bryant asked. 'I know you don't like the timing but everything points to it being an untimely accident.'

Kim took a look around. She knew that if anything had been caught on CCTV, Stacey would find it.

In the meantime, she couldn't help wondering at Rachel's state of mind. Yes, her family had just been horrifically murdered. Had the full realisation of that suddenly hit her while sitting and sipping a latte? Had the grief led her into the path of an oncoming truck, or had she been thinking of something else entirely?

FIFTY-SEVEN

Potential fathers were like buses, Penn thought. One minute you had none and then they were queuing in the reception.

He'd barely finished the process with Warren Cox, Rozzie's ex-boyfriend, when Reece Porter had turned up.

Unlike Warren, who had been accompanied by both parents, Reece was sitting in reception on his own. From what the boss had said about Della Porter, he was surprised the woman wasn't sitting right beside him.

Once everything was ready on the interview table he went to reception and beckoned the man through.

He followed with his hands buried deep in his pockets.

'This ain't gonna hurt, is it?' he asked as Penn closed the door.

'Not at all and thanks for coming in. If you could just fill out your details on that form and we'll have you out of here in no time.'

'How many guys are you testing?' he asked, taking a seat.

'There's nothing to worry about,' Penn reassured.

'Yeah, you folks say that,' Reece said, filling out the form.

'If you didn't sleep with Rosalind Daynes there's no issue, is there?'

'Yeah, sure, cos there's no chance of you folks mixing up the results, is there? Ain't nobody innocent in prison.'

Penn could sense the nerves coming from him in waves. The man was worried about something.

He waited until Reece put the pen back on top of the form.

'Can you take your cap off for me, Reece?' Penn asked, putting on the latex gloves.

'Sure,' he said, taking it off and placing it in his lap.

Penn hid his surprise. He hadn't seen the man without his baseball cap and had aged him late twenties. Without the cap, the thinning hair and receding hairline added a good seven or eight years to that. Definitely too old to be living with his parents.

'Okay, Reece, open your mouth for me.'

'You're not gonna shove it right at the back, are you, and make me gag?'

Bloody hell, the guy was a baby.

Warren Cox was a kid in his teens and hadn't made a bit of fuss.

'I'm going to swab the inside of your cheek. It's not invasive or painful in any way. Are you happy for me to continue?' he asked. No way was he going to be sued for taking a sample without consent.

'Go ahead,' he said, opening his mouth.

Penn angled the swab in and stroked at the inside of his cheek.

It was over in seconds.

'Okay, you're all done,' he said, once the swab was sealed in the bag.

Both samples were being expedited to the UK's Forensic Science Service which prioritised on request and obtained a result in around eight hours.

'That's it?'

'Yep. Told you it was nothing.'

He smiled as he put his cap back on, as though he was proud of himself for surviving the ordeal.

'I wouldn't hurt her, you know,' he said, heading for the door.

'Rozzie?' Penn asked.

'Yeah. Well, any of them. They were all pretty decent,' he said, closing the door behind him.

Penn shook his head and collected together the sample and the completed form.

He frowned at a detail that he hadn't noticed.

'Oh shit,' he said, grabbing everything before bolting from the room to head back upstairs.

FIFTY-EIGHT

'I'm sorry, he's not up yet,' Gavin said as he opened the door to their small apartment.

Kim stepped inside, aware that she was constantly at war with her own opinion about Zachary Daynes.

Bryant waited until Gavin had moved towards the living-room door before he entered the space and closed the front door behind him.

'He's not got out of bed since we came back yesterday.'

'It's quite a shock he had,' Kim said, more to herself. It was almost nine and Kim had to remind herself that he had lost pretty much every family member he had in the last seventy-two hours. And yet there was something about him that disappointed her; a lack of backbone, courage, conviction. She wondered if that was how his parents had felt. Again, she chided herself. She didn't know the man well enough to make a judgement on his whole character.

'I'm sorry, Gavin, but we're going to need to speak to him,' she said firmly.

'Okay, I'll get him,' he said, pointing towards the lounge.

Kim headed into the small space, which now appeared even

smaller. The tiny coffee table had been pushed to the side and three packing boxes were half filled in the middle of the room. Thank goodness Leanne had stayed in the car.

She scooted around the boxes to take the single chair by the window.

'He'll be right out,' Gavin said from the doorway.

'Having a sort-out?' Bryant asked, nodding towards the boxes.

'Zach wants to go and live back at the house,' he said, shrugging. 'Asked me to start getting our things together.'

Kim was shocked at the speed of such a decision. Especially since most of his family had been slaughtered there.

'And you?' Kim asked, wondering if Gavin always did what Zach asked.

'He's been through a lot.'

'I asked about you. Do you want to live in that house?'

He hesitated and shook his head.

'It's too big, and given recent events, well, let's just say there are a lot of ghosts.'

Kim could feel his discomfort at showing disloyalty to his husband, but she wasn't quite finished with him yet.

'How are you processing your feelings about Rachel?'

'Mine are unimportant, Inspector,' he said, shifting uncomfortably. 'I lost a sister-in-law. I didn't grow up with Rachel; nor was she my wife.'

'But the two of you were close once,' Kim said, feeling that they still were. Something had remained between the two of them.

'Right now I need to be strong for Zach.'

'Do you always do that – minimise your own feelings to make way for someone else's pain?'

'Let me just go and see where he is.'

He left the room, and Bryant raised an eyebrow at her.

'Not in any great rush to talk to us,' her colleague noted.

'He's coming,' Gavin said, stepping back into the room.

'We'll wait,' Kim said. 'Please tell us how you met Rachel.'

'I actually met her at that coffee shop,' he said, wincing in pain.

'The one where she...?'

'Yes, Inspector. A few times a week I'd treat myself to lunch away from the office. Just for a breather, and there she was, doing the same thing. She'd have her Kindle, a sandwich, and a bowl of chips that she never ate.'

His face softened as he savoured the memory.

'Every time she was there I promised myself I'd speak to her. Just strike up conversation, and every time I failed miserably. In the end she spoke first.'

Kim said nothing as his body relaxed into the memory.

'It was a sunny day. She took off her sunglasses, placed them on the table and turned to me and said, "Okay, is it the chips or me you keep looking at?" I was too stunned to speak. "Either way just ask and the answer will be yes." So I asked her if I could take her out for a drink. We met two nights later, and it was as though we'd known each other our whole lives. We never struggled for—'

'Regaling the officers with the great love story,' Zach said from the doorway. No one had heard him approach. 'But of course, it wasn't love, was it?' Zach said, squeezing Gavin on the shoulder as he passed. 'You didn't know that until you met me.'

As subtle as the gesture was, Kim felt a sense of propriety behind it. He still felt like a love rival despite the fact his sister was dead.

Kim bit down her growing dislike of the man.

Bryant sat forward. 'Zach, may we once again offer our condolences for your loss.'

Somehow her colleague always managed to utter the words that were going to stick in her throat as though attached to barbed wire. The man didn't appear all that perturbed by his own loss.

Objectively, Kim could understand Gavin's instant attraction to Zach. Rachel had been attractive, but it was as though even in the womb he had stolen more of the good looks he was entitled to. Had Rachel taken Zach's share of backbone at the same time?

'We do understand that you'd like to be left alone at this time, however we just need to ask you about the visit to your parents' house on Saturday afternoon.'

Gavin turned to face his husband. Clearly, they had not had that conversation in the intervening hours. Was that part of the reason Zach had taken to his bed? Did he not want to face any difficult questions?

The grief-stricken-twin option wasn't ringing true in her ears.

'Oh, it was nothing. I just happened to be passing so I thought I'd nip in for a cuppa.'

The imperceptible frown on Gavin's face told her that wasn't true.

'Passing from where?' she pushed.

'Sorry?'

'Where had you been or where were you going?' Timbertree was almost four miles from Pedmore.

'I'm not sure. I can't remember.' He rubbed at his head. 'So much has happened, I don't even know what day it is.'

'It's Wednesday,' Kim said, knowing she'd caught him in a lie. Whatever the reason, it had prompted a special journey and one he'd chosen to make alone.

'Can you share what you talked about?'

'Many things.'

'Did you talk about Jonathan Pike?' she asked.

'I think the subject did come up,' he said, as though searching his memory.

'In what context?' she pushed.

'I think I expressed my concern at them taking on such a responsibility at their age.'

'They were fit and well, I understand.'

'Always questionable with my mother, Inspector,' he said, referring to her mental health. 'But physically, yes, they were both well.'

'So your objection was based on?'

'Well, by all accounts the young man is troubled. I worried about the effect that might have had on my parents. I mean, who knows what kind of relative he might have had lurking in the background?'

Gavin had the grace to look shamed on his husband's behalf. Zach possessed total conviction in his judgement.

'And your mother's response?'

'She insisted they were going ahead with it.'

'So you actually asked them not to?' Gavin asked, trying to keep the accusation out of his voice.

Zach frowned at his husband's question. 'Of course.'

Kim understood the displeasure on Gavin's face. There was a world of difference between expressing concern and actually asking for the foster agreement to be cancelled.

'My mother was desperate for something to love. She'd always tried to replace the child she lost, and goodness knows where that would have ended if he'd got into the house.'

'He's seven years old,' Kim said, unable to help herself. 'And your parents were only fostering him.'

Zach laughed. 'Oh yes, but my mother loved a project. I wouldn't have been surprised if they hadn't adopted him at some stage. Another sibling.'

Zach's face fell as he realised what he'd said and that he no longer had any siblings left.

The conversation was not helping the unease that was growing in her stomach.

'Did Rachel share your concerns?'

'We didn't really talk about it, but I think she was okay with it. Rachel was very live and let live. She didn't always consider the wider implications. She thought it was commendable, which of course it was, but caution should be exercised when there are long-term implications.'

'Financial ones?'

'Of course.'

Kim already had a sense of how Zach might feel if someone was taking what he felt was his.

'And that's all you discussed?'

'I think so. As I said, it was just a flying visit.'

No. He had made a special journey to convince his parents not to foster a troubled child. And his sole mission had not been successful.

'Did the discussion get heated?' Kim asked.

'*Lively* I think is a better description.'

'Did it turn physical?' she asked, remembering the way Zach had grabbed his sister's wrist and a similar mark being present on Helen Daynes.

Both Zach and Gavin looked aghast.

'Excuse me, Inspector.'

'I have to ask, Zach,' she said, making no apology. She had seen his response with her own eyes.

His gaze met hers. His was cool and unwavering. She didn't break the eye contact, and she didn't retract the question. She waited for an answer.

'Of course it didn't get physical. I would never lay a hand on my mother,' he said, belying his words. She hadn't asked if *he* had become physical; he had assumed that, and she hadn't mentioned specifically his mother.

In that moment she knew that much more had transpired on that Saturday afternoon than she was being told. He was lying to her about events that had happened just hours before their murder.

'I think I'd like you to leave now, Inspector,' Zach said, standing.

His eyes were alight with a fire she hadn't yet seen.

'We'll see ourselves out,' she said, heading for the front door. She had no wish to be fed more lies by the weak, ineffectual man.

And yet there had been something in that final expression – a flame of anger, a heat of aggravation – that left her with one final question.

Did Zachary Daynes possess more backbone than she'd thought?

FIFTY-NINE

'Bloody hell, Penn, you're right. The Porters don't have any children,' Stacey said, sitting back in her seat. They had all assumed that Reece's last name was Porter, and Penn had even written it on the statement ahead of time before speaking to Reece the day before. And the man hadn't corrected him.

'Where the hell did they find him?' Stacey asked, wondering why the Porters had appeared to unofficially adopt him.

'Didn't the boss say Mr Porter worked in some kind of social care role?'

'Yeah but I'm pretty sure there are strict rules against getting too involved with your cases, especially taking them home and passing them off as your own child,' Stacey answered. 'May be why Mrs Porter was so against him coming to the station.'

'To be fair, they appear to have done the guy a lot of good.'

'Living with his not parents in his mid-thirties, odd-jobbing for neighbours and obsessing over a girl half his age?' Stacey queried.

'It's all relative. Reece Gordon, as we now know him, was

thrown out of the care system at sixteen. He took no exams and did his first time in prison two months before his nineteenth birthday.'

'For what?'

'Burglary. Next was breaking and entering, two more stretches for burglary, and his last and longest stretch was for assault and battery almost ten years ago. Not a peep since.'

'Okay, call me psychic but I'm gonna guess that Alec Porter was involved somehow.'

'He was one of the visiting social workers to the halfway house where Reece was placed after the last prison stay. Not a sniff of trouble since,' Stacey answered. 'And I just can't argue with that. If he was robbing and beating people before the Porters took him in and now he isn't, I don't really care what ethical lines Alec Porter blurred to do it.'

'But we don't know that for sure. Burglary and assault are not petty crimes. He knows how to access a property, and he can be violent.'

'Does he know how to use a gun?' Stacey queried, playing devil's advocate.

Stacey pulled her keyboard back towards her. She had appreciated a break from the various CCTV leads she'd been asked to follow, but now it was back to it.

'Not sure you can put it off any longer, Penn,' she said without looking at him.

This news was not gonna go down well with the boss. She was gonna be seriously pissed off.

SIXTY

'Penn, are you kidding me?' Kim cried. 'The Porter house –
now,' she said to Bryant. 'I repeat: Penn, are you fucking kidding
me?'

Penn assured her he wasn't and went on to explain how the
error had occurred. Not really listening, she was focussing on
containing the explosion that was brewing in her mouth.

She didn't really know who she was angry at. She just knew
that assumption was a dangerous tool in their line of work.

'I have good news as well,' Penn offered once he'd finished.

'It'd better be really good.'

'McGregor and Co called. Herbert McGregor has handled
the Dayneses' financial concerns for almost forty years, and the
man himself will see you at midday.'

'Okay, Penn,' she said, ending the call.

'What?' Bryant asked.

'Reece Porter is not Reece Porter – he's Reece Gordon and
is not related to Della and Alec in any way, shape or form.'

'You have to be joking. How many times has Penn met with
the guy and not worked that out?' Bryant asked, shaking his
head.

'Almost as many times as we've met with Della and haven't worked it out either,' she snapped.

She remained silent until Bryant pulled up on the drive of the Porter home.

Bryant followed as she strode to the front door. He appeared to be considering saying something when the door was opened by Alec Porter.

'The jig is up, Mr Porter. We know that Reece is not your son.'

'Please come in,' he said, standing aside.

Della was sitting in the same armchair as the day before. She fiddled with her handkerchief nervously.

Kim was annoyed at them. No, they hadn't outright lied, but they had done a nice job of skirting around the truth.

'Please don't blame my wife,' Alec said, standing behind her. 'She misled you to protect me. I understand you might consider that obstruction, but other than that she's done nothing wrong. I'm the one you should arrest.'

'For what?' Kim asked, feeling the anger ebb out of her. 'If there was a charge in the books for being overly dramatic, I'd consider it, but there isn't. What exactly are you afraid of?'

'Alec could get into a lot of trouble,' Della said, reaching over her shoulder for his hand. 'His actions were inappropriate, unethical and against protocols.'

The gravity of Della's voice suddenly explained something. Della and Alec had never been in any real trouble in their lives. None of what they perceived to be Alec's wrongdoings were of any interest to the police. To her they were indiscretions, but this pair were just terrified of breaking the law.

'How did it happen?' Kim asked, prepared to hear their story, which she felt sure would bear out her revised opinion of the couple. They were good people who were scared of authority.

'Alec used to do weekly visits to a halfway house in—'

'I can tell it, Della,' Alec said, patting her hand before taking a seat.

'I got into social care for adults because I wanted to do some good. I wanted to help people, make a difference in their lives.'

Kim noted that Della looked on proudly.

'I've never been the ambitious type, so my job changed almost monthly. Over the years I got relegated to visiting and checking on vulnerable people who had been released from prison.'

'Was Reece one of those people?' Kim asked.

'He wasn't one of my cases, but that's where I met him. He just sat, staring out of the window alone. Every time I visited he was sitting in the same place, just staring. It was like he was contemplating his next move in life; as though he was deliberating some big decision. After a few weeks I struck up conversation. I just asked him if there was anything he needed. He said no and thanked me for offering.' He paused. 'I knew what he'd been in prison for, but his politeness and manners struck a chord with me. Despite his past, he could still manage to say thank you. It gave me hope that he could turn his life around; that there was something in him that wanted to do better, be someone else.'

He took a breath. 'The next time I went I made a point of starting a conversation. He told me some of his past, and he wasn't a victim about it. He didn't blame anyone but himself for the way his life had gone. For once I felt that I could do something; that I could help and guide a young man down a different path, offer him an alternative. I asked him if he'd like to come to dinner and he politely accepted.'

Kim turned to Della. 'You weren't worried about having a convicted criminal in the house?'

'Of course. Until I met him. He reminded me of a little boy I'd know briefly some years ago. Reece was charming, polite, well-mannered and helpful. I felt an instant connection to him, and him to us. He began spending more time here, and it seemed so natural to ask him to move in. We know we over-stepped boundaries, but we really do love him like our own, and he's not been in any trouble since.'

'Which is a credit to you both,' she said, choosing not to mention having found him lying under the bed of a teenage girl while it was an active crime scene.

'Della, please be honest,' Kim said, feeling comfortable using the woman's first name. 'Did Reece have a thing for Rozzie?'

Della took her time before answering.

'I know he liked her at one time. I think it was just a platonic thing. She was nice to him, always made a point to pass the time of day, but there was one time he came back, and he was in a bit of a state. He'd been doing the guttering, I think. I asked him what was wrong, but he just said something about there being some things that you just couldn't unsee. I didn't press him.'

Kim stood. 'Okay, thanks to both of you for your time and for—'

'Danny,' Della called out suddenly.

Kim frowned.

'The little boy Reece reminded me of. It was many years ago now, before the twins were even born. I used to talk to him at the edge of the garden. He was a lovely little boy. His name was Danny. He was Helen's nephew.'

'Thanks again, Della,' Kim said, heading out of the front door.

Della must have been mistaken.

As far as she knew, Helen Daynes had never had a nephew.

SIXTY-ONE

Stacey placed the latest video-footage clips into two separate files. In the first file were three clips from along the high street where Rachel had had her fatal accident. None were directly on the event, though she had a clip from a hardware shop opposite, a clip from the same side of the road and another from the end of the high street.

In the other file she had hours of footage from a convenience store a hundred yards from the end of the footpath that then disappeared onto the Dayneses' land.

She glanced over at Penn, who hadn't said a word since ending his call with the boss. She knew he felt as though he'd missed something and had let her down. It wasn't the case, but she didn't have time to give him a pep talk. A pile of mundane tasks were mounting up on her desk.

She grabbed the pile of statements to her left and pushed them towards him.

'Here – these are the financials for the family since the twins were born. See if there's any clue in there.'

'Jeez, thanks, Stace.'

She shrugged. In the absence of a reassuring chat, it was best just to take his mind off it.

She decided to take a look at the convenience-store footage first. If there was a chance the camera had caught someone accessing the land to harm the family, that took priority.

She opened the newest file, which was a night-time view of the pavement from the hours of 11 p.m. on Saturday night to 7 a.m. on Sunday morning. The camera was motion activated so she was able to scroll from one activation to another. The first couple were people walking past after a night out. They went nowhere near the stile that led to the Dayneses' land. There were no further activations until three when the camera caught a fox sniffing round the bins. Nothing further until dawn where the birds were activating the cameras by flying into the road for crumbs of food scattered by the fox.

She closed the file. A wildlife documentary but no suspect.

She opened the file previous to the one she'd just watched. This was another eight-hour stretch from 3 p.m. until 11 p.m. on Saturday. Immediately she could see a lot more activations of the camera. People in and out of the store.

She hit play at 11 p.m. then pressed the rewind button. She sat back and watched, moving her gaze between the foreground and the background.

At 10.36 p.m. a figure passed by the camera that caught her attention. After watching the natural gait and demeanour of people in and out the shop doing nothing wrong, this figure stood out.

The man was dressed in stonewashed jeans and a green jacket. On his head was a denim-type baseball cap. His body was hunched and closed, his head down as though protecting himself against a cold wind, but it hadn't been cold that night.

She stopped the footage and went back to where he first stepped into view. His hands were thrust deeply into his pockets, his arms stiff against his sides, his head lowered.

She rewound and watched the first part of the clip over and over, but she couldn't make out one facial feature.

She continued watching and noticed in the very last second his left foot step off the kerb. She waited a few seconds to see if he'd moved to the side to allow someone to walk past from the opposite direction. There was no one.

She watched it again. He had to be crossing the road.

There was nothing on the other side except a hedge line and a stile at the end of the footpath that led to the Dayneses' home.

SIXTY-TWO

'Thank you for seeing us, Mr McGregor,' Kim said, stepping into the man's office.

Herbert McGregor wasn't the youngest seventy-year-old she had seen, and the speed with which he stood to offer his hand did nothing to add vitality to his image.

'You're welcome. Anything I can do to assist with finding the monster that hurt William and Helen, although I'm not sure how a stuffy old accountant can offer anything helpful.'

His gaze held a devilish glint, and Kim couldn't help wondering why he was still around. He owned the company which had seven other nameplates on the wall. She couldn't imagine he needed to work.

From what she understood, he'd been sitting right here for over forty years, and the office reflected it. What might have once been bespoke, quality oak furniture was now dark, heavy and unloved.

'I don't like change, Inspector,' he said, peering over half-rimmed glasses.

'We understand that you took care of the family's financial matters for many years.'

'Thirty-eight and a half to be exact. From the moment William needed to file tax returns for his new business. If I remember correctly, he had a turnover of a hundred thousand pounds, which was pretty healthy in 1981 when you could buy a house for ten thousand, and the average house price was around nineteen thousand, as opposed to the almost quarter million it is today. His gross profit was nine thousand pounds. Again, not bad, but he made a net loss of almost two thousand pounds. Not so good.'

Kim burst out laughing.

'And that's why they keep me around,' he said affably. 'That and the fact that with some good advice, William never made a loss again.'

'May we talk to you about the couple's wills?'

'Of course. There was nothing strange or obscure. Both left everything to each other with ourselves as co-executors for the finances and the same for health.'

'Health?' Kim asked.

'A provision normally included if one party should become unable to make financial decisions.'

'Like Alzheimer's?'

'Amongst many others.'

'And you were co-executors?'

'Absolutely. Such arrangements preclude either party from making arbitrary decisions about the other's health and well-being.'

'Not a member of the family?'

Herbert shook his head. 'Let's say the executors for Helen's health had been William and Rachel. Let's say William tired of Helen and decided he wanted her out of the way, in a home perhaps. A family member may be easily swayed into going along with such a dastardly plan. An objective co-executor would ensure that any arrangement was in the best interest of the subject. We're talking doctors reports, expert testimonials, specialist advice.'

'And both William and Helen agreed to this?'

'Insisted upon it. They didn't want any of their children to have the responsibility of such decisions.'

'And if they died together?'

'We remain executors of the estate, and everything was to be divided equally between surviving children.'

Penn was wrong. There was nothing here. The wills were straightforward, and given recent tragic events, everything now went to Zach.

'Were the Dayneses making any alterations to the will?' Kim asked, thinking about the burned piece of paper.

'A very small change to the wording. Nothing major but something Helen was keen to do. It was just the removal of one word.'

'What word?' Kim asked.

'The word natural. The will stated that the estate be divided amongst all surviving natural children. Helen wanted that word removed.'

'Did you know that the couple were about to foster a seven-year-old boy?'

He frowned. 'No.'

'Could the foster child have had any claim to the estate?'

'You'd have to speak to a lawyer about that one.'

'But could Helen have been trying to make provision for a foster child?'

'I honestly don't know.'

'Do you think they could have been planning something long-term?'

'With what?'

'The little boy. Do you think they might have been planning to adop—'

'No, that would have been imp— I mean... no, definitely not.'

'Mr McGregor, you went to say that would have been impossible.'

'Improbable,' he said as his face tightened. 'Given their age, I would have thought that would rule them out as adoptive parents.'

He looked at his watch pointedly. 'If you have no further financial questions.'

Kim paused, wondering if there was anything else she could ask him. It had seemed so straightforward, but given his response to that one question, she wasn't quite so sure.

'No. We're done. Thank you very much for your time.'

There was no doubt in her mind that the man knew something he wasn't sharing, and she wondered how many people were keeping this couple's secrets.

What she had learned was that Helen had wanted to open the purse strings possibly to include seven-year-old Jonathan Pike. The bigger question in her mind was whether Zach had been aware of that when trying to persuade his mother to change her mind.

SIXTY-THREE

Stacey watched the video clip another twenty times before accepting that she was getting nothing more from it. There was no point calling the boss to say that an unidentifiable male appeared to have crossed the road about six hours before the murders took place.

She opened the folder that held the footage from Rachel's accident in the high street.

'Hey, Stace, got any more of these?' Penn asked.

'What, ten years of bank statements isn't enough to see if there's anything dodgy?' she asked, reaching for another pile off the printer.

'Nope. I need more.'

'You got something?' she asked.

'Not sure yet,' he said, taking the pile from her.

Even that was way more than she'd had.

She looked at the first file, which was the video taken from across the road. The top edge of the footage caught only the legs and feet of the people sitting at the tables outside the coffee shop.

Jeans and ankle boots landed at the middle table at the

exact moment she was expecting to see Rachel appear. A bag
Stacey recognised as a Michael Kors was placed by her feet.

Within a minute, another set of legs appeared, and Stacey
could just make out the lower hem of an overall. The waitress
taking her order.

Rachel retrieved her handbag from the ground and put it
out of sight on the table. Her hand appeared, resting on the arm
of the metal chair. The street was growing busier, and Stacey's
view was often obscured by passing traffic and pedestrians, but
she was able to see the cigarette in Rachel's hand.

The overall returned with what she assumed was Rachel's
order. Another cigarette just minutes after finishing the first.
Stacey found herself trying to look around the people and cars so
she missed nothing, but the image was not three dimensional, and
no amount of shifting in her seat was going to give her a better view.

There was always something eerie knowing you were
watching the last moments of a person's life, almost like you
knew something they didn't, even though it was in the past.

Some part of you still wanted to shout a warning back in
time.

Stacey kept her eyes glued to the screen as the overall reappeared. Based on the time, she suspected that was a second
drink. Eventually she saw the movement of the legs that indicated she was about to leave. Again, she tried to look around a
pair of stonewashed jeans to catch any detail.

'Ah, careful,' she called out as Rachel's foot caught the leg of
the chair.

'I'm only searching bank statements,' Penn quipped.

She ignored him. Even though she couldn't hear anything,
her mind had supplied the tinny sound of metal hitting metal.

There was no question that Rachel had stumbled badly.

She rewound and watched again in slow motion. Her toe
caught the the leg of the chair, which crashed into the table, and

Rachel's hand appeared on the back of the chair for support, which sent it screeching further into the table.

She continued watching the next five seconds before the offending lorry hurtled into the frame, cutting off her view and, as they now knew, Rachel's life.

She cringed as her mind again supplied the sickening sound effect of metal against flesh. She swallowed down the nausea that came with the knowledge of what had just happened out of view.

She took a breath and watched that telling five seconds again. And again. There was no doubt in her mind that Rachel had righted herself after the stumble and had walked away perfectly fine.

She sat back in her chair, wondering which camera view to try next.

'Hang on one second,' she said, sitting upright.

'Okay, do you want me to be careful or to hang on?' Penn asked.

Stacey again ignored him. He knew full well she talked to herself.

Stonewashed jeans. She'd seen them recently.

She went to the footage from the council that was at the top of the high street. The siting of a bus shelter prevented her from having the perfect view of where the incident had taken place, but she wasn't only looking around that area. Her gaze was searching the whole High Street.

'Gotcha,' she called out as she spotted a familiar figure in stonewashed jeans, a green hoodie and a denim baseball cap. There was no doubt that this was the man who had been close to the public footpath on the day of the murders, and here he was again, in the area where another member of that family had been killed.

She rubbed her hands as the figure moved towards the

camera. He wasn't walking with the same demeanour. His body was open and relaxed, and his head was up.

'Come on – show me who you are,' she said as he was about to disappear beneath the camera.

She paused just at the last second and let out a whoop.

This image had a face that she recognised. It was staring at her from the wipe board.

She picked up her phone.

Now it was time to call the boss.

SIXTY-FOUR

The roller shutter to the premises was half down when Bryant pulled up outside.

Kim got out of the car and had no compunction with ducking underneath it.

She could see that the last items of stock had been taken, and the reason for her visit was sweeping shavings into a pile.

Davey Burston dropped the broom and walked slowly towards her.

Bryant had followed her under the roller shutter, and she could see Leanne's legs on the other side of the door.

'Mr Burston, you appear to have omitted a few details from the chat we had yesterday.'

He wiped his hands on his trousers. 'I don't know what you're talking about.'

Roy Burston appeared from a side door that led to the office.

'You went to see William Daynes on Saturday night,' Kim said, calling his bluff.

Roy frowned first at her then at his son.

Davey began to shake his head.

'We have CCTV,' she said, not divulging that it was a poor

quality, obscure image of someone that looked like him a quarter mile from the house.

'You used the public footpath that leads from the road,' she said, taking a leap.

'Son?' Roy asked.

He swallowed. 'Yes, okay. I walked that way. I considered knocking on the door to ask William to reconsider, to give us the business back.'

'Oh, Davey, it was way too late for that,' Roy said, shaking his head.

'I had to at least try, Dad. They took everything from us. I just wanted to talk to him.'

'And did you?' Kim asked.

Davey shook his head, looking miserable. 'I bottled it. I carried on walking. I followed the footpath into Stourbridge, got a pizza and went home.'

'Alone?' Kim asked. With a few more details, it was a checkable story.

'Yeah, alone,' he said, pushing his hands into his pockets.

'Were you still angry?' Kim asked. There was nothing to have stopped him trying again later.

'I was angry at myself for not having the bollocks to knock on the door.'

Roy shook his head.

'I didn't do anything, Dad, I swear. I was just trying to help,' he said, stung by his dad's disapproval.

'It was all gonna be mine,' he said, looking around at the empty space.

'I know, son, but it was my mistake. I shouldn't have relied—'

'No, it's their fault. If that wanker hadn't turned William's head...'

'Daryl Hewitt?' Kim asked, reacting to the venom in his voice.

'Who else?'

'And what about Rachel? Were you angry at her for not stopping her husband?'

Colour flooded into his face.

'What's Rachel got to do with this?' Roy asked. 'They've been friends since they were kids.'

'Rachel Hewitt died yesterday afternoon, Mr Burston. She was killed by a speeding lorry on Brierley Hill High Street.'

Kim waited to see if Davey would offer anything. Stacey had sent her the image and this one was unmistakeably him.

'You were there, in the high street. You walked right past her.'

'Wait a minute,' Roy protested. 'Don't even suggest—'

'Did you see her?' Kim asked, ignoring his father.

Davey nodded.

'Did you speak to her?'

'No.'

'Why not?' Kim asked. 'If the two of you were friends, why didn't you stop and offer your condolences, ask her how she was?'

'I was angry with her,' he admitted. 'I tried weeks ago to reach out to her. She blew me off. Told me she didn't get involved in the business. Our friendship counted for nothing,' he spat.

It was clear to Kim that the young man was still full of rage and that he was happy to dump it anywhere.

'Something doesn't seem right with what you're telling us.'

'You want the truth? She was crying. She didn't see me cos she was crying, and if you must know, I was glad she was upset. I know how that sounds after what she'd lost, but I was pleased that she was hurting.'

Cold, uncharitable, uncaring; Davey Burston was all these things. He was being eaten alive by the rage at the injustice of his family's loss. His anger was all over the place, waiting to settle on someone. He was fizzing like a shaken bottle of pop. That made him unpredictable. It made him volatile and dangerous, but did it make him a murderer?

She was prevented from asking any more questions as her phone rang.

She excused herself and headed for the roller shutter where Leanne stood sentry outside.

'Go ahead, Penn.'

'Court order is through for the doctor,' he said.

'Okay, thanks,' Kim said, heading for the car. Finally, they could look at the treatment records for Helen Daynes.

'One other thing, boss,' Penn said quickly, before she ended the call. 'I've been going through the Dayneses' accounts and, before you go in there, there's something you should know.'

SIXTY-FIVE

Kim had said little in the car after sharing what Penn had told her.

'Got himself out of the shit with that one then,' Bryant had said.

'He wasn't in any shit,' she'd answered.

She'd spent the rest of the journey in silence while her mind computed everything she'd learned about Helen Daynes. There was a sadness growing within her as they headed back towards the office of Doctor Raymond Cutler.

He opened the door before she'd knocked it.

'So you're back,' he said resignedly.

She nodded as the man stood aside for her and Bryant to enter.

'I have the file ready,' he said, pointing to a folder on the desk.

It was two inches thick and detailed Helen Daynes's mental health from the time she was pregnant with the twins.

It also contained her secrets.

'I don't need it,' Kim said, taking a seat.

Bryant turned her way in surprise.

Her silent time in the car had borne results.

'Helen and William adopted a child before she fell pregnant with the twins.'

Doctor Cutler nodded as he took a seat. 'Yes, they'd tried two rounds of IVF which had failed. Helen was distraught at not having a child. They were the perfect couple for adoption, and they chose a seven-year-old boy named Daniel.'

Seven years old. Just like Jonathan.

'He'd been with them for about six months and was a bit of a handful, but they decided to have one last go at IVF and were successful. It wasn't an easy pregnancy.'

Kim already knew where this was going. 'She gave him back.'

Doctor Cutler shook his head sadly. 'You make it sound like a simple decision. It wasn't.'

'I didn't say it was, but ultimately that's what she chose to do.'

'It was a difficult pregnancy,' he repeated. 'She was fragile. She needed lots of bed rest, and Daniel's behaviour deteriorated. She couldn't cope. To continue was putting everyone at risk.'

'It doesn't alter that she chose to give him back.'

'It was painful. He was like her own child.'

'But he wasn't, was he?' Kim snapped, feeling her stomach react to his defensiveness of Helen's actions. 'She had to choose between children that were naturally hers or the one that was hers on paper. What would she have done if Daniel had been naturally hers? Would she have still given him up? How would she have chosen then? That's what adoption is supposed to mean, that the child is yours. He's not some filler until something better comes along.'

'Guv,' Bryant warned.

'It wasn't like that,' Doctor Cutler offered.

Kim knew her composure was slipping, but her heart was

hurting for the seven-year-old boy who had been dumped back in the system. How many times had he been told what adoption meant? How many times had social services, William and Helen assured him that he belonged to them? That he was their child now, that he had a family who were going to love him and take care of him, unconditionally. Had he lowered his guard and let them into his safe, private world? Had he believed them?

She had been that close herself once. Her foster parents had been trying to adopt her when they'd been killed in a car crash. She understood what it was like to allow the feeling of safety, of permanence, to work its way in, even when you weren't looking.

She also understood being sent back to the place where you meant nothing to no one except people who were paid to take care of you, all made worse because you'd dared to hope and, more importantly, dared to trust. How exactly had it all been explained to him?

'She never forgave herself.'

'Which helps no one,' Kim offered cuttingly. Her sympathy lay with the little boy.

'And this is the reason she kept it a secret,' Cutler explained, holding up his hands.

'I'm sure she tortured herself for years,' Bryant said, trying to bring a little objectivity back to the conversation.

'She never stopped torturing herself. It's the single reason for her mental-health problems. She tried to get him back. She agonised over the decision, and once it was made, she instantly regretted it.'

'Was she trying to replace him with Jonathan?' Bryant asked, taking over the questions, having decided she couldn't be trusted to speak.

'If you want the truth, I think every child thereafter was an attempt to replace Daniel. Of course, it almost killed her when she lost a child all those years ago. It brought it all back.'

'Social services wouldn't allow her to take him back?' Bryant asked.

'Absolutely not. They couldn't be sure she wouldn't do it again. So they closed the case file and sealed it.'

'And yet they were willing to let her foster Jonathan?' Kim queried.

'The UK has around ninety-seven thousand children in care and approximately fifty-six thousand foster families. Both figures increase every year but at totally different rates. Kids needing foster homes increases by around ten per cent and foster families by maybe three or four per cent. You do the maths.'

'But her history with Daniel had to be considered surely?' she pushed.

'I'm sure it was, but given the figures I've just quoted, would you have turned Helen and William Daynes down?'

Kim could see his point.

He continued. 'They would never have been allowed to adopt Jonathan, but social services will take all the help it can get.'

'But you can't un-adopt a child in the UK, can you?' Kim asked, her thoughts turning back to Daniel.

Cutler shook his head. 'The adoption is only voided if the child is adopted by someone else.'

'And was he?' Bryant asked.

'We'll never know.'

'I think not,' Kim said. Penn's discovery of the monthly payment to social services had continued for eleven years, until Daniel had reached the age of eighteen. As Daniel's parents, they had been liable for child support until he reached adulthood.

Kim stood. She'd heard enough.

'Inspector, I'd really like you to understand that she—'

'I understand as much as I need to, Doctor Cutler. Thank you for your time.'

She headed for the door, not wanting to hear any more about the suffering of the woman.

She understood perfectly what it had done to Helen but, more importantly, what had it done to Daniel?

SIXTY-SIX

'Wasn't there a little Russian boy adopted by an American woman that was in the news some years ago?' Stacey asked.

Penn nodded. 'Yeah, if I remember correctly, she put him on a plane, alone, with a note saying she'd made a mistake or something.'

Stacey shook her head. 'That's beyond me. How could anyone do that?'

'Desperate measures, Stace. I think he was violent, threatening to kill her or something. She said the orphanage in Russia had misled her about his mental condition.'

'Are you excusing her actions?'

'I don't judge anyone if I haven't lived their life.'

'But she took responsibility for him, Penn. She signed a piece of paper committing her to being his mother. His mother. It's not like buying a pair of boots that leak the first time you wear them. A child is not returnable.'

'What should she have done?'

'Get him help, understand him, love him and do everything she would have done if he'd been her natural child, and not return him like a faulty iPad because it didn't work the way she'd thought. It undermines the whole adoption process.'

Penn sighed. 'There are families that give up their parental rights to natural children too. It's never as simple as—'

'Nothing about having kids is simple. When did your mum know that Jasper had Down's syndrome?'

'Pretty early. Mum was known as a geriatric pregnancy with Jasper, so the doctor ordered all kinds of tests. I think it was a CVS – chorionic villus sampling or something – that picked it up.'

'You ever hear her talk about terminating the pregnancy or giving Jasper up because he wasn't what she'd originally expected?'

Penn looked horrified. 'Bloody hell, Stace.'

'Exactly. You can't imagine a life without your brother, and your mum didn't even consider another option.'

'People give up children all the time. And there are times when it's the right thing to do.'

'And all I'm saying is that I feel some decisions are made easier when the child is adopted, and they shouldn't be.'

'I wonder whatever happened to the Russian boy,' Penn said, pulling his keyboard closer. It was Penn's way of saying they fundamentally disagreed and that he didn't want to discuss it further.

Stacey accepted his position.

'What are you typing, seeing as you don't know his name?'

'You know my feelings about Google. Just tell it what you know and allow it to fill in the blanks.'

Stacey chuckled. 'So you're asking it about an adopted child sent back to Russia by an American mum.'

'Pretty much word for word there, Stace.' He laughed. 'Absolutely nothing I can find on the child,' he said, scrolling through the articles. 'Everything is about the mother and the court case. His name was Artoyem or Artem or sometimes Artyem. His name was changed by—'

'Hang on,' Stacey said, sitting bolt upright. 'Artyem?'

Penn nodded.

'Jesus, Penn, could that be an anagram of Martey?'

Penn began to nod slowly.

Surely not. She was reaching. But what if she wasn't? What if Martey was a nickname, a jab? What if the person terrorising Rozzie was the child Helen gave away?

SIXTY-SEVEN

'You know what I've been thinking about?' Kim asked as Bryant parked the car close to the Golden Arch sign. It had only been as they'd left the grounds of the hospital that she'd realised it was almost three and none of them had eaten a thing. She'd instructed Bryant to pull in. They'd ordered burgers and coffees.

'What, guv?' Bryant asked, unwrapping a Big Mac. Strict instructions from Jenny prohibited him from having fast food more than once a week. As he liked to bend the rules a bit, he made sure his one burger was a big one.

Kim unwrapped her plain cheeseburger, took a bite and then put it aside.

She pulled out her phone and glanced sideways to see a look of pure ecstasy on her colleague's face.

'Jesus, Bryant, get a room.'

'You have no idea how good this tastes.'

'You having the same type of experience back there with your Filet-O-Fish, Leanne?'

'You know, I just don't get it,' Leanne said, giving her burger a puzzled look. 'What's the fascination? I haven't had one for years and I probably won't again.'

'Doesn't compare to your number nine from Jade Palace, eh?'

'Nothing compares to that,' she said, wiping her hands.

'Keep talking to each other and leave a simple man in peace,' Bryant said, taking another bite.

'Yeah, right,' Kim said, scrolling through the photos on her phone. 'Take a look at this, Bryant.'

'On my lunchbreak, guv.'

'Be serious and take a look.'

He leaned across the handbrake. 'It's a photo of the Dayneses' house.'

'You know, surprisingly, that wasn't the question. You see that guttering along the wall there. Is that above Rozzie's room and the family bathroom?'

Lewis's room was at the gable end of the house.

'Think so.'

'Remember what Della said. Something about Reece being in a bad mood a few months ago after working on the guttering. Maybe he saw something in Rozzie's room. Maybe he can tell us who the father of Rozzie's baby is.'

'Worth a shot,' he said, swallowing the last of his Big Mac. 'You gonna finish that?' he asked, eyeing up her cheeseburger.

'Nope, and neither are you. You know Jenny's rules,' she said, throwing it into the paper bag.

She took the lid off her coffee and scrolled to the contact number for Della Porter.

The woman answered on the second ring.

'Is Reece there, Della?' she asked.

'He was, but I think he's gone out again. Why? You're not still—'

'I just want to ask him something. It's just about what he might or might not have seen.'

'Oh, okay. He's gone next door. He made a call and said something about meeting someone to tie up something. Not sure exactly what he said because the kettle was boiling next to me.'

'Did he say who he was meeting?' Kim asked as a feeling of unease began to steal over her.

'No, he was gone before I could ask.'

'Thanks, Della,' Kim said and ended the call.

Who could he be meeting over at the house? It could only be a family member. She quickly scrolled down to Zach's number. She called but it went straight to voicemail. She called Gavin. His phone rang for twenty seconds before voicemail kicked in. Finally, she rang Daryl Hewitt. Like Zach's phone, it went straight to voicemail.

Why was no one answering their phones, and who was Reece meeting at the Dayneses' house?

She gave Bryant urgent instructions to head towards the house.

Something was about to happen there, and she had a feeling it wasn't going to be anything good.

SIXTY-EIGHT

Symes allowed a car into the car park to maintain his safe distance of one car between him and them.

He knew they wouldn't be looking for the Kia Sportage he was driving now. The owner would not yet have reported it stolen. He was bound, gagged and folded in the back. Though it was a hatchback, a large picnic blanket and the parcel shelf was covering him nicely.

It wasn't a bad ride, and he hoped not to have the car owner on board much longer. Once he had the person he wanted, the guy would be chucked overboard into the nearest body of water.

He approached the machine. He didn't want anything and was tempted to shout 'fuck all' in response to the machine's questions, but he didn't want to draw attention to himself. Not at this stage.

'Nuggets,' he called at the speaker and continued along.

The car between them must have ordered something big. It waited at the window ahead long after Stone and her posse had pulled away.

He paid for his nuggets and collected them at the next window. He realised that he couldn't stay in the car park. The mid-afternoon lull preceded the after-school rush and there were too many spaces.

Luckily, they had pulled into a parking space bonnet first so were staring at a fence when he sailed past. He took a left off the car park and pulled into the entrance to the Halesowen Harriers football club. From here he could see if they turned right and headed back towards Halesowen. Anywhere else and they were likely to go straight past him and he could pick them up again.

There was an excitement building inside him, the flames of which were being fanned by playing this cat-and-mouse game of shadowing her every move. He was feeling the intimacy of being this close to her: knowing everything she was doing, everywhere she was going and the knowledge that she had no idea he was even here.

So far, they had been either lucky or clever. Either it hadn't been the right time, or she'd been in the company of either her lapdog or her guard dog. He smiled at his own intelligence as he saw her colleague pull out of the fast-food car park. The car turned left. They were coming his way.

He lowered his head and turned away from the window. By the time he was back on the road, a handful of cars had come between them. That was okay. He'd soon make up the space.

Whatever it took, he wasn't letting that car out of his sight until he had what he wanted, and he had just one more gift to give.

SIXTY-NINE

'Two cars?' Kim asked as they pulled onto the drive.

'That's Daryl Hewitt's car,' Bryant noted, pulling up behind it.

'What the hell is he doing here?' she asked as the foreboding in her stomach got worse. The other car she knew belonged to Gavin and Zach.

The house had been released back to the family late last night, and she no longer had the legal right to come and go as she pleased.

'One sec,' Kim said as her phone began to ring. 'It's the control room.' They only normally alerted her to bodies and crime scenes, or made contact if she was ignoring Woody's calls.

'Stone,' she answered.

'Marm, we have Symes on the line for you. He will speak to you only. He has something—'

'Put him through,' she said as heat engulfed her whole body.

'Marm, DCI Woodward will be listening in on—'

'Connect him,' Kim instructed.

She heard a click and then a change in background.

'Symes, I swear—'

'No talking, bitch. Just listen.'

She switched to loudspeaker. Bryant and Leanne leaned closer.

Her heart nearly leaped from her chest when she heard the girls crying. Every muscle in her body wanted to turn the phone off, but she couldn't. She sat and listened while two little girls cried, screamed and begged for their lives. She sensed that Bryant and Leanne were looking at each other, but she couldn't take her eyes from the phone, as though she could convey some kind of message back to the girls.

She swallowed down the emotion as the recording ended.

'Symes, if you hurt one hair on their—'

A click sounded in her ear. The call had ended.

Her own horror was reflected on both Bryant's and Leanne's faces.

'How the hell am I not supposed to respond to that?' she cried. 'What the fuck am I supposed to do?'

Bryant took a deep breath. 'Guv, you gotta deal with what's right in front of you. Maybe once we've seen what's going—'

'Did you just hear the same thing as me?' she asked incredulously. The picture of Emma's broken mother forged into her mind. Her worst nightmare was coming true and there was nothing she could do to stop it.

'I heard it, guv, and I also know that the control room and Woody have now got everyone possible trying to find where that call came from.'

'Jesus Christ,' she called out in frustration as she got out of the car. 'Fuck's sake,' she growled, kicking the Astra's front tyre. Just the sound of the terror in their voices, their pleas punched her right in the solar plexus.

'As soon as we're done here, we'll—'

'Then let's get done, Bryant,' she said, knocking on the door. No answer. She knocked again.

'Okay, anyone else finding it a bit weird that there are

supposedly four guys in there and not one of them is answering the door?'

Bryant nodded his agreement.

She tried the door handle. It opened.

'Bryant, you take upstairs, I'll take downstairs and Leanne you—'

'Will stay right here and do my job.'

Kim ached to scream in her face that she was a police officer first and foremost, but she suspected it wouldn't do her any good. As ever it was her and Bryant, and God only knew what they were walking into.

SEVENTY

'It's in,' Stacey shouted, clapping her hands.

'The DNA?' Penn asked.

'Yep,' she said, opening the email. 'Oh,' she said, reading the results. 'No match. Not for either one of them.'

The lab had outdone themselves on speed and efficiency, but it had all been for nothing. Neither Reece Gordon nor Warren Cox was the father of Rozzie's baby.

'Where the hell do we go now?' Stacey asked, wondering who else they could test.

'Just run it,' Penn suggested. 'You never know.'

Stacey entered the details into the NDNAD. The National DNA Database had been created in 1995 and originally only held the profiles of convicted criminals or people awaiting trial. But by 2008 they'd been allowed to take samples, without consent, from anyone arrested for all but minor offences.

When she'd finished, Stacey sat back. 'I mean. I'm not really sure what this has to do with the murders anyway. You really think the father of Rozzie's baby would do this? And what about Rachel? If she was murdered, how does— Blimey O'Reilly,

Penn,' she said, sitting up. 'We just got ourselves a positive hit within a minute.'

SEVENTY-ONE

Bryant heard the crash of something falling at the top of the stairs. He took them two at a time and instinctively headed for Rozzie's room.

'What the hell? Get off him!' Bryant said, rushing over to the bed where Reece Gordon was poised with his fist ready to crash down on the figure sprawled across the bed.

Daryl Hewitt held up his forearm in defence.

'Step away from him, Reece,' Bryant instructed calmly.

'Do you know what this bastard did?'

Like most police officers, Bryant was able to gather all the information at his disposal and make a reasonable deduction in a couple of seconds.

'He's the father of Rozzie's child?'

'Yeah, so tell me why I shouldn't just pummel him right now?' he spat.

During their conversations, Bryant had never seen the man like this. His face was twisted with rage and hatred.

'Because then I'll have to arrest you instead of him. Have you hit him yet?'

Reece shook his head.

'Then you're not in any trouble, but one punch witnessed by a police officer and you're in the shit.'

Reece released him with disgust and then wiped his hands on his trousers as though he'd been touching something repulsive.

Daryl sat up. Relief and gratitude shone from his eyes.

'Thank you, Officer. I'm—'

'An absolute pig is what you are. A seventeen-year-old girl? The sister of your wife?'

Bryant struggled to get his mind around how many lines this man had crossed. Was there nothing he hadn't taken from this family?

'It was just the one time. We'd both had a couple of drinks. Things with Rachel were—'

'Please stop,' Bryant said, holding up his hand. He didn't want to hear any kind of justification for his actions. Especially when both women concerned were lying dead in the morgue. 'You knew Rozzie as a child. She was little more than a child anyway, but you knew her from when she was eleven years old. If I didn't have a warrant card, I'd have let him beat the shit out of you.'

'He's only jealous anyway,' Daryl said, nodding towards Reece.

'You know it's taking me all my effort not to leave the room, lock the door and let him do what he intended when he called you over here, so I wouldn't bait him any—'

'I didn't even like her in that way, you sicko. She was young enough to be my kid. I just liked her. She was nice to me. We had a laugh sometimes, and she deserved someone a lot better than you, you despicable excuse for a man.'

Bryant couldn't argue with a single thing Reece had said.

'What was it about this family that appealed to you so much?' Bryant asked. 'You married their daughter. You moved in on the business, and you slept with their other daughter? Why would you do all that?'

'You wouldn't understand.'

'Try me,' Bryant said, folding his arms.

It appeared he'd found all the drama.

The guv was probably already having a cuppa with Gavin and Zach in the kitchen.

SEVENTY-TWO

Kim walked into William's study and right into the barrel of a gun.

Too fucking late she realised the truth of what had been staring her in the face all week.

'Close the door quietly behind you,' Gavin said, taking one step back.

She did as she was told. Gavin nudged her forward with the end of the rifle.

Zach stood by the fireplace looking bewildered.

'What the hell is going on, Gav?' he asked as his husband positioned himself behind the desk.

Damn it, she had no chance of getting to him before he had the opportunity to take a shot, at either or both of them.

She kept her eyes on Gavin as she opened her mouth to explain to Zach the realisation that had just smacked her in the face.

'Zach, meet Daniel Daynes. Your brother.'

Gavin's upper lip curled in a half-smile as every ounce of colour dropped from Zach's face.

'What the hell? Are you... my b-brother?'

'Not by blood,' she clarified, taking Gavin's silence as permission for her to answer his question.

Hurry up, Bryant, she silently prayed.

'Go ahead, continue. He deserves to know the truth before I finish this once and for all. Unfortunately, there'll be a murder I couldn't prevent, as well as the inevitable suicide of a grief-stricken man, but there is only us in the room, and with you two dead, there'll only be my version of events.'

He nodded towards Zach, urging her to continue.

'Your parents adopted a child before you were born, before your mother was even pregnant with the two of you. It was a difficult pregnancy. She couldn't cope. Her mental health suffered. She sent seven-year-old Daniel back to social services in favour of her natural children.'

'No... it's not true. Gavin is my h-husband.'

'It is true, and legally he is your brother. You can't annul an adoption unless the child is adopted by someone else, which never happened, did it, Daniel?'

'Gav?' Zach implored, desperate for any denial.

'Carry on. You're doing great so far.'

Gavin appeared to be enjoying himself immensely.

'Gavin was determined to be a part of this family. He targeted Rachel initially and, I'm sorry to say, he met you and you became the easier target. I think he knew Rachel would suss him out eventually.'

Kim didn't mean to be unkind. Zach had been as much a victim in this as the rest of his family.

'He infiltrated your family by any means necessary.'

'Is that why you took every opportunity to come here alone?' Zach asked. 'Just to spend time with my parents?'

'Ask her. She has all the answers.'

'Yes. He wanted his rightful place in the family. He wanted

to be first son; the elder, the one to be looked up to, to be admired, to be steady. He married you for your family.'

Kim recalled his question in the morgue. *Oh, Helen, what did you do?*

He hadn't been talking about Helen shooting her family; he had been talking about what she'd done to him.

'He loved them, and he killed them.'

Zach's mouth fell open. 'Rachel?'

Kim nodded. 'He knew Rachel was still in love with him and would go to the place they met. Did he not pop out while you were minding the baby?'

'For nappies. He said the ones in the bag were too small.'

'And did he have any nappies when he returned?'

'I never gave them a thought, and then we got the call to go to the hospital.'

He shook his head as though trying to sort his thoughts into order.

'It's all true, Zach. I know you're trying to find a loophole, but he killed Rachel because the whole family now has to die,' she insisted.

'But he was with me all night when my parents were killed,' he said, forcing back the tears that had come into his eyes. Some part of him was accepting the truth and another part was still rallying against it, despite the fact the man in question was pointing a gun in his direction.

'Are you sure, Zach? You came home on Saturday afternoon and repeated the conversation you'd had with your parents?'

'Of course.'

Kim remembered the strong smell of alcohol on Zach's breath the day after.

'And then what?'

'We had a few drinks.'

'Both of you or just you?'

Zach narrowed his eyes, searching his memory.

'I passed out. We were drinking shots. He put me to bed. and I woke up beside him. I assumed...'

'That he'd been there all night?'

Zach nodded.

'He killed your family and staged it to look as though Helen had done it, started a small fire by the kitchen window, then hid until the emergency services arrived, and sneaked out when they turned their attention upstairs.'

Zach said nothing, as though waiting for Gavin to deny any part of it.

Gavin continued to stand there with that smug half-smile on his face.

Kim couldn't believe the depth of sympathy she'd been feeling for this man just hours ago.

'What changed?' Zach asked, as though the penny was finally dropping.

'Jonathan,' Kim said simply.

'Thank you, Inspector, but I can take it from here.'

Gavin turned towards his husband and, although his focus was now in that direction, Kim dared not make a move. If she spooked him in any way, that gun could go off and someone could get killed.

She had to play for time. Any second Bryant was going to realise she was nowhere to be found.

'I was always going to be part of your family, Zach. I was the first child. I was chosen and then thrown away because of you. I still belonged in this family, but how could I tell them who I was when they'd made it clear they didn't want me?'

He paused and regarded Zach's bewilderment for a minute.

'You weren't so bad to be around. Less challenging than Rachel but easier to handle. Less fire, less passion but less complications.'

Kim could see that Zach was wilting with every cruel word.

'As I grew up, I only ever thought about destroying you all. That was always my goal, but then you took me to Sunday lunch and it felt right. Me being there with all of you. My plan was still there, but there was less urgency. I had the chance to enjoy what should have been my life. And then you told me about Jonathan, and I knew she was trying to replace me.'

Zach shook his head as though remembering something. 'You deliberately wound me up and wound me up about that kid, about how he was going to spoil everything. You urged me to go see them on Saturday and beg Mum to reconsider.'

'And you failed again, didn't you? She wouldn't listen to you. She didn't care about your wishes at all. She was still going to bring that little bastard into our family. I bet he wouldn't have been sent packing after a year. I mean, do you have any idea what it was like for me being sent back to that home? To have two mothers that gave you away? They gave me a nickname. They called me reject, and that name stayed with me until I was free to leave. I had a family, Zach. They told me they would take care of me forever, and I believed them. You just can't play with people like that.'

Kim saw the irony in his words after what he'd done to Zach, the man who now stood before him, crushed.

He literally had lost everything in the space of four days.

Kim heard footsteps approaching the door.

'Quiet,' Gavin instructed, pointing the gun at her.

She could see that with the gun turned away from him, Zach was having the same thoughts she had. It was good to see that there was some spirit left inside him, but he was too far away, and he knew it.

'Guv?' Bryant called through the door.

Her gaze met Gavin's. His eyes were cold and hard. He had every intention of walking away scot-free. His expression told her he wasn't playing. She had to be quick.

'Guv,' Bryant repeated, knocking on the door.

'Gavin did it,' she cried out. No matter what he did now, her colleague knew who was responsible. It wouldn't take long before he put it together, if he hadn't already.

Gavin raised the rifle.

'Wait,' she said, holding up her hand. 'You think you know everything, but you don't. There's a lot about Helen you don't know.'

She adjusted her breathing as he lowered the gun. She knew she was playing for time. Now that Bryant knew where she was, he wouldn't rest until he had her out. Zach was also watching her closely, wondering what else he was going to learn. His self-esteem had taken a battering after his husband's revelations and what she had to say wasn't going to help him one little bit.

Gavin nudged the gun at her to continue.

'Helen regretted her decision pretty much as soon as she made it. Within days she was trying to get you back.'

'I don't believe you. I was still theirs. Social services have a legal obligation to return—'

'Social services have a legal obligation to protect the well-being of the child. Helen was now on antidepressants and viewed as unstable. She had given you up and then she wanted you back. Social services don't play like that.'

'Are you lying?'

Kim shook her head. 'She began therapy as soon as you were gone. We've seen her records. She wanted you back. She loved you. She made a mistake and paid for it for the rest of her life.'

In saying the words, Kim felt herself come to terms with Helen's actions. She had made a mistake and then punished herself for over twenty-nine years.

'It's all in black and white,' Kim said, delaying for a moment the words that were going to hurt Zach even more, even though they would help him understand the distance that had existed between him and his mother.

'Every child she had was an attempt to recapture you. You were her first child, natural or not, and the guilt and regret tortured her. She never stopped thinking about you, missing you, wondering where you were. She lost a child to cot death nine years after having the twins. The loss brought it all back. It was like losing you all over again.'

Zach appeared to be lost in his own thoughts, as though events over the years now made sense to him.

'Fostering Jonathan was all about you. She was still trying to fill that space in her heart reserved for you.' She lowered her voice. 'She never got over losing you, and she was in the process of still trying to take care of you.'

He frowned as his brain tried to resolve what she'd told him. Kim heard soft footsteps around the door. She had to keep talking so that Gavin didn't realise how close they were. The second he did, he would shoot that gun, and she had no idea which way.

'Helen and William were in the process of changing their wills. They had taken out the word natural and that had nothing to do with Jonathan. He was never going to be more than a foster child because social services would never have allowed Helen to adopt again. She was changing her will because she knew by law you were still her child. She was still trying to make it up to you once she was dead.'

He stared as though seeing through her.

'She didn't believe me,' he said, choking back tears. 'I told her who I was, and she didn't believe me. She looked horrified, scared, disgusted.'

Kim didn't remind him that she had just witnessed him shooting her husband to death.

'She just kept shaking her head, her eyes full of fear.'

Kim could still hear the whispering outside the door. She had to cover it up.

'Gavin, you have to understand that—'

Her words were cut off as the heavy oak door crashed open and two figures fell into the room, just as a single gunshot rang through the house.

SEVENTY-THREE

'Jesus Christ,' Bryant said as Kim checked herself over for injuries.

She didn't feel hurt. She followed his gaze to the blood spatter on the window.

'Fuck, fuck, fuck,' Leanne said, standing up and holding her left arm at a strange angle.

Zach appeared to be rooted to the spot, staring at where Gavin had stood just seconds earlier.

Bryant shot behind the desk as a siren wailed in the background.

She looked to Leanne as her colleague disappeared behind the desk.

'Police and ambulance as a precaution,' Leanne said, nodding towards Bryant.

Kim approached Zach and gently took his forearm.

'No, no, I have to stay,' he said as his lower jaw began to chatter.

Kim removed her jacket and put it around his shoulders. The fact that the man was still standing after the onslaught of revelations he'd heard in the last half hour was testament to a depth of strength she hadn't known he possessed.

Regardless, his body was going into shock.

'Don't look,' she said, guiding him towards the door.

'Still alive, guv,' Bryant said as his head appeared above the desk. 'He's unconscious but breathing,' he said, tracing a line from his chin across his cheek, indicating the shot had gone diagonally instead of vertically.

'Thank God,' she said, continuing to guide Zach away.

Leanne stood against the wall, cradling her elbow. Her face was pure white.

'I'll be back,' Kim said, needing to get Zach away from the scene.

'I'm fine,' Leanne said before groaning.

Kim was at the front door when two paramedics came rushing towards her.

'Second left,' she advised as a second ambulance and a squad car came screeching onto the drive, followed by a breathless Reece.

'Flagged 'em down at the road,' he said, glancing at a glassy-eyed Zach. 'Is he okay?'

'He's had a few shocks, but he'll be fine,' she said, realising there was no one left to call to come get him. His whole family was dead.

'Is there anything else I can do to help?' Reece asked, looking around.

'No, you've done enough.'

Kim had no clue what Bryant had encountered upstairs but it was clear that Daryl Hewitt's car was no longer on the drive.

'Take your coat back,' Reece said, removing his own.

'What are you...?'

'I'll take him next door. Della will look after him. He knows us.'

Zach offered no objection as Kim took her coat and Reece wrapped his around the man's shoulders.

'Come on, mate, let's get a strong cup of tea inside you,' Reece said, taking Zach's arm and guiding him gently and slowly down the drive.

'Reece,' she called out.

He turned.

'Thank you,' she said sincerely.

They weren't family but Zach had known the Porters all his life.

The second paramedic team rushed to the front door.

'If you're not needed with the gunshot victim, there's a woman standing against the wall, pretty pale and incredibly stubborn, who appears to have dislocated her shoulder.'

Kim wondered what body organ it had cost Bryant to prise Leanne away from the door to help. Clearly, they'd used the technique of one at the top and one at the bottom, which took a good few tries to perfect without serious injury.

As she re-entered the study, Gavin was being placed on a stretcher. A low groan told her he was still alive.

Leanne was still against the wall, arguing with the paramedics.

'I'm not going,' she said emphatically. 'Just pop the fucker back in and send me on my way.'

'So Gavin was Daniel?' Bryant asked as the paramedics negotiated the furniture in the study to wheel him to the ambulance.

'Yep, the prospect of Jonathan tipped him over the edge,' Kim explained.

'Jeez, and he seemed like such a nice guy. In other news, Daryl was the father of Rozzie's baby.'

'Ugh,' she said, wrinkling her nose in distaste.

'Yeah, exactly what Reece was thinking when he had him pinned down on the bed.'

'Fair play, Reece,' she said as they followed the trolley out of the door into the hallway.

Leanne had been persuaded to take a seat in the ambulance while they popped the fucker back in.

'You'd best get after the ambo,' she said to Bryant as they put Gavin in the back. 'You need to get a guard duty set up and be there if he's ready for questioning.'

'You not coming?'

She nodded towards the second ambulance. 'I'd best stay with her. We'll get a lift to the hospital once she's sorted,' she said, nodding to the squad cars.

'You sure?' he asked, frowning.

'Got more coppers here than an EDL protest. I'll be fine, and my very own superhero will be good as new in about twenty minutes.'

'Okay, see you there,' he said, leaving her standing in the doorway.

Kim had the sudden urge to call him back, say something, share something, but she didn't. She stared at the ground and swallowed the emotion down in her throat.

As soon as he'd disappeared, she collected herself and headed to the back of the ambulance.

'She okay?' Kim asked the paramedic standing at the front of her shoulder.

'As stubborn as you said. This should be done at hospital.'

'Just get on with it,' Leanne growled.

Kim adjusted her position for a clear view.

'Okay, take a deep breath – one, two, three.'

Kim winced at the sound of the joint being popped back into place. She watched as the last splashes of colour left Leanne's cheeks and her eyes rolled backwards and she folded against the guy supporting her.

The paramedic turned to her. 'She'll be back in a couple of minutes.'

That didn't give her long.

'Take care of her,' Kim said, before moving away. The plan was formed firmly in her mind, and she just needed one more thing to execute it.

She approached a young-looking police constable halfway down the driveway.

'You got your phone on you?' she asked, holding out her hand.

'Err... yes, marm, but—'

'Mine got trashed inside and I need to make a call.'

She kept her arm outstretched to show she wasn't moving away without it.

He dug in his front trouser pocket and handed it to her.

'Thanks, I'll be back in a sec,' she said, heading towards the gate.

She walked away from the strobing blue lights and into the darkness of the road then paused behind the brick pillar and took her own phone from her back pocket. She switched it to silent and placed it down the front of her jeans. The borrowed phone was placed into her back pocket.

Despite everyone's best efforts, they had been unable to find Symes or the missing two girls. There was only one way she had any chance to keep them alive. Not one person would have sanctioned her plan, but she knew there was no other way. To save the girls, she had to give him something he wanted more.

Her.

There was no street lighting on the lane. A beam of light activated as she walked past the driveway to the Porters' house.

If Symes was as determined as she thought he was, she wouldn't be alone for very long.

She tried to keep her body relaxed as she heard the hum of a car engine behind.

Her heart started hammering in her chest, the blood was

rushing to her ears, but she maintained her speed and composure.

She took a deep breath as the car stopped.

She tensed her back as she heard the footsteps nearing behind her.

She didn't turn around and she didn't cry out when the searing pain in her head turned the world black around her.

SEVENTY-FOUR

'Bloody hell, how long was I out?' Leanne asked, sitting upright.

'First or second time?'

'What?'

She had no recollection of coming round at all after that searing pain had rendered her unconscious.

'You were out for a total of seven minutes. How's the pain?'

She tried to move it.

'It's a ten,' she groaned as stars floated across her eyes.

She looked around the paramedic, surprised that Stone wasn't gloating from the doorway.

She looked to the other paramedic as the first readied an injection.

'Can you grab that mean-looking, short-haired police officer and tell her I'm almost good to go?'

The first paramedic frowned as he held the needle close to her arm.

'The one in the leather jacket?'

'That's the one,' she said as the needle sank into her skin.

'She took off ages ago,' he said, nodding towards the gate.

Leanne reached for her phone and dialled Kim's number.

She'd had gangsters that were easier to handle than this police officer. The number rang out until voicemail.

'I'll bloody find you,' she muttered, realising Stone must have gone to the hospital with Bryant. She wouldn't want to miss any of the action.

She swallowed her anger as she called Bryant's number. Stone knew she was under strict instructions to stay with Leanne at all times. Her next call was going to be to DCI Woodward. That was a fact.

'Hello,' Bryant said breathlessly.

'Put her on,' Leanne barked without pleasantries.

Silence. 'Put who on?'

'Your bloody hoppo. Don't mess with me, Bryant. I know she left with you the minute I passed out.'

'She's not with me.'

'Bryant, I'm not joking so—'

'She's not fucking with me,' he shouted, and Leanne's blood ran cold.

Leanne got herself out of the ambulance and looked around. There were squad cars and officers milling around but no Inspector Stone.

'She's gone. She's legged it,' she said, holding her shoulder in place until the pain medication kicked in.

'Leanne, you had better be joking?'

'She waited, Bryant,' Leanne shouted down the phone. 'She waited until I passed out,' she said, running down to the road. She knew it was pointless. If Symes was anywhere close by, he'd now had a ten-minute head start.

'I'm coming back,' Bryant said.

'No, stay at the hospital,' Leanne said, thinking ahead. 'I'll come to you. It'll be quicker.'

She ended the call, ran back to the ambulance and grabbed her jacket.

'You a driver?' she asked one of the police officers.

He nodded.

'Grab a buddy and get me to Russells Hall right now, and use every siren and light you've got.'

SEVENTY-FIVE

The sensation of her phone vibrating silently against her stomach brought Kim out of the darkness of her own consciousness.

It took only seconds for her to remember what she'd done. She knew her body was moving but not by itself. She was in the back of a car and every bump sent a wave of pain to the lump that had already formed on the back of her head.

She could feel the roughness of some kind of blanket covering her and resting against her cheek. She was lying on her right side with her arms and legs hog-tied behind her, preventing her from any kind of movement. She had no idea how long she'd been unconscious or how long she'd been in the car, but the plan of escape had formed in her mind the second she heard that recording of Symes terrorising the girls.

She needed to know if the first part of her plan had worked. She couldn't feel the bulk of the borrowed phone in her back pocket, so she was hopeful he'd taken the bait.

She prayed that he was taking her to the girls, that she had called it right and they were still alive. Her plan was no more in depth than that. Get to the girls and save them.

Whatever happened after that was in the lap of the gods.

SEVENTY-SIX

'So what the hell do we do now?' Bryant asked, getting into the back of the squad car beside Leanne. His own car would remain parked at Russells Hall.

'Head towards Himley,' Leanne said to the driver as she checked her phone. 'Sirens off.'

'Leanne...' he said as the car pulled away at speed.

'Have you called your boss?'

'Not yet. I've instructed Penn to get to the hospital for Gavin, and Stacey to await further instructions.'

'Call him and let him know what's going on. Tell him we want another two squad cars to join us but not on the blues.'

Bryant took out his phone 'But what are we...?'

'We're tracking her. She knows I put a tracker in her phone. While it's still switched on we have a rough idea where she is.'

'So don't we want every resource available screaming its way towards her?' he asked, confused. Surely they should deploy the army, navy, air force and every squad car in a twenty-mile radius. She was with a psychopath who wanted nothing more than to kill her.

'Not until she stops moving. The last thing we want is a

high-speed chase and to show Symes our cards. Someone might get killed and then we'll never find the girls. Once they stop moving we need to be ready.'

'How far ahead are they?' Bryant asked, scrolling to Woody's direct line. It was for emergencies only and he'd never used it before.

'I'm guessing about twenty minutes.'

'Shit,' he said as Woody answered the phone.

'Exc—'

'Sir, it's DS Bryant,' he said hurriedly. 'It's DI Stone. Symes has her.'

Silence fell and for a second Bryant wasn't sure if they had lost connection.

'Bryant, if this is some kind of untimely April Fool's—'

'She gave Leanne the slip at the Dayneses' property.'

'How the hell did Leanne allow that to happen?' he bellowed. 'She had one job, which was to stay with her at all—'

'Sir, to be fair she was unconscious after having a dislocated shoulder pushed back in,' Bryant defended. 'I think once she heard that recording she knew what she was going to do. Walking away from the Dayneses' house was a deliberate act to lure Symes to her. She knows—'

'That it's the only way to find the girls,' Woody finished.

'Sir, Penn is on his way to the hospital, and Stacey will update you fully from the office on the Daynes case, but we need—'

'Name it.'

'We need two more squad cars to join us. We're heading towards Himley.'

'And?'

'That's it for now,' he said, trusting Leanne's judgement.

'One second,' Woody said, covering the phone.

Bryant took a second to glance over at Leanne's phone. The green dot was still pulsating.

'Okay, Bryant. Get your officer to call his location into the control room. The cars will be with you in minutes.'

Bryant did as he asked, and the officer offered his location to dispatch.

'Tell me again that's all you need,' Woody said.

Bryant knew he was fighting the urge, like himself, to throw every resource he could muster at their direction of travel.

'Just until we have a location and then we can throw the works at it.'

'Stay in touch, and Bryant?'

'Yes, sir?'

'Bring her back.'

He was prevented from saying anything further when the line went dead in his ear.

He would have said that he fully intended to, because any other outcome was not an option.

'What's happening?' he asked Leanne, who hadn't once taken her eyes from the phone.

'Still moving.'

'Jesus,' he said, wishing they could do more. 'Can't we move any faster?'

'We're gaining on them with every minute that passes.'

'You're saying she knew about this tracker?'

'Yep. I put it in there Sunday evening. She fought me on it but nothing new there.'

'She never told me,' he said, which made him think she'd had something like this in her mind all along. Failure from the search team to find the girls would have grown the notion, Symes's recording would have cemented the idea in her head, and Leanne's timely injury had played right into her hands.

He knew beyond a shadow of a doubt that she was perfectly prepared to exchange her life for theirs.

'We've got company,' said the driver, nodding to his rear-view mirror.

Bryant looked out of the rear window to see a second squad car behind them.

'And another,' the driver said as a third pulled out of a side street.

Bryant still couldn't get his thinking beyond a twenty-minute delay.

He was sure the boss was expecting them to track her, which was all well and good while her phone was working, but what if it went dead or through a no-signal zone? She might know they were coming but she didn't know how long it would take. Twenty minutes. What damage could Symes do to her in twenty minutes?

He swallowed down a wave of sickness as Leanne raised her gaze.

'Good timing,' she said. 'Her phone has stopped moving. Start heading towards Shipley,' she said to the driver. 'And you and your buddies now need to make as much noise as you can.'

SEVENTY-SEVEN

Kim felt the car come to a halt. It wasn't a pause at a set of lights or a junction. The engine had stopped.

She felt the car shift as Symes got out of the driver's side of the vehicle.

A rush of cool air circled her as the back of the car was opened.

She felt something being cut close to her wrists before her arms became separated from her feet. Her joint muscles cried out at the sudden freedom.

A meaty hand grabbed at the back of her neck.

'Out you get, bitch,' he said, pulling her out of the car. She landed in a heap on what felt like gravel. 'It's just you and me now. That tracker they probably put in your phone is about thirty feet away from where I grabbed you, so you're pretty fucked.'

Thank God he'd taken the bait and believed the borrowed phone to be hers. Everything about saving the girls hinged on her being able to use her head. Physically, he was right. She was fucked. Her wrists were still bound behind her and her ankles tied together.

'Get up, bitch,' he said, using her arms to pull her to her feet.

He ripped the blindfold from behind her head and there he was, as ugly and foul as she remembered him.

Despite the beating of her heart, she tried to employ all of her senses, as she had no idea where she was and daylight was fading fast, so it had to be around 6 p.m.

She couldn't hear any traffic, and she was standing before what looked like a row of six or seven derelict cottages.

'Welcome to the place you're going to die,' he said, grabbing her right arm.

'You'll never get away with it,' she said, returning the hatred in his eyes.

'See anyone around, do you?'

'They'll find you.'

'I don't give a fuck,' he said, dragging her forward. She had no choice but to hop to keep up with him. The time to fight him hadn't come yet. First, she had to make sure the girls were safe.

'You gotta understand, Stone, that they can give me the fucking electric chair once I'm done with you. All I want is your last breath. I want to watch the life fade from your eyes and for me to be the last thing you ever see.'

'So let the girls go,' she said as he pushed open the front door of the middle cottage.

'Oh no. I have big plans for those two little girlies.'

Kim's stomach turned at the anticipation in his voice.

'And you're gonna watch every single minute cos I know how badly that will fuck you up while you wait for your turn. You're gonna die with a broken body and a broken head.'

He pushed her into a room on the left.

Her legs were still tied together, and her hands were behind her back.

She had no choice but to fall. She twisted herself slightly so she fell on her right arm and not her face.

She heard a small squeal as she fell. The sound was music to her ears. They were alive.

'Over there,' he said, nudging her to the far wall.

He moved to the corner and switched on a high-beam torch. It lit up the room, and once her eyes adjusted to the glare, she saw two young girls huddled together against the wall behind the door. They looked dirty, pale and terrified. But they were alive. She'd take frightened over dead any day of the week.

She fought down her rage at their tiny wrists and ankles bound by tie wraps. Their mouths covered with duct tape. The corner of one had come loose, which is why she'd heard the scream.

A single empty bottle of water stood a few feet away from them. There was no evidence of food. He'd done only what was necessary to keep them alive. She remembered the state in which she'd found Edna. Why would she be surprised? Why would he treat two little girls any differently when his plan was to beat them to death anyway?

The fact that their mouths were covered only highlighted the terror in their eyes.

'It's okay, girls,' Kim said, trying to sound reassuring.

'Is it fuck,' Symes said, punching her in the side of the head. She blinked away the stars to keep eye contact with the girls.

'The girlies don't know what's gonna happen. I've been saving that pleasure for your arrival,' he said, walking perilously close to them. They recoiled and tried to push themselves further against the wall.

She fought every urge inside her to scream out not to touch them, knowing he would use them to torture her more.

He walked backwards and forwards in front of them.

'Our little girlies here don't know that I'm going to break every bone in their little bodies.'

He kneeled down and touched the cheek of the smaller one, who tried to burrow further into the other girl.

Kim ached to get his filthy hand away from her.

'I'm going to punch them and kick them until they flop around the floor like rag dolls. I'm going to cause them unimaginable pain and suffering until their tiny little organs give up on them and they die.'

Kim could hear their moans of terror, and they were visibly shrinking before her as the excitement built in his eyes.

Symes truly was the most despicable psychopath Kim had ever known.

'And the poor little luvvies don't even realise that it's all your fault. You condemned them to a horrifically slow and painful death when you took my reward away.'

'It's me you want, Symes,' Kim said, trying to get his attention back to her. She was powerless physically, but she had to play for time. Even if it was to annoy him. One kick for her was one less for them.

'Oh no, bitch, you are not going to fool me again. You distracted me last time with your clever mouth, and I lost my payment.'

'How many hours, Symes?' Kim asked, determined to bring his attention back to her. 'How many hours of your life have you dedicated to getting revenge on me?'

'I've planned this from the minute I was in the slammer. Every day and every night I've thought about this moment and what I'd do to you.'

He had turned her way. Good.

'You wanna know how many hours I've spent thinking of you? Fuck all.'

She had no choice but to speak to Symes in a language he understood. 'Oh no, actually, I lied, there was this one time I was laughing my head off while telling a group of guys how I single-handedly took you down and blinded you in one eye.'

She could see the rage colouring his face.

'They were a bunch of chauvinistic pigs who couldn't

believe that a woman had done that alone. Still hurts, doesn't it, your ego?'

She was rewarded with a kick to the left side of her ribcage. She groaned and swallowed down the pain.

'Did you tell them in prison that you were taken down by a woman? How hard did they laugh? I mean, there are some proper hard men—'

She stopped as a second kick to the same spot sent her sideways.

'Of c... course you're going to win this time. You've got me tied up and that's the only way you can win this. Y... you'd better hope your mates in prison don't hear about th... this.'

The pain was making it increasingly difficult for her to speak, but while there was breath in her body she'd carry on.

'I'm not surprised you don't plan on going back. They'd laugh you out of the fucking place.'

She readied herself for another kick, but what she saw coming her way chilled her to the bone. A smile.

She had lost him.

'Oh, Stone, you're fucking good,' he said, giving her a little clap of appreciation. 'You know how to get under my skin, but I'm not falling for it, and I know just how to shut you up.'

He took a roll of duct tape and walked back towards the girls.

He kicked the nearest one in the knee. She screamed out in pain. He smiled wider as he turned around and approached Kim.

'Now, you're gonna have to listen without speaking and watch the screams and the agony I'm gonna cause.'

He ripped off a piece of duct tape and leaned down to place it over her mouth.

Kim knew she was out of time. He had caught on too quickly. She was powerless to fight him physically. She had only one weapon left.

'If you do that you'll never have time to get to me,' she said, playing her very last card. 'Take out my phone. Front of my trousers.'

His face darkened. 'I threw your fucking phone away.'

'Decoy. Mine is still here.'

'Stop trying to waste my fucking time.'

'You'll regret it, Symes. You were right about the tracker but not the phone.'

He roughly reached into her waistband. 'You fucking—'

'Take the back off. You'll see a tiny green chip. That's the tracker.'

'You're fucking lying,' he said, prising off the back under the torchlight.

'They're not going to be far away now. You can spend your time hurting them, but you'll get caught before you get to me.'

He found what he was looking for.

'You've got time to get away with the person who you've fantasised about for years, but you've got to do it now. It's them or me.'

He hesitated for just a second before striding across the room and hauling her to her feet.

He threw the phone to the floor and stamped on it. She heard the sickening crack as parts flew out of it.

He pushed her out of the cottage and towards the door. She heard the sound of multiple sirens in the distance. They were coming. The girls were alive. The girls were safe.

And she was now on her own.

SEVENTY-EIGHT

'What do you mean it's gone off?' Bryant said as Leanne reloaded the app.

'The light stopped flashing before it faded completely.'

'You said we were less than a mile away?'

'We were. We are,' she said, going to the app menu.

'Which way?' the driver asked at a crossroads.

'Go straight over,' she said, tapping in some codes.

Bryant fought the urge to stop the car, get out and call Kim's name.

'What are you doing? Do you realise that every second counts? He could be beating the bloody shit out—'

'I'm accessing the data files. The program does an update, a backup to file every ten seconds. If I can look at the exact distance there was between us, I can get us back on track, and you shouting at me isn't going to make me do it any quicker.'

Bryant decided to shut up. Explaining was slowing her down.

'Got it,' she said, looking at the time on the screen, the map and then out the window.

'Go back,' Leanne instructed. 'Back to the crossroads and turn left.'

The driver radioed in and then turned in the middle of the road. Bryant watched as the accompanying cars did the same thing.

'About a third of a mile down is another left turn. She's there somewhere, and that's the closest I can get,' she said as the car approached the lights.

'Nothing down there,' Bryant said. 'Just some— Oh shit.'

'What's down there?'

'A few derelict cottages. Bought by a developer over ten years ago. Couldn't get insurance to cover the build cos of subsidence.'

'Perfect place,' Leanne said as the car made the left turn. 'Shelter, quiet, unused buildings.'

Bryant had the car door open before it had stopped moving. The lights and sirens continued from all three cars.

'There's no other car here,' he said across the roof to Leanne.

'I think it's the spot,' she said, heading towards the middle cottage.

'Check 'em all,' Bryant called to the officers who had all now been briefed as to what they were looking for.

The absence of a vehicle was scaring the shit out of him. Had Symes finished with them all and, despite not caring about dying, had chosen to scarper anyway?

'Where the—?'

'Shush, did you hear that?' Bryant said as they entered the cottage.

'Use your phone,' she whispered, switching hers to torch.

He did the same and wondered if he was destined to be bossed around by strong women. Just the thought ripped through his gut. Where the hell was Kim?

'In here,' Leanne called out at the top of her voice.

He ran in to find Leanne's harsh torchlight resting on two terrified little girls.

'Jesus, Leanne,' he said, knocking the phone to the side so the glare was gone but the light remained.

'It's okay, girls,' he said, lowering himself to the ground. The younger girl, Chloe, pushed herself closer to Emma, the first girl that had been taken.

He turned to Leanne. 'Carry on looking.' His boss could be lying somewhere unconscious. Or worse.

'We're police officers. No one is going to hurt you now. You're safe.'

They didn't move, and he knew better than to rush them.

'Is there anyone else here?'

Both slowly shook their heads.

He pointed to his mouth.

'Can I try and take that tape off?'

There was a hesitation before a small nod from one followed by the other.

He could hear officers talking outside the door to dispatch, others to supervisors. Finding the girls alive was big news. There would be two families sleeping better tonight.

They were both shivering either through cold or fear.

'Get me a knife, some blankets and water,' he called to the voices outside the door.

He wanted to ask the girls a hundred questions. He was beyond relieved to have found them alive and safe, but that wasn't the end of the story for him.

'This might hurt a little bit,' he said, holding the corner of the tape. 'Just squeeze your eyes shut and I'll peel it back slowly.'

Emma nodded and squeezed her eyes tightly shut.

He tugged gently but it was stuck firmer than he'd thought.

'Okay, I'm going to have to do this quickly. Can you be brave for me?'

Her eyes widened but she nodded. Chloe started to cry.

'Okay, close your eyes again, both of you.'

They did and he took the tape off as quickly as he could.

'Good job,' he said as tears filled her eyes. 'You were so brave. Do you think you could help your friend be brave too?'

Emma nodded and swallowed back her tears. He could have hugged the life out of her.

'Right, I'll be as gentle as I can, okay?' he said, turning to Chloe.

'I-It's okay. It's b-better off,' Emma said, trying bravely to reassure the smaller girl.

Chloe blinked rapidly as though bracing herself.

Bryant worked a corner of the tape free. She nodded. He pulled.

She let out a little yelp.

'Are you hurt?' he asked.

Both shook their heads, but Emma rubbed at her knee.

'Did he hit you?'

'Kicked,' she said.

A fresh wave of hatred and loathing coursed through him as an officer appeared with two foil blankets and two bottles of water. A second officer handed him a knife.

'Can you put your hands out for me?'

They both thrust them forward at the same time. He cut the tie wraps quickly and then freed their feet.

He unscrewed the tops of the water bottles and handed them a bottle each.

They each took a drink immediately and, while they did, he wrapped the foil blankets around them.

Secure in the knowledge that everything necessary was being done, he felt comfortable in asking some questions.

'Was there a lady here?'

They both nodded.

'Did he hurt her?'

They nodded, and Bryant felt sick to his stomach.

'Where?'

Emma pointed to her side. 'He kicked her, twice,' she said, holding up two fingers.

'He said he was going to hurt us, break all our bones, but the lady stopped him.'

Of course she did, Bryant thought.

'He hurt her instead.'

Bryant's heart ached.

'Did he say where they were going?'

They both shook their heads.

'Do you remember anything else they said?'

'The lady showed him her phone. Said there was a choice,' Emma offered.

Damn it. She had deliberately shown him the tracker to get him away from the girls. She'd shown her only hand to save two innocent lives and, damn her, it had worked. He felt the emotion pricking at his eyes.

'Nothing else, Bryant,' Leanne said, coming back into the room. 'Parents are on their way.'

The girls surprised him by turning and hugging each other tightly.

'It's over,' he said again as they cried in each other's arms.

Leanne took a step backwards and they both heard the crunching underfoot.

Leanne shone her torch down to reveal a mobile phone smashed into a hundred pieces. That was why the green light had gone out.

He looked to the woman holding the torch.

'What the hell are we gonna do now?'

SEVENTY-NINE

Kim knew that he had driven away from the sirens. It had been her last hope that he would run into the approaching vehicles and that someone would spot him. Her hopes had faded along with the blaring sirens.

She'd achieved what she'd wanted and got him away from the girls. If Leanne was any good at her job, they were now in safe hands and would be reunited with their families. It was the one thought she had to keep in her head.

The car stopped and Kim guessed they had been driving no more than ten minutes. She had tried to listen for any revealing sounds, but the noise of the car and her efforts to keep her ribcage steady had taken most of her attention.

She felt herself being pulled out of the car by her bound feet.

The whole front of her fell to the ground, her face hitting the door frame on the way down.

He laughed out loud as he heard the thud.

He hauled her to her feet. Her legs were starting to feel like jelly.

He'd brought her to what looked like a burned-out warehouse. She looked around and saw nothing. She could hear nothing. A sense of finality began to seep through her bones.

She fought it away.

'You don't even want a fair fight, Symes?' she asked, trying to pull at the tie on her wrists.

'It's not a fight, bitch. It's an annihilation, and you're not gonna get up to your usual tricks.'

He took the roll of duct tape from his pocket, tore off a fresh piece and roughly covered her mouth.

'Much better,' he said, grabbing the powerful torch from the passenger seat.

He dragged her across rough gravel and into the building. She adjusted her breathing to use only her nose and tried to ignore the pain coursing through her ribs.

He pushed her down to the ground. She fell backwards, her wrists still tied behind her so her hands landed on the cold concrete first. She felt something snap in her left little finger. The pain was immediate but she still tried to pull her wrists apart. If she could get one thing free, she could fight back.

The torch suddenly illuminated, and it was fixed firmly on her. She could see nothing behind or around the harsh glare.

She didn't know if she was in a corner or the centre of the space.

More importantly, she didn't know from which direction he was going to strike.

She tried pulling her wrists apart and felt a trickle of blood run down her thumb. The repeated efforts of trying to escape the wraps had cut lines in her skin that were starting to bleed.

The futility of her efforts tried to wash over her, but she fought it.

She felt the air change around her and a boot landed in the right side of her ribs. Again, she spluttered as she moved across the ground.

The groan of pain was absorbed by the tape as she heard his laughter.

Although her feet were locked together, she tried pulling them up and kicking out, hoping she'd catch his ankle.

But he was protected by the darkness while the spotlight was on her like a solo stage performer.

'Oh, Stone. I've dreamed about this for so long,' he said, landing a punch to the side of her head. She blinked away the stars and tried to focus on the air around her for change, for warning.

'But this is even better than I could have imagined,' he said, kicking her in the back.

She tried to move like a spinning wheel as her body cried out in pain.

'I swore to myself I'd make it last, that I'd savour every second, but it's too tempting to just beat every last breath from you.'

Kim felt a rush of rage as his foot met with the back of her neck. If only she could get either of these ties off. She could either fight back or try to avoid the blows.

She used her thighs to try and yank her feet apart. The tie wrap barely budged.

'Nice try, bitch,' he said, taking a good kick at her left hip. The pain shot down her leg and back up through her pelvis.

'So many body parts,' he said, using his foot to roll her fully onto her stomach. He brought the sole of his foot down forcefully onto her left kidney.

She tried to roll away, but he pushed her back and repeated the move on the other side. She coughed up something wet that got caught against the tape across her mouth.

Every movement was excruciating. There was no part of her body that wasn't contributing to the overall agony coursing through her.

'Okay, enough pissing about – let's get to it,' he said, kicking her in the face. With her arms tied behind her back, she couldn't shield any part of herself.

The pain tore through her body like fire running through her veins.

The hits kept coming, one after the other – his fists, his feet, faster and faster as his momentum grew. Blow after blow. Kick after kick.

No one was coming. She'd given up her lifeline for the girls and she thanked God she had. She knew she'd done the right thing, and she knew she was going to die.

She closed her eyes and tried to put herself outside the pain. She thought of her brother and all the years she'd spent without him. There was comfort in the knowledge they would be together again soon, and if God would grant her one last wish, she would get there before her mother and he would never be alone again.

She wasn't sure how much more her body could take, and every blow now took her closer to him.

She thought of the people she'd leave behind. Stacey, Penn, other colleagues, and people she'd known. They would grieve and they would miss her for a while, but they would go on. Leanne might feel guilty for a short while, but she'd be on to the next.

For a moment she considered her mother, lying on her own deathbed, being eaten alive by the cancer that now consumed her. Kim felt no loss and only the sense of relief that she'd be there to protect her brother just as she'd always been when he was alive.

I'm coming, Mikey, she thought as she felt her eyes begin to droop. She wished she could take him news of their father, but his identity was held by the one person who would not occupy her final thoughts.

Her body travelled towards unconsciousness. Despite the pain, she could feel her toes and fingers growing cold. The time between her breaths was growing longer, and yet she could hear her breath louder.

She knew her body was shutting down.

A picture of Barney came into her mind. Her companion and in some ways her saviour. He had absorbed every part of her: her fears, her joy, her regrets and asked for little in return. Charlie would keep him. Charlie would love him and take care of him for the rest of his life.

As the blows continued to rain down on her, she felt herself travelling towards the darkness that was grabbing at her, trying to enfold her.

She suddenly thought of Bryant. He would feel her loss most. He would never forgive himself for not being there to save her. He would live with that for the rest of his life. Her death would weigh heavily on her one true friend, and that saddened her to the core.

A single tear fell from Kim's eye as she took her long, final breath.

EIGHTY

Penn glanced across the grave at Bryant, who was probably having the hardest time of all of them. The car carrying the coffin was slowly ascending the hill to their current location.

Given the circumstances, he was touched that the man had taken the time before the service to pull him aside and tell him he hadn't fucked up by not identifying Reece's real last name earlier. He appreciated it, but he didn't believe it. He pushed away the thoughts of what mistakes had led them to this moment. There were too many to count, and they would all second-guess their actions for years to come.

This case aside, he had felt the thin line of tension between them from the day he'd joined the team. It wasn't overt or particularly obvious. The man was innately pleasant with impeccable manners, which prevented him from appearing hostile, but the easy relationship Bryant had with Stacey was nothing like the relationship with him. There was genuine warmth when he spoke with the detective constable, an under-lying fondness that had grown over time. When Bryant conversed with him, there was an edge of tolerance, a slight tightening of the jaw. He had never addressed it and had accepted that they were never going to be friends.

But recent events had made him question whether or not he should address it. Had Bryant opened the door for an honest conversation by approaching him before they'd entered the service, and was now really the time to have that talk?

He hadn't worked with the boss for as long as the others, but in that time he had learned more from her than he had from any other superior officer. Her actions over the years had taught him lessons on integrity, passion, drive and, most importantly, courage. A small voice told him that the boss would want him to do it.

Before he even realised what he was doing, his feet were moving him towards his colleague.

Bryant lifted his eyes from the hole in the ground and blinked away the emotion before frowning.

Penn followed his gaze and swallowed. He couldn't stop now.

'I know this probably isn't the time to—'

'It's not,' Bryant said, cutting him off. 'You do know what we're doing here today?'

'Yes, but I need to say something before we can put it to bed,' Penn pushed. Today was all about bravery, and now he'd started, he couldn't stop.

'There's nothing to put—'

'I'm sorry I'm not Dawson,' he blurted out, addressing the only thing he thought it could be. He cursed his own bad timing at mentioning the death of one colleague while standing beside the freshly dug grave of another, but now he'd started, he couldn't stop, despite the puzzlement that now shaped his colleague's face. 'I know everyone was close to him and that I took his place on the team. I'm sorry I'm not him, and if I could bring him back, I'd do it in a—'

'Not even close, Penn,' Bryant said, shaking his head. 'We

all had individual relationships with Dawson. Mine wasn't a particularly close one, but he had his moments of brilliance, and I'll always respect that the man gave his life to save a child.'

The irony of the reason for them standing where they were right now was not lost on him. He knew he couldn't have picked a worse time. They were all hurting, but he had to get to the bottom of this antagonism Bryant held towards him. He'd always assumed that it was taking the man longer than anyone else to come to terms with Dawson's death.

'Jeez, Bryant, I just wish you'd tell me what I've done wrong,' Penn said, running his hand through his curls.

'You want the truth?' Bryant asked.

'Of course. If I didn't want—'

'You're strange,' Bryant said.

'I'm wh-what?' Penn asked, stunned.

'I don't get you. I don't understand you. You listen to nothing through headphones, you enjoy post-mortems, you can quote facts about serial killers at the drop of a hat. You have a brilliant mind that scares the shit out of me, and your social skills leave a lot to be desired. I don't know how to relate to you.'

Had it not been for the gravity of the situation in which they currently found themselves, Penn would have laughed out loud.

'You don't like me cos I'm weird?'

Bryant's eyebrows drew together. 'I didn't say I didn't like you. I said I couldn't relate to you, and I didn't want to hurt your feelings by broaching the—'

'Hurt my feelings?' Penn asked incredulously. 'Do you wanna guess how many times I've been called weird? My school years were a blast, but you're right and there ain't a damn thing I can do about it. We have little in common, but the one thing we both share a passion for is work. How about we relate on that?' Penn asked.

He saw the ghost of a smile touch the corner of the man's lips.

'Okay, Penn, that seems like a good place to start.'

Both men fell silent, fighting to control their own emotions as the hearse finally came to rest beside them.

There were no words left for either of them.

EIGHTY-ONE

Symes watched the scene at the graveside and allowed a sense of peace to steal over him.

He had known all those years he had waited and planned and plotted that it would be worth it. He'd always felt that he would actually know contentment once she was dead. And he did.

The added bonus was that he was still free.

When he'd escaped from prison, he'd been totally prepared to accept his fate once he'd killed her. Part of him had considered suicide by cop. Problem was he'd been enjoying himself. He'd forgotten just how sweet freedom was. As he'd seen the last breath leave her body, he'd realised he could have it all. He'd avoided the police for almost two weeks, and he'd continue to do so.

But first of all, he'd needed to see her coffin enter the ground. This was his cherry on the top of the cake. Once she was lowered into the dark earth, he would hotfoot it out of the nearest exit and disappear for good.

As sparse as the gathering was – of colleagues, as she had no family – it was still touching to see so much genuine emotion at her passing. He laughed. Was it fuck! Every tear, sigh and brave smile gladdened his heart more. The bitch was finally dead, and he was as free as a bird.

He felt a hand tap him on the shoulder, heard a voice in his ear.

'You looking for me?'

He whipped around and felt his stomach drop to his knees.

Kim Stone was standing right in front of him.

Her face still bore the marks of his labours, and her smile wasn't even close to reaching her eyes. There was a coldness, a detachment he'd never seen before.

'You had your chance, Symes, and you blew it.'

She stepped closer, out of earshot of the police officers behind her.

'Get out again and I'll be waiting. Next time I'll kill ya,' she growled.

The last words went straight into his ear and the ruthlessness chilled him to the bone. They were not the words of a police officer. They were the words of someone with nothing left to lose.

He was still reeling from the shock when two officers appeared behind him. How the hell had this happened? He'd seen her take her last breath. Her death had been plastered all over the news for days.

She stepped back.

'Take him,' she said, folding her arms.

Symes considered trying to run but he knew he was surrounded.

He'd achieved nothing. It had all been for nothing.

The rage started to build in him, and the bitch recognised it immediately. Her eyes glinted dangerously, daring him to make some kind of move, anything to give her an excuse to hurt him. He could see the hunger for violence in her face.

He held up his hands, and four officers surrounded him.

They turned him around as her colleagues came walking down the hill. He took one last look at the woman he thought was dead.

It was over and he knew it.

EIGHTY-TWO

Kim waited until Symes was out of sight to lean back and use the wall of the crematorium to support her.

Woody had wanted her to take no part in his elaborate plan to flush Symes out, which he'd formed immediately. There had been a press conference to announce her death while her body lay in an induced coma for three days. No one had been allowed to visit her, and her whole team had been instructed to maintain the pretence. Woody had been sure Symes would resurface to make absolutely sure she was dead, and so the crematorium and cemetery had been staged accordingly, with a total of twenty-seven police officers in plain clothes keeping watch on every inch of the site. She had been waiting in the office for the right moment after insisting to Woody that she had to see it through.

Seeing his face again had brought it all back – the physical beating, the futility of her escape attempts, the vulnerability at not being able to defend herself, the pain and feeling of wanting to die when she'd been brought out of the coma.

The surgeons had said she was very lucky. She was full of pins and metal, and permanent damage had been done, but to them she was alive and somewhat mobile and a roaring success. The cocktail of drugs had helped with the agony while her body had started to heal, and she'd been told that it would be months until she was almost as good as new. Right now, the 'almost' was like a get-out clause, a loophole for the doctors because quite frankly they didn't know.

Her team was growing closer, and she was running out of time. She had to find the strength within herself to reassure them she was fine.

It had been on her third day out of the coma that Woody informed her that her mother had passed away peacefully in her sleep. The only emotion Kim could muster was resentment.

After her chat with Leanne, she had resolved that she wasn't going to visit her on her deathbed. There was no forgiveness in her heart, and her only course of action would have been to scream in her face and let all the hatred and rage out of her. Not a good move for a dying woman with a mental illness. So the hate would continue to live where it always had, deep down inside her.

As the team approached, she tried to fix a smile to her face.

There was an awkwardness once they were standing before her. Penn was checking her over physically, Stacey had tears in her eyes and looked like she wanted to hug her, and Bryant wasn't removing his gaze from her face. Leanne looked around.

She had to try and pull this off.

'Come on then – debrief time,' she said, adjusting her position against the wall.

'Boss, how are you...?'

Kim silenced Stacey with a shake of the head. They weren't going there.

'Symes is in custody, and he'll never get to hurt anyone again. Now tell me about the case.'

'Gavin confessed,' Bryant offered. 'Once his cheek had been sewn up where the bullet exited, Penn went to work on him.

Spent two days presenting him with evidence of how much Helen still loved him and had never forgotten him. He did a great job.'

Penn smiled at the compliment, and Kim was glad to hear it.

'Zach's been busy. Been spending a lot of time with Reece making plans on what needs doing to sell the house. I think the Porters have kind of adopted him. He's also removed Daryl from the business and installed a manager to oversee the day-to-day running of it. He's made financial arrangements so that Mia will always be taken care of, but he wants no further contact with Daryl. He's broken the contract with the lumber supplier and taken the business back to Roy and Davey Burston. He feels it's what his dad would have wanted. He won't speak Gavin's name, and it's like he's going to cut that time of his life out and pretend it never happened, although he seemed very relieved that Gavin would be entering a guilty plea and there would be no trial.'

'Good. And the girls?' she asked.

'Alive, traumatised, both in counselling, but they'll be fine.'

Kim already knew that Edna was on the mend and would make a full recovery.

That left just one question to ask.

Woody had filled her in on the details of how Leanne had used the tracker device to lead them to her and the girls, as she had known they would. What she hadn't known about was the second tracker that had been fixed in the heel of her boot that first day when Leanne had stayed up all night. That second tracker had led them straight to her.

'I'm guessing I know what a number nine is now,' she said, addressing Leanne. It wasn't a Chinese takeaway at all.

'Yep, it's designed for people who can't be trusted to follow the rules and do what they're told.'

And of course, Leanne had known that she would be one of those people.

And that brought her to her final question.

'So who was it?' she asked, casting her gaze between Bryant and Leanne. One of them had brought her back from the dead.

'It was Leanne,' Bryant said. 'She didn't hesitate, just threw herself down and started pumping that chest.'

Kim focussed on her. 'Thanks, but I still don't like you.'

'And I still don't give a shit, but in some cultures, if you save a life, you own it.'

'Yeah, right, and I'd like to own a toaster that's not in bits on my kitchen table, but that's not gonna happen either.'

Silence fell and Bryant stepped forward.

'Listen, guv, we've all—'

'Okay, show's over for today, folks. Time to get back to the day job.'

For them it was but for her not so much. Right now, she had no idea when she'd be signed off as fit and healthy enough to return to work, and even less idea what arrangements would be made in the meantime.

She gave them all a nod before heading slowly towards where Charlie awaited her with Barney.

As she turned away, she allowed the expression to fall from her face. The effort to try and exude normality was exhausting. And she'd had enough for one day.

Kim closed and locked the front door behind her. The cameras were still there, and the app had been downloaded to her new phone. All other traces of Leanne were gone apart from the deconstructed toaster on the dining table.

Without removing her jacket, she lowered herself down to the sofa. She'd pushed her body and her mind to end this. Yes, she could have left it to the team to execute Woody's plan, but just like Symes had wanted to see her body lowered into the ground, she had needed to see him back in custody.

She had made the effort to achieve three things. Firstly, to get Symes safely back behind bars. Done. The second thing had been to find out who had saved her life. Done. The third was to convince her team she was okay, and two out of three wasn't bad.

The truth was that since the moment she'd regained consciousness, she'd been fighting a numbness that was trying to steal over her. A veil of paralysis was trying to descend somewhere in her mind like a roller shutter door that couldn't be stopped, and yet somehow she kept managing to wedge her foot underneath and send it back up. It was constant and it was exhausting.

Everyone she met greeted her with the same question or a variation. How are you? How are you feeling?

Nothing. She felt nothing.

She wasn't angry, sad, regretful, joyous, grateful. Just fucking nothing.

How the hell was she supposed to feel?

She'd given herself to a madman. She had knowingly offered her life to save Emma and Chloe. She had made that deal. She had accepted it. Every inch of her body had been subjected to a brutal attack, and she had kept her side of the bargain and died. And then due to the actions of others, she'd been forced to renege on the deal she'd made. Her life was owed to someone. Not Leanne, but someone, somewhere was owed the debt of her existence.

Barney stepped up onto the sofa with reticence instead of his usual gambolling buoyancy. It had been a while since it had been just the two of them together in this house.

He didn't look at her. He stared forward as though waiting for an invisible boundary line to be lifted.

She slipped her arm around him and pulled him close.

'We'll be okay, boy, won't we, eh?' she asked as the numbness came for her again.

A LETTER FROM ANGELA

First of all, I want to say a huge thank you for choosing to read *Six Graves*, the sixteenth instalment of the Kim Stone series, and to many of you for sticking with Kim and her team since the very beginning.

I thoroughly enjoyed researching and writing *Six Graves*, and if you enjoyed it, I would be forever grateful if you'd write a review. I'd love to hear what you think, and it can also help other readers discover one of my books for the first time. Or maybe you can recommend it to your friends and family... And if you'd like to keep up to date with all my latest releases, just sign up at the website link below.

www.bookouture.com/angela-marsons

Most authors have news stories that stay with them long after they have vanished from the public eye. The case of Artem Saveliev was one of those incidents that stayed with me long after it was making headlines. My heart couldn't forget the image of a young boy having been plucked from everything he knew to begin a new life only to be returned like a faulty appliance.

I understand that this would not have been an easy decision to make, but it got me thinking about the difference for some people between an adopted child and a natural child and difficult choices between the two.

I firmly believe that for many parents the difference

between an adopted child and natural does not exist, that they could give no more love or devotion to either, but there are others for whom the contractual bond doesn't equal the blood tie.

As ever, I like to keep Kim on her toes, and although her final battle with Symes was difficult to write, I think it was long overdue.

And I'd love to hear from you – so please get in touch on my Facebook or Goodreads page, Twitter or through my website.

Thank you so much for your support – it is hugely appreciated.

Angela Marsons

www.angelamarsons-books.com

facebook.com/angelamarsonsauthor

twitter.com/WriteAngie

ACKNOWLEDGEMENTS

Oh, this was a tough one to write for many reasons but not least due to how much I enjoyed writing *Six Graves*. This one caused me more than one sleepless night as I doubted everything about it. There was much coffee, cake and reassurance offered by my awesome partner, Julie, especially when I abandoned an entire plot line a third into writing the book. There is no problem too big that she doesn't offer me a logical, measured approach which pops a pin in the balloons of doubt that float all around me. I am as grateful as ever for her honesty, passion and enthusiasm.

Thank you to my mum and dad who continue to spread the word proudly to anyone who will listen. And to my sister Lyn, her husband Clive, and my nephews Matthew and Christopher for their support too.

Thank you to Amanda and Steve Nicol who support us in so many ways, and to Kyle Nicol for book spotting my books everywhere he goes.

I would like to thank the growing team at Bookouture for their continued enthusiasm for Kim Stone and her stories.

Special thanks to my editor, Claire Bord, who allows me the freedom of my ideas, even when those ideas cause horrified silence at the other end of the phone. Regardless, she encourages me to explore every storyline and character development that I throw at her. I am honoured that she trusts my judgement as much as I trust hers to make sure that between us, we publish the best possible version of the story.

To Kim Nash (Mama Bear), who works tirelessly to promote our books and protect us from the world. To Noelle Holten, who has limitless enthusiasm and passion for our work, and Sarah Hardy, who also champions our books at every opportunity.

A special thanks must go to Janette Currie, who has copy-edited the Kim Stone books from the very beginning. Her knowledge of the stories has ensured a continuity for which I'm extremely grateful. Also need a special mention for Henry Steadman, who is responsible for the fabulous book covers which I absolutely love.

Thank you to the fantastic Kim Slater who has been an incredible support and friend to me for many years now, who, despite writing outstanding novels herself, always finds time for a chat. Massive thanks to Emma Tallon who keeps me going with funny stories and endless support. Also to the fabulous Renita D'Silva and Caroline Mitchell, both writers that I follow and read voraciously and without whom this journey would be impossible. Huge thanks to the growing family of Bookouture authors who continue to amuse, encourage and inspire me on a daily basis.

Thank you to Suzanne Jane Daphne Adams who generously offered money to Equine Market Watch horse sanctuary to be a named character in this book. Your generosity is appreciated, Suzi.

My eternal gratitude goes to all the wonderful bloggers and reviewers who have taken the time to get to know Kim Stone and follow her story. These wonderful people shout loudly and share generously not because it is their job but because it is their passion. I will never tire of thanking this community for their support of both myself and my books. Thank you all so much.

Massive thanks to all my fabulous readers, especially the ones that have taken time out of their busy day to visit me on my website, Facebook page, Goodreads or Twitter.